# THE STRENGTH OF EGGSHELLS

# THE STRENGTH OF EGGSHELLS

Kirsty Powell

CLOUD INK

First published in 2019
Published by Cloud Ink Press Ltd, Auckland
P.O. Box 8988, Symonds Street, Auckland, 1150
www.cloudink.co.nz

ISBN 978-0-473-47420-1




Cover design: Robin Charles (www.robincharles.com)

Cover photographs reproduced with permission of the family of David Sandford and Doug Houlbrooke

Internal design and typesetting: Craig Violich (www.cvdgraphics.nz)
Printed by Ligare, Auckland

To Witi Ihimaera – who encouraged me to get started
and told me to twist the knife harder.

# One

# Kate

Our flat is just past the lowest point on Dominion Road, a shapeless box above a shop. I bang the showroom door shut and run up the stairs hoping for Ian but it's only Ursula. I know exactly what she'll say.

'Hello, darling.'

I sprawl on the couch, the bit where the springs don't poke through and try not to watch Ursula at the stove. She cracks an egg with a hollow knock against her false boob and slips it into the pan.

'One egg or two?' She turns from the stove, her pleated skirt fills our kitchen. 'Protein-building for your big date with Eric?' Ursula points her spatula down the stairs. 'I've found you the perfect dress, the cutest sandals.'

I snort, curl my legs underneath me on the worn-out couch and look away. 'Not sure I'm going yet.' I pull my ponytail across my face and bite into the coarse blonde hair.

'Not sure?' Ursula marches across the kitchen. 'It's never helpful to be unsure.'

I sink deeper into the couch, bite harder on my hair and refuse to look at her. But I know that won't stop Ursula.

'When do I get to meet this man?'

The question hangs unanswered between us.

'Does he want babies?'

I put my fingers down my throat and pretend to gag.

She pretends not to notice. 'Good farming stock and you've got the hips for it. That'll be two eggs if we're about to commence procreation.'

She cracks another egg into the pan. 'Isn't he crazy about you? What's there to be unsure about?'

I lower my eyes and pick at the hole in the couch. 'Isn't that obvious?'

Ursula turns and raises her glittered eyebrows. 'No, darling, the obvious is escaping me.'

I draw myself up off the couch to my full height and glare down at Ursula across the kitchen table. 'Look at me, six foot without my shoes on, size 11 feet and born in a nuthouse. Would you want kids?' I slump back down on the couch.

Ursula clucks her tongue. 'Why don't we just rephrase that?' She lifts the limp green spinach out of the pot. 'You're five foot twelve inches tall and you could look like that blonde model Jerry Hall if you'd just stop dragging your knuckles around like some Neanderthal woman.'

Ursula raises pauses to let the drops of water fall away, then lowers the spinach down onto the toast. 'That's no reason you shouldn't have kids. Is there anything in your life that you are NOT unsure about? Poor wee Kate would rather just sit here on the couch and…'

I jump up again and slam my fist down on the rickety kitchen table. The carton of eggs spills open onto the floor.

'You overstuffed peacock. I'm not the one who hangs Ursula up in the wardrobe and trots out Ian to his hunched-over job in the IT world. No opinions, no friends, no one notices…ouch!'

I pull my hand away and rub the red mark that Ursula's spatula has left across my knuckles. 'How dare you.'

*BRRRRING.* The doorbell on the showroom door rings out below.

Ursula throws the spatula in the sink and snatches off her apron. 'You'll keep.' She marches past me, her high heels clacking down the stairs.

'Bloody Ursula.' I rub my hand again, turn off the stove and find the dish cloth to scoop the shell and tendrils of yellow yolk up off the cracked lino. When the last of the egg is in the bin, I find a felt tip pen in the tangle by the phone and write on the empty carton. *SORRY – gone to get more eggs.*

My motorbike helmet is lying by the door. I grab it on my way out and sneak down the stairs through Ursula's showroom, trying to stay out of sight behind a rack of dresses.

'Goodbye, darling,' Ursula calls after me as if nothing has just happened between us, then turns back to her customer. 'Don't you think my flatmate looks fantastic in that little T-shirt and jeans I chose for her? I just wish she'd stand up straight and pull back those shoulders so we can see her bust. She'd look so much better with a little more butt and a bigger bosom, don't you think? As I was saying before, it's all about the foundation garments we choose. But some people just remain unsure.' Ursula raises her eyebrows at me over the rack of dresses. 'Some people just aren't ready to listen.'

I shut the door, harder than it needs.

At the corner I stop and dial the number I know by heart. It rings and rings, as I know it will. A woman's voice answers, asking me if I'd like to leave a message after the beep.

'Message for Dr Heng. Eric, it's me, Kate Whyte. I can't make it – Mum's not well. Got to go down to the farm for a few days and help out. I…' I pause and the message cuts off before I can finish.

With the eggs balanced in my helmet I push open the showroom door and stand aside as Ursula's customer edges his bulging shopping bag out of the shop. Ursula and I both watch from behind the door as he loads them into the boot of his late model car and pushes down the pink tulle overflowing out of one of the bags.

'So nice when I meet someone prepared to be their true self. I'll be able to retire from my day job soon.' Ursula snips shut the showroom door and we both climb up the stairs in silence. She picks up the egg carton and reads my note before firing it into the bin. 'I'm sorry too,' she mutters. 'We need to talk.'

I turn away from Ursula to the stove and switch the pan on again. 'I'm heading home for a few days.'

'You've cleared that with the long-suffering Eric?'

'Nope, just left a message. Mum needs me.'

'And does she?'

I shrug and smash a couple of eggs against the side of the pot and splash them in to poach in the lukewarm water.

'White lie, huh?' Ursula throws out the cold toast, puts in some new bread and thumps down the knob on the toaster. 'The kiss of a white butterfly makes the biggest hole in a cabbage.'

Bloody Ursula. White butterflies storm around in my stomach.


*ooOOoo*


On work mornings it's never Ursula who wakes me. With Ian there's no need to set an alarm. At 7.00am he's shaving. At 7.15am he's dressed in a dark suit with a white shirt and a striped tie, subservient in colour and width. The jug always switches on at 7.20am and he makes coffee. I stumble out of bed when he knocks on my door and grab an Afro comb to part my hair enough to see my way to the couch. Ian hands me a coffee and the front section of the paper. He sits at the kitchen table with the business news. At this time of day neither of us speaks. There has always been a quiet peace between us – we both like it this way. Best friends since primary school, that's what I say when people ask how I came to flat with Ian Dunn.

I never tell them how my mother Ginny had gone up the road to his cold house, picked him up, brought him home and warmed him back to life by the fire. Just as she would a mismothered lamb, she fed him, bathed him and nursed his bruises. Like a pet lamb my best friend Ian had mothered onto our place. He never went back home to his father after his own mother left.

I hardly knew Mrs Dunn way back then. I only remember her laughing mouth blowing cigarette smoke down at the local hall.

'Why are your teeth broken, Mrs Dunn?'

Ginny shushed me, pulling me away, promising she would tell me later, but she never did.

'Has Ian come to live with us in case he gets his teeth broken too?'

Ginny put a hand to her lips, her sign for me to stop asking. 'Not now Kate.'

'Where do babies come from?' Ginny shushed me; she'd tell me when I was older. But how will I know when I was old enough to ask again? I never did. There were things that children learned not to ask adults about.

Ian gathers up the front of the paper; he'll read the rest of it on the bus.

I tell him I'll be away, down at the farm for a few days to help with the shearing.

He gathers his satchel and the egg sandwiches he's made. He pauses mid-plastic wrap. 'About Eric, is it true what you told Ursula?'

The white butterflies are back. I nod without looking up from the paper, trying to remember what I had said to Ursula. The moment passes.

'Give my love to Ginny and John.' Ian is gone out the door to catch his bus.

It's my job to clean up the dishes. I always leave things the way Ian likes to find them.

My gear thrown in a backpack, I head down the stairs and out through the showroom. The dresses hang on the long racks like a sequinned rainbow.

'Bloody Ursula.' I slam the door shut behind me.


*ooOOoo*


Past Tuakau, my motorbike plunges down onto the river flats beside the Waikato River, past the willows, over the lumpy bridge. Rather than turning right onto the sealed highway to the port, I turn left and head up the Klondyke, a shingle road. I stand up on the pegs, open the throttle and let the bike have its head. The bike is part of me, we buck across the washouts and oversized rocks, tipping into the corners. I push my weight over the outside peg to dig in the back tyre, leaving a tell-tale weave in the thickest patches of shingle. Over the apex my bike and I drop back down onto the sealed road. I wave to the old lady who lives on the corner at the port and then hit the shingle again, climbing up into the limestone country.

Nearly home, I stand up on the pegs again and leave a fishtail behind the bike as I progress at speed. I steer the bike along the heavy snake of shingle in the centre of the one-lane road. The bike revs between my knees and slews backwards and forward, spewing the stones up behind us. My ears are roaring, my lungs are filling and I'm singing *Hallelujah* higher and higher. Soaring above us now, I look down…

*My mount forms a plume of dust ripping up the valley, a vast cloak that spreads out behind a warrior princess. My long dark hair is flowing backward. My breasts are clad in spirals of steel. The mane of my horse is rising and falling. My sword is slapping against my thigh with every foot fall. The last corner is before me.*

'Shit.' I pull my warrior woman back into the moment. A cow stands in the middle of the road just beyond the apex of the corner. She stares at me; neither of us blink.

'Look where you want to go,' I mutter, dragging my eyes away and throwing my bike into the gap between the cow and the bank. My brake slews the back wheel around in a half circle of scattered stones. I pull up behind the old girl, blocking her path. She turns around and we eyeball each other again. An old Hereford with a calf bulging out both sides of her ginger flanks and piggy eyes under her curly white top knot. She should know better than to bust out onto the road. The cow breaks our gaze first and turns away. I turn the old girl around and shoo her back along the road towards the paddock where she should be. Back on my bike, I speed past her to open the gate, then herd the cow backward and forward. Her sides heave, she bellows, her head weaving from side to side, getting wild now. I rev the throttle at just the right moment to push her through the open gate. Udder swinging, she trots back in her paddock and drops her head to eat. I shut the gate behind her.

At the cattle stop, I pull up by our mailbox and wait for my father, John Whyte. He rides his bike down off the ridge above the road, his team of dogs streaming out behind him. Neither of us mentions the cow, but I know he saw what happened by the way he shrugs his shoulder and the wrinkles at the corners of his mouth deepen upward. It's never his way to praise his kids to their faces.

'School holidays for teachers, huh?' He kicks his bike into gear. 'Good to see you home.'

We ride together past the woolshed, and stop at the killing house to feed the dogs.

John hands me the axe and turns to look at my bike.

'Are you looking after her?' John kicks my front tyre and nods when he finds it tight. He squats down and pulls the bike up off its stand to vertical and checks the oil glass down by the footbrake.

I nod, knowing the oil is full. I always do these things just the way he showed me. Rub the 'wet n' dry' sandpaper through the sparkplug and check the gap using the gauge he gave me.

He grunts his approval, drops my bike back down onto its stand and calls the dogs in.

The axe handle is slippery with mutton grease. I lift it high to chop chunks off the dog-tucker carcass that is hanging on the gambrel, an overfat wether. We throw the meat to the dogs, locking each one into its kennel and then ride on up to the house, past the macrocarpa hedge whose tops sway dark green in the westerly. The last cattle stop chatters me welcome and there is my home, nestled in the shelter of the wind break and the warm glow of the late afternoon sun. Sixties weatherboard, it's not much to look at. Extra rooms, still not fully painted, added on when the family took in two extra strays: first me and then Ian. We ride past the vegetable garden.

There's my little mother, Ginny, bent over amongst the runner beans. She hears the bikes clatter by and stands up to see who it is. She has an apron full of beans, which drop to the ground as she runs out the gate to greet me.

'So nice to see you.' Ginny reaches up to pat my ponytail as I lift off my helmet.

*ooOOoo*

The runner beans have been top and tailed. The mint leaves make a green stain on the wooden chopping board. I cut the mint fine, almost to a pulp, then add a little sugar, boiling water and vinegar. The table is set. Ginny lifts the roast out of the oven; the gravy is stirred. I step outside to call the men in off the deck. They stand shoulder to shoulder against the railing, nursing a beer in the crook of their elbows, arms crossed over lean bellies. Son, like father, Robbie and John, both nuggety built, olive-skinned with eyes that crinkle into deep smiles. Their freshly-showered hair stands up on end: Robbie's rich brown, and John's the same but a dusting of grey showing through at the temples. They have both changed for dinner into clean Stubbies shorts and unironed T-shirts straight off the clothesline, the peg marks showing at the shoulder seams. Their bare feet and ankles are stark white below the gumboot line.

We take our usual places at the long table. John sits at the head; Ginny, the little red hen, perched beside him; me opposite Ginny; then my brother Robbie feeding the baby because his wife's working in town on the evening shift; and three empty places with the younger boys working away on farms. At the far end of the table there's the usual clutter. Wind-fallen fruit, bright orange rubber rings, yesterday's farming magazine with advertisements for drench and unopened bills in their crisp white envelopes with tell-tale clear windows with the name of our farm, West Hills, RD2, showing through. At West Hills the calendar on the wall is always marching towards the 20th of next month. On that day John will pull open the bills, scratch his head and Ginny will dip into her school bus driving money. The table is only ever fully cleared if there are real visitors for dinner – a rare event. Stock agents, family and neighbours know to take a spare seat and push back the debris of the day to day.

When the bottle is empty, Robbie drapes the baby over his shoulder and reaches across the table with both hands for the silverbeet. The baby nuzzles the hair on my brother's sunburnt neck, burps milk down the back of Robbie's T-shirt and relaxes to sleep.

'It's been a while.' Robbie raises his eyebrows at me as he stands up to plonk the sleeping baby in the carrycot in the corner of the dining room. 'Any news from the big smoke?'

I shake my head and watch as the baby stirs for a moment in the old cot. Was it the same carrycot that took the previous generation of Whyte babies up to the docking yards in the Land Rover and down to the local hall in the back of the station wagon? Baby John, who is named for his grandfather, stretches and continues to sleep; another farmer in the making, nothing surer than that the sun will set each day over West Hills. I look out that way, through the doors opening onto the deck. Our hills in the distance above the shelter belt are getting thick with gorse, grown back since the government took off the subsidies and the wool prices fell away. The last of the sun is sparking off the yellow flowers.

John smiles my way as he carves mutton off the leg. 'There must be something happening up there in the land of asphalt?'

Ginny stands to pass the roast vegetables around, holding the oven cloth underneath the hot dish. She pats John on the head with the platter as she passes. 'You're a great one to ask.' She plonks the dish further down the table. 'The man who never ventures north of the Tuakau Sale Yards.'

John helps himself to beans, well cooked to a sludgy green with the purple bits showing through, just the way he likes them. 'Didn't I buy you some new gumboots in Pukekohe just the other week?'

'I rest my case.' Ginny smiles at John and shakes her head.

'I just prefer to shop where I can park my ute in the yard.' John nods at me across the table. 'Shearing Saturday if this weather holds – could do with a hand to muster.'

I nod my reply.

Robbie reaches for the dish of beans. 'What's Ursula up to this weekend? We got our best ever shearing tallies last year with her on the cheese scones at morning tea.'

'What about Ian?' John taps his fork on the table. 'Forget the scones – I'd rather have another man on a shearing handpiece.'

John ducks as Ginny makes a swipe for his head with the gravy spoon. He grins at her, making a grab for the spoon. 'Mind you, nothing wrong with Ursula's scones, but this Ian/Ursula thing is confusing and no help when I'm planning my sheep work. Couldn't he just stick with being one thing or the other?'

I rise up out of my chair. 'Butt out, Dad.'

Ginny reaches across to soothe me back down into my seat and shakes her head at John. She turns to me. 'It's ages since we've seen either Ian or Ursula out here.'

I nod and shake my head at the same time. 'It's Ursula at the weekends and she has to stay home and run her dress shop and Ian is still doing the hard slog during the week.'

Ginny drops her head on one side to admire the simple cotton dress I'd put on for dinner. 'Did Ursula pick this one? Has she thought up a name for her shop yet?'

'Chrysalis Clothing.' I sniff and look down at the dress. Bloody Ursula.

John nods his approval. 'Nice frock but don't get too la-dee-da. I still need my wool girl at shearing time.' He drops the spoon back into the gravy boat, sending brown splatters across the tablecloth.

Ginny sighs as another tablecloth is assigned to an early wash. She gets up from the table. 'That reminds me.' She fishes through the papers on the end of the table until she finds a damp scrap of envelope that she waves my way. 'Eric rang for you while I was doing the washing.' She hands me the scrawled number.

I slump down in my seat and screw up the note. 'What did you say to him?'

'I just asked him how you were, dear.' Ginny looks across the table and holds my eye longer than she needs.

Bloody Ginny. I shrug. 'What did he say?'

'Well, funny thing – he asked me how I was. Told him I was fighting fit, of course.'

I slump further down in my seat, accompanied by several white butterflies.

'Who's that?' John nudges Ginny's arm. 'Is someone chasing a date with our Kate?'

'No, dear, it's nothing like that. Just that doctor chap Kate's supposed to see each month for her medication, wants her to give him a ring back.'

'You don't say.' John scratches his head and looks at Ginny. 'Didn't you tell me he was a little fella? He'd be a bit on the short side for our Kate, wouldn't he?'

Ginny stretches herself up to her full five foot five and a quarter. 'You can talk, John Whyte.'

John grins. 'Yep, us Whytes are all a bit short – except for Kate, of course.' He looks over at me. 'How about we get you married off to a two metre Peter, like Rodney down the road? I could borrow you back for the mustering as well as breeding some decent All Blacks.'

I poke my tongue out at him.

Robbie laughs. 'Don't you think our Baby John here could make the grade?'

'Well, no offence, but you did marry a squirt of a girl. Your kid's never going to be a Pine Tree.' John bangs the end of his fork on the table. 'It's a crying shame, these giant All Blacks marrying themselves off to skinny little blonde things. Imagine the kids they'd have if one of those really big forwards were to marry our Kate. Line breeding – we do it all the time with stock.'

Robbie winks at me. 'Lanky kids with sticking out ears if they turned out like Rodney.'

John roars with laughter.

I stick my hands over my ears and stand up to clear the table.

Ginny rises to help me. 'What a lot of nonsense. You've been reading my *Woman's Weekly* again?'

'Only a quick glance.' John pats Ginny's rump as she carries the leftovers past. She stands on his foot and he pretends to howl in agony.

ooOOoo

Baby John is sleeping in the carrycot, his hands striking an origami pose in mid-air, lips pursing as he suckles while he dreams. The dishes are done and John and Robbie are settled in front of the telly in the lounge. Ginny slips into the darkened dining room and sits beside me on the couch. We both watch Baby John in silence for a while.

'So nice to have a baby in the house again. Such a long time since we brought you home in that carrycot.' Ginny rubs her eyes. 'Such a pretty baby – I used to sit like this and watch you sleep.'

I slump further down the couch and speak through my ponytail. 'Wasn't much of a girl though? All those dresses you made that I wouldn't wear.'

Ginny sighs. 'Yes, you running around in the boys' hand-me-downs out there on the farm.' Ginny pushes her worn wedding ring up and down her finger. 'It's a pity I didn't have Ursula on my team back then. She's better than I ever was with girlie things.'

I scowl in the dark. 'Ursula thinks I'm pig stubborn.' I curl my legs up against my chest on the couch, wrap my hands around them and bury my chin. We both watch Baby John.

'Is that really the carrycot you brought me home in?'

Ginny nods.

We both look down at the old dark canvas with the shiny metal elbows that let the hood fold back around the sleeping baby's head.

The next question is obvious but I never ask. The words are stuck in my throat, punched down and stamped on by those kids at primary school who used to chant:

*Kate Kate, knickers in a state, that's what you get with Kingseat Kate.*
*Kate, Kate, mother took a skate, lock her in the nuthouse, Kingseat Kate.*

The Whyte boys of course had dealt to those girls and their brothers as well, and Ginny had soothed over the upset mothers. It stopped happening to my face for a while, but there were always the whispers and giggling about '*Kingseat Kate*', the girl who played in the sandpit with a boy, while the rest of them whirled around showing off their undies on the shiny bars of the jungle gym.

*Kate's a Dumb Head, Kate's a Dumb Ted, Kate's a Dope Ted...*
*Kate's ADOPTED from the NUTHOUSE.*

The last triumphant line was shouted out across the playground and then subsided to an anxious giggle as they looked around to see if any Whyte boys had overheard before they started all over again.

My friend Ian would put his fingers in his ears and nod for me to do the same. We would sit there in the sandpit and start to sing, '*Harr lay lu yar, Harr lay lu yar*'. Higher and higher we would sing, louder and louder until the girls gave up. Then Ian would pull my fingers away and we would get back to building our tunnel, breaking through, our damp fingers touching deep under the sand. Up to our armpits in the cold sand we would link our little fingers the way you pull on a wishbone and try to forget about those dumb girls.

Ginny Whyte is still looking down at the baby. I can feel her breathing beside me, bursting to talk about it.

Ursula says I already know the truth about my birth mother being in Kingseat Hospital, so it's just plain stupid not to ask and get the details straight in my head.

There was a time when I had wanted to know. I'd filled out the form when I was old enough and ridden out the back when the envelope arrived, the official looking thing a dead weight in my pocket. On the side of a clay hill at the estuary I'd sat to open it. With shaking hands I'd split the seal with my thumb and drawn out the single page of heavy parchment paper, and stared at the brief additions made to the standard form. My name spelt correctly. My mother's name 'Vetoed'. Through my tears I had stared at that one harsh word, a road block, a message from a mother who didn't want me. A small kernel in my chest had shrunk back into its half-formed shell. But what of my father? The blank line stared back at me, a hole in the document. Worse than a veto, my father, just a blank space. I had crumpled the paper around the kernel.

Ian had found me there, picked up and read the crumpled paper and then tossed it into the stagnant water. We had both watched until the small bundle had sunk beneath the surface. Without a word he'd rubbed my tears away and then raced me home on our bikes at breakneck speed, which required all my concentration. Thank God for Ian. We never spoke of it again.

I sit on the couch and ignore Ginny. I'm not sure, I may never be sure and why do I need to know? Baby John is sucking in his sleep. The world about me is warm and safe.

Ginny puts her hand over mine. 'Your old carrycot reminds me – isn't it time…'

Not bloody Ginny as well!

Veto. I pull my hand away, fingers in my ears and begin to hum, '*Harr lay lu yar, harr lay lu yah*'. The dining room roof is blowing away. I try to blow her words away as well, but they won't go.

Ginny is gently taking my fingers out of my ears just as she did when I was a child and the battle was too important for her to lose. 'You're not thirteen anymore. Don't you think it's time we…?'

Veto. Where's Ian when I need him? I grab my hands away from Ginny and run to my room, pull on my leathers, jam on my helmet. Gone out the door, I spin my motorbike around on its stand and ride away hard, back to the city.

# Two

# Beanstalk

How peculiar. He'd never thought as an old man that this cancerous thing would still be with him. Yet here he was, still staring at the ceiling at 3.00am, still thinking about Jane. Beanstalk prided himself on being a man of order even in retirement, and yet how quickly his mind slipped into disarray at the thought of Jane Stanley. She a mere patient and he the physician charged with her care all those years ago.

A hapless Medical Officer, or that's what his colleagues had thought when he'd taken the post at Kingseat Hospital. A mental hospital position best suited to an eccentric. 'Professional hara-kiri' is the way they'd described his future, behind his back of course.

Was he eccentric? Wide awake now, he clambered from his single bed and took down the box from its shelf. The poetry book was still there, of course, and the white feather as well. Just as it had been when he'd retrieved the box from the final place Jane had hidden it all those years ago.

Beanstalk lifted out the notebook and held it up to his nose but there was only the smell of musty paper and the feather, odourless after all these years. He cast his mind backward to remember how life had smelled then. The years offered nothing olfactory until he reached the late summer of 1965, still rendered with salt and the rot that happens on the edge of an estuary. Yet it was not so much the smell of the thing but the words that helped him to recall the detail in the middle of the night. Beanstalk opened the poetry book and it all came back.

At first, he'd only known Jane as a mummy covered in bandages, a quiet nun sitting amongst the grotesque, refreshingly still amongst the floodway that was psychiatry at Kingseat. Unblinking green eyes behind white bandages reading a book, or maybe his thoughts. He hadn't meant to, of course, but he'd formed a habit of bringing her more books. Frivolous volumes that a young woman wrapped in mummy bandages might enjoy.

But the first time he saw her face? He remembered it exactly, moving through the dayroom, the banging, rocking, shrieks and gesticulations that followed his usual progress across the room and then suddenly a small hand slipped into his. He looked down and drew breath. The nurses had removed the bandages. Too late – the green eyes had seen how he had recoiled from the angry burnt-monster mask that stared up at him as Jane had walked by his side. He had failed her already.

How could you describe Jane? Beanstalk shuddered. Even now, here in the darkness of his small home, so many years later, still the image was just as fresh and just as terrible. Her features burnt completely, just raw surgical slits refashioned to show the orbs of her green eyes. Her ears melted away with the stubs that remained glued back against the angry redness of her skull. Her mouth an unclosable hole that marked hoarse breathing between sparse teeth. What was left of her hair was clumped in uneven patches, finely spun gold but lifeless and unbrushable amongst the open scars. Even the maddest of the patients steered clear of the tiny monster that lurked on the dayroom windowsills where she would sit and read behind a drawn curtain.

It became his habit to take her outside, away from the dismal dayroom, smoke-filled with looming walls and broken chairs. It seemed best to match her muteness with space and silence. The medical notes said that Jane never attempted to speak. Was her oesophagus too burnt or was it just her inclination? Beanstalk could never be sure with Jane.

She would hold his hand and they would walk together down through the grounds to the tidal creek out the back of Kingseat. He would take her away from the staff and the inhuman cries of daily psychiatric despair.

What possibly could he speak of with this silent young woman who made no attempt to reply? He spoke of what they saw, he named the plants and they watched for birds.

He had no clue at first what she thought, or how much she could take in. The history had been vague. A discharge from Middlemore Hospital when her burns had become stable, Kingseat a dumping ground and a home for lost souls who had ceased to communicate with the world. A place to hide away those who could no longer front an image of robustness.

After the scars had healed to a point where the bandages could be discarded it became his habit, when the tide was right, to take the small boat and row her down the creek behind the hospital. Jane would lie against the gunwale and trail her hand in the water. To get her attention, he would splash a little with the oar and after a time she would splash him back. At first just a little and then in buckets. Beanstalk would laugh and shake the drops off his thinning hair, hardly orthodox, but they'd developed a language of sorts. When he said something that pleased her, she would nod her head by a tiny degree that only Beanstalk could see. When she was not pleased she would turn away. He found himself, a grown man, becoming desperate to please her.

Not ethical he knew, Beanstalk had every intention of stopping this behaviour. He promised himself, just one last boat trip before they resumed their meetings in his dreary office, an unproductive hour each week where Jane had refused to communicate, wrestling against her scars to turn away from him in the chair he had placed next to his desk.

This day had started out with rain, but after it had dissipated, they set out under heavy cloud in the small boat. Jane lay with her scarred cheek resting on the wooden side, running her fingers through the sky-coloured water as he rowed. There was no splashing that day, just the dipping and dripping of oars in and out of muddy water.

In the distance, Beanstalk spied a white heron, standing alone, its stillness reflected in the greyness of the day. He touched Jane and pointed it out. They rowed closer, both of them mesmerised by this lonely figure.

The bird was still etched in his memory all these years later: the set of its neck, the beak, the whiteness of the feathers. Then, lifting off, it was gone. They glided across to where the heron had been and Jane spied a feather floating. She grabbed it off the surface and touched it to her face. Beanstalk whispered to Jane of the kōtuku, such a rare gift bestowed on them both. He gave her his doctor's notebook and suggested that she draw what they both had seen. She wrote a poem instead; she wrote of the heron.

He could hardly contain his haste to reclaim the notebook and read what she had written there. Finally, he had found what he had always hoped for in his jaded psychiatric career. At last, gold in his hands. Jane was communicating, just with him.

## Finding Kōtuku

Before us lonely water
A heron stands
White statue in mud
Observing the surface
Which never runs clean

Thrusting a bill beneath
To dredge what's better left
Unseen, unclean
Never touching
Untouchable memories

The bird startles and lifts away
Trailing muddy feet
Our boat draws forward
Towards my prize
I seize the white feather

Beanstalk read and reread her poem about the kōtuku, an amateur attempt, of course, but Jane was communicating at least. He begged her for more, to write in sentences, to tell him how she felt. Jane handed him the notebook and turned away.

Beanstalk became even more desperate to please her. He watched the tides and planned to take her out again in the dinghy as soon as he had the opportunity. How could he groom this talent; how could he give this young woman back some sort of a life?

The day dawned clear, the tide was right. He hurried through his usual patients then took the opportunity to slip away during the afternoon, the notebook ready and the pencil sharp.

As usual Jane was nowhere to be seen in her villa, but the pulled curtain in the corner of the dayroom was a sign. Sure enough, she was there, curled up over a book. Some children's tale by Enid Blyton. Beanstalk took it from her hands, tossed it back on the shelf and made a mental note to get her started on proper literature. Another mistake. In his haste to get to the dinghy he didn't notice her dragging her feet as he gabbled on about poetry and all that he would share with her. The brim of her hat hid Jane's face. Even if he had looked, her burnt features would have given no clue to her thoughts.

The dinghy pulled away from the edge of the hospital grounds onto the estuary and Beanstalk presented her with the notebook and urged Jane to write. He thought later, how he must have looked to her, a grinning idiot.

Jane took the pencil and bit the end. She moved as if to cast the notebook in the water and Beanstalk stood to remonstrate, snatching the book back. The boat rocked and the notebook slipped from his grasp into the bilge as they both held onto the sides of the boat until the dinghy settled.

Beanstalk retrieved the notebook and handed it back to her. 'Please, Jane, dear Jane, please write for me.'

Her green eyes held his for a moment, and then she had opened the book and busied herself with the pencil. He'd held his breath, excitement growing. Had he looked like a panting schoolboy? With trembling hands he'd lightly rowed, his eyes never leaving the bent head and the hand that moved across the notebook.

## Riding in Beanstalk's Dinghy

A tidal creek stalks the boundary
A water rat stalks the nest
Dr Bean stalks the dinghy
Frog marches me along
Pulling and pushing
The flotsam of this place
Sucked out leaving only mud
Returning the jetsam
Throbbing heart of madness
We row together with the tide
Fingers sieve murky water
He passes me his notebook
Watching over a quiet bird
I write the words that come
But not for Beanstalk

# Three

# Meredith

The last hen has gone clucky again. Meredith slips her hand beneath the sitting chook and pulls out a warm brown egg. 'That's my Lucky girl.'

Lucky flips her red comb to one side, fixes Meredith with an unblinking eye and settles again on her empty nest.

Meredith picks up the fierce little chook, pulls her close and feels the warmth of Lucky's back against her stomach. The hen squawks and paddles her feet in mid-air. Meredith opens the gate to the chook enclosure and lowers the hen down into the garden. The chook stalks off, eyes intent on the ground and disappears from view into the vegetable patch.

Meredith gathers a few sprigs off the remaining parsley that hasn't yet gone to seed. She carries her small bounty up the path, past the outhouse to the back door and into the quiet darkness of the kitchen. It feels odd to be taking her time. She stands still for a moment and listens to the silence. Gone is the rasping saw of curdled lungs and the banging of the walking stick on the wall. Bang, bang. The stick had constantly called her back to the closed-up front room, which smelled of urine and decay, back to the clock on the front room wall that ticked slowly. Ever so slowly, the clock had drowned the lungs of her querulous Aunt Gwyneth.

But now it's done, just Meredith and the vicar at the gravesite, the precious Edwin not troubled to make the trip from Wellington for the funeral.

When Aunt Gwyneth had first come to the inconvenient truth that death was near, she would fuss over her numerous pillows and then sit back and regale Meredith with her funeral plans. How Edwin would be there to arrange everything. Darling Edwin, who wrote short abrupt notes in a tight unlinked hand but never appeared in person.

Looking back now it seemed to Meredith that Aunt Gwyneth's impending death had really just been about reducing the pillows. The clock ticked as the patient sank further down in the bed. The last pillow was discarded when her aunt became a curled-up but still breathing foetus, a rasping carcass of bones wrapped in skin around a heart that refused to stop keeping time with the clock. Of course, the clock won out in the end. Meredith had burnt the offensive mattress in the backyard and aired the front room. After that she'd stopped winding the clock. The front room stood still.

The egg and parsley are arranged on the crust of last week's loaf. There's no butter left. Meredith spoons on some red plum chutney instead and carries her plate to the table. Three letters are there from this morning's post. Has she ever received three letters before, all addressed to Meredith Innes and all arriving on the same day?

Of course, when Peter had written she had got lots of letters but that was different. No letters, no letters, no letters, and then finally three or four all tumbling through the slot on the same day, long dreamed of gemstones all the way from France. But that was long ago.

Meredith places her plate down carefully next to this morning's post. She cuts across her egg, the yellow yolk leaking out and spreading across the plate. She pushes the crust into the yolk, takes a mouthful and scrutinises the letters. Each is written in a different hand, with a different style of envelope and different quality of paper. Which one to open first, as if the order she reads them could affect the outcome? She mops up the last of the yolk with the parsley, which is past its best and tastes coarse and bitter in her mouth.

There's a knock on the back door and Phyllis puts her head around it. 'Just popped over to make sure you're alright, dearie. How was the funeral? I would have come you know, but for that brisk wind up at the graveyard. Did Edwin show?'

Phyllis sidles into the room, pushing her sharp little nose over Meredith's shoulder. 'Oooh, gosh that was quick – a letter from his lordship already, and one from that posh lawyer Mr Mason down on Victoria Avenue. Who's the third one from?'

Meredith snatches up the letters and puts them behind an ornament on the mantelpiece. She collects up her finished plate from the table. 'Cup of tea?'

'Of course, dearie.' Phyllis settles her thin shoulders onto the couch without needing to be asked. 'Gosh, it's quiet around here without herself banging that stick every five minutes. You know, I could hear her banging away over at my place when the window was open on this side of the house.' Phyllis puts her hand to her mouth. 'Not that I listened, of course. All your hard work looking after that tyrant all these years and I bet you don't get a word of thanks from darling Edwin. She spoiled him rotten as a child. Whatever was she thinking?'

*ooOOoo*

*Dear Miss Innes,*                                    *4th March 1932*

*As you are aware, further to the death of my mother, Gwyneth Andrews, the house in which you currently reside has been willed to me in its entirety and is now my personal property. My wife's sister and her family will be moving in at their earliest convenience, which is two weeks hence. I trust you will leave the place immaculately presented and settle any outstanding bills on your own account. I have notified Mr Mason of Mason and Partners of my wishes. There will be no charge for your prolonged lodging under my generous mother's roof. I wish you well for the future.*

*Yours faithfully,*
*Edwin Andrews*

*ooOOoo*

*Dear Miss Innes,* *4th March 1932*

*My sincere condolences at the recent loss of Mrs Gwyneth Andrews, whom I understand was your mother's sister. My client Mr Edwin Andrews has asked that I would inform you of his requirement that Mrs Andrew's property in Wicksteed Street be vacated within 14 days of receiving this letter. Mr Edwin Andrews has also asked that I would close all accounts in the name of Mrs Gwyneth Andrews and he states that you will settle these by your own account. It appears that these accounts have remained unpaid for some time with a total owing of £23 10/6. I am aware this is a considerable sum. I suggest you make an appointment to meet at my rooms to discuss this detail.*

*Yours sincerely,*
*Richard Mason*

*ooOOoo*

*Dearest Meredith,* *28th February 1932*

*Fancy me spotting your aunt's death notice in the paper. Reg says I'm quite the detective. I'm not sorry the old duck's dead. You may be sad because blood is thicker than water, but I'd have to say some blood needs a little thinning and I would put your Aunt Gwyneth in that category. You know me, Meredith. Never one to put my words through the mincer.*

*It seems like such an age ago since our childhood days and how the times have changed for us both.*

*Anyway, we have been up here in the Mangapurua Valley for quite a few months and the time has shot by. We had to walk off Reg's father's farm – went broke when the wool prices bottomed out. We needed somewhere to go where we could at least be together. I didn't want Reg having to go off to one of those work camps. So, we took a lease on some land up here where a returned soldier had walked off his block. Just the tough ones still farming up here.*

*Hard going but at least we can feed ourselves. There are no shops for miles so we don't need to spend much. We live like kings on wild pork, butter, cream, eggs, and not forgetting all the fruit and veg we can grow in my little garden.*

*Luisa plums grow really well up here and we have taken up making the most delicious yellow plum wine, and the local dances are great fun. Reg says he has as much wine, woman and song as any man could ever wish for. When we arrived here, there was no bath and the dear man built me a beautiful wooden one. He measured my posterior and had to build it two boards wide. Now don't go thinking this is due to my ample proportion, just that the boards were on the skinny side! I keep trim up here running around after our little ones and getting my garden going. Proud to say, after three children I can still fit my best tailored skirt. Only problem is, not many outings up here for our Sunday best.*

*We live in a bush house – it was just a slab hut when we arrived. Imagine that, with Michael our baby only 16 days old. Just two rooms and you could see daylight between the corrugated iron pieces on the cooking chimney but Reg, bless his heart, has fixed it up. He's divided the bedroom in half and cut more shingles to add another room and there's a whare out the back if we have a visitor and not to mention our fancy new bath in a little alcove off the kitchen…even if we do have to use a potato for a plug!!*

*But enough of my waffling. Why don't you come up here and stay a while? Free board and as much as you can eat. It would be great if you could help me with the little ones. We could have some fun like we used to all those years ago.*

*I am wondering if you are over Peter yet. I know he was keen to be a farmer. If he'd made it home from the war this is just the sort of place you'd have ended up living anyway.*

*If you do come, can you please bring some sheets? I have used up all my spare ones. Dyed them bright yellow with onion skins and hung them up under the tin roof to stop the drips falling on the beds when we have a big frost. Very bright and gay they are, even if I say so myself.*

*By the way, there are still bachelors up here who need a good farm wife. So make sure you bring <u>double</u> sheets, just in case. You know me, Meredith, always a keen nose for a <u>good</u> <u>match</u>!*

*Hope you can come soon. Had best sign off as Teddy the mail man will be riding by any minute. You'll love the trip up on the riverboat – makes you feel quite the lady staying at Pipiriki House.*

*Got to go. Drop me a line soon.*

*Love from your dear old friend, Agnes*

*ooOOoo*

The album is kept on the shelf by her bed – not many pictures but all his letters. Here is Peter with his cobbers in uniform before he went away, laughing smiles and a cigarette stuck to each bottom lip. And here the picture of just the two of them, the only one she has. Meredith in a green velvet hand-me-down dress, poorly fitted but Peter not caring, swinging her around. The only boy who had ever told her she was pretty in a way that she could believe.

She can't see his face in the photo as he's looking down at her but she knows he's smiling. The corners of his eyes are crinkling just for her and, for once, Meredith is smiling as well, not for the camera, just for Peter. He had taken her dancing and my, how he could dance, tipping her this way and that, spinning her around and pulling her in close after every dizzy circle, then letting her go with a bow.

He had shaken her father's hand and taken second helpings of her mother's plum duff. Mother had pronounced him a dish.

'He'll do right by you, girlie,' Father had said after Peter had come to help them milk the house cow. A timid thing who didn't usually take well to strangers, yet the old cow had leaned her flank on the young man's shoulder while he stripped her out. Father had checked with a bloke he knew who said that Peter treated his dogs well. 'You do well if you stick with this one, girlie.'

Peter, so keen to get home from the war, just hankering for a quiet, green New Zealand valley tucked in under the hills. Astride a farm hack with dogs at his heels, a warm fire and Meredith, *as pretty as a picture to come home to*. He'd written that in his letters, how it would be. They wouldn't have much to start with, *hardly two sticks to rub together*, but Meredith knew there would have been a warm stew in the pot and babies coming on. They would have made it through.

Agnes is right, of course. Mangapurua or some other lonely valley is exactly where they would be now, she and Peter together somewhere on a farm. If only Peter had come home from the war, things would have been different. Right now, they'd be somewhere out there on a soldier's settlement block.

Meredith kisses the picture, closes the album and for the first time in a long time, she sleeps through the night.

*ooOOoo*

The young woman at the typewriter turns and stares as Meredith walks into the chambers. Her lipstick puckers and Meredith watches as the secretary's made-up eyes sweep down just once over her home-sewn cotton shift, knitted cardigan and the brown lace-up shoes with flat heels. The woman's eyes slide away and she wrinkles her nose as if there's an unpleasant smell in the room. Meredith has seen this look before and knows what the secretary is thinking: clean enough, but plain, penniless, and on the shelf. The secretary turns away. She flings the shiny lever back across her typewriter and settles to type. Meredith can see the young woman is pleased to have a job, money to buy lipstick, high heels and a young man with prospects to walk out with. A young man never tainted by war.

Richard Mason stands as Meredith enters the room. By habit he moves to turn his back to the empty fireplace, not lit at this time of year. He waves her into a well-upholstered chair and carefully reviews her features, running his eye over her in a business-like manner. 'How are you, Miss Innes?'

Meredith senses that he does not need her to reply.

He begins to pace; Mr Mason is a man who likes to think before he speaks. He stops for a moment and looks directly at her and then continues to walk. 'I knew your mother. You look a lot like her, same dark hair, same piercing blue eyes.' Mr Mason stops pacing and addresses the far wall where his certificates hang, now yellow and mildewed. 'Your mother was quite a different woman to her sister Gwyneth and I see the offspring have turned out quite differently as well.' Mr Mason sighs. He clasps his hands behind his back and resumes pacing backwards and forwards across the large, handsome room.

'Now, the matter of these accounts.' Mr Mason stops and takes a seat behind his dark polished desk. He opens a file, picks out a sheaf of papers and wraps his wire-framed glasses across his nose and behind both ears. 'Ah yes, store bill, coal, butcher, hardware. Mrs Andrews would take care of these before she became ill?' Mr Mason stops and looks up over his glasses.

Meredith nods.

'And you nursed her to the end with never a penny coming your way?'

Meredith nods again.

Mr Mason sighs, takes off his glasses and turns away. Again, he is addressing the wall with the certificates. 'I will take care of these bills and here is a small token of Edwin's unrealised appreciation.'

Mr Mason stands up and hands Meredith an envelope. He ushers her out of the room without shaking her hand. 'Spend it wisely, Miss Innes. I wish you well.'

*ooOOoo*

Meredith grasps the brown neck, which is bony under the feathers. She stretches and twists in one fast motion. Lucky lies limp in her arms. The disconnected neck and head flop across her elbow. Meredith sits down on the back step. She plucks off Lucky's feathers, saving the soft down to plump up the pillow she plans to take up the river. With a sharp knife she cuts the puckered white skin around the back passage and carefully pulls out the lower gut without getting any chook manure on the meat. She narrows her hand and slips it inside Lucky's warm little body. Carefully, she pulls out Lucky's entrails. There is a long tube full of eggs. The first ones are nearly formed, with pliable skin instead of shell. She handles the eggs. They feel like parchment, soft beneath her fingers. Meredith lays the biggest of the partly formed eggs aside on the step for her breakfast. She examines the remaining eggs. Further down the tube they become smaller and smaller to just a tiny clot where they have been formed deep inside Lucky.

Next to come out is the liver, a rich layered brown, and the tiny heart, a dull red elongated structure, still warm. Meredith tears through the diaphragm and pulls out the lungs, delicate pink froth, so soft. She takes the axe and chops off Lucky's head and feet, dropping them into a hole she has dug in the garden, along with the innards. She smooths the earth back over with the spade.

There is still the last of yesterday's bread to use up. She will add some sage and thyme from the garden and one of the nearly formed eggs for stuffing. She will sew the back cavity closed and roast Lucky tonight. If she's careful, there will be just enough chicken to get through until she leaves, maybe even enough for a sandwich on the steamboat.

Meredith walks into town and buys three brand new double sheets and a length of fine cream Viyella. The woman behind the long wooden counter glances at her left hand. 'For your hope box, dear?'

Meredith nods to the woman and gathers up the packages. Fine thing, if she had a hope box.

*ooOOoo*

At 5.30am Meredith locks the front door of Aunt Gwyneth's house for the last time. The steps down from the front porch are damp in the gloom of an early morning river fog. She picks up her leather suitcase and the paper bag that contains her chicken sandwich and doesn't look back.

On Wicksteed Street most of the houses are still sleeping. There are only a few with lights on as working men prepare for their day, or mothers tend to woken babies. Meredith takes a side street to cut through to Victoria Avenue.

The main street of Wanganui is quiet at this time, apart from one man sweeping the street. He leans on his broom as she walks by and glances at her suitcase. 'Heading for the river boat are you?' He touches his cap. 'Weather's looking good for it.'

Meredith nods and hurries on down to where the sturdy paddle steamer is tied up on the quay. *Wairere* is already starting to puff as her boiler is fired into life by the engineer stoking below.

The captain oversees the loading of luggage, mail sacks, tea chests filled with grocery orders, tins of kerosene and a few live pigs and chickens with their legs trussed. Two strong young Māori boys laugh and joke with the passengers on the wharf as they toss, catch and tie down the goods on the back deck of the little boat.

A woman hands her luggage over for loading and nods to the captain. 'Thank you, sir. A bonny day for the river?'

'Yes, Mrs Bettjeman, a corker day. How come you're leaving town already?' He winks. 'Missing those bairns and that husband of yours?'

The woman's warm Scottish brogue rolls down the wharf towards Meredith. 'Aye, Captain, funny thing – always looking forward to a trip down the river, and then no sooner I'm here than I'm hankering to get home again to our quiet wee backwater up the Mangapurua.'

Meredith's ears tune to the name of Agnes' valley. She moves close to hear the captain's reply.

'Aye, this river gets in yer blood. Give my best to Fred.' Captain Stewart turns to greet his next customer as the sturdy woman walks across the plank to the steamer.

It's Meredith's turn. She nods to the captain and watches as her suitcase flies free for just a moment between the two sets of strong brown hands that toss and retrieve it between the wharf and the riverboat. She steps down onto the boat and stands at the lower rail. The lazy brown Whanganui River stretches wide. To her right is the sea, and somewhere to her left on up the river is Agnes and the Mangapurua Valley. She takes a deep breath. She does not belong in this town. She turns to face up stream where the sun is now showing above the hills on the eastern side of the river.

The captain opens up the throttle and there is a graunch of metal as the drive shaft meshes with the paddle wheels. Water droplets cascade off as they begin to turn. The ropes are thrown clear and the wharf is receding. There are cries of 'hurrah, goodbye, haere ra, give my love to…' – voices bouncing backward and forward across the lengthening divide of silted water. The farewell is done, and the thud of the steamer blocks out all else.

The *Wairere* threshes out and under the town bridge and past the last of the small houses on the town side that huddle together on the hill. The sun has risen now and its warmth reflects off their windows like farewell kisses touched to a waving hand. Meredith cannot make out Wicksteed Street.

On the outskirts of town, the steamer threshes past tall stately houses set back from the river. The homes of the wealthy town fathers are large wooden affairs where oaks and sycamores cross arms and well-kept lawns run down towards to the river, each with a small paddock on the river bank where a contented house cow looks up or a horse sleeps. A young boy waves and runs barefooted along the river bank, keeping pace. Meredith waves back until the child is blocked from view behind a tangle of debris in a fence strangled by too many floods.

A kererū wood pigeon flies low between tall trees, his fat white chest and purple green wings beating to keep time with the chuffing of the paddle steamer. Meredith counts the beats until he finds a new tree.

At the Upokongaro settlement, a small girl stands on the bank beside an older woman, perhaps her grandmother. Just above them a crooked cottage clings to the bank above the silt line. The old lady holds the child up to wave as the steamer passes by. Meredith waves until the small girl is out of sight, then hugs herself, arms crisscrossed around her body. Not that the day is cold, just to feel a small touch of human warmth for her own departure.

The church spire slips away. The river banks become less populated. The willows are crowding in now. A solitary farmer stands with his horse, an extra pack horse and dogs down on the muddy bank, ready to catch the mail sack and whatever else he had ordered from town. The farmer's face is weathered and patient under a battered wide-brimmed hat.

What would Peter look like now if he'd made it home? Could he be this man? Meredith looks hard at the farmer, trying to remember Peter's features. Creases are starting to show on this man's brow and crinkles are around his eyes, which are accustomed to squinting against the sun: eyes trained to look out for stock or signs of wild pigs across broad gullies.

The steamer noses in and out, crisscrossing to both sides of the river, stopping by a muddy bank or a small outcrop of papa rock. Always the mail sack, sometimes a box of fencing staples and an order of groceries.

A new double bed with a wire woven base is lifted overboard to where a farmer and his small tribe of children are standing on a small rocky outcrop ready to receive it. Someone shouts from the boat. 'Give the Missus a break or you'll wear this one out as well.' Good-natured laughter fills the air from both sides as the steamer pulls away again.

The Māori settlements are even louder, with never just one person on the landing: horses, dogs, children leaping and shouting, nosing their canoes around the steamer. Old Māori women on the deck with black shawls about them remove their pipes and keen a greeting to the cluster on the bank who are calling back. The plump round heads of brown babies peep over the edges of the shawls. Humanity washes on and off the steamer at every stop. Hatrick's boats have become the lifeblood for people of all hues on this river. Always folk standing, watching, waiting for the steamer to arrive. They never turn their backs until the boat has gone out of sight.

Captain Stewart is, above it all, a deft hand on the large wooden wheel. He stands tall, feet widespread, in front of the funnel, which warms his back. A man at ease in this world; a man who has mastered the river.

Mrs Bettjeman joins Meredith at the rail. 'Where're you going, lass? Have you done this trip before?'

Meredith shakes her head. 'You know the river?'

'Aye lass, you're in for a treat. Forty-four rapids between here and Pipiriki. But Kenny Stewart up there, he's a safe hand on the wheel.' Mrs Bettjeman waves up to the captain who tips his hat to them both. 'Are you staying at Pipiriki and going on up the river tomorrow?'

Meredith nods.

'That bit's even better. We have to hold onto our hats on those rapids.' She smiles and waves to the men lounging on the luggage. 'The Māori boys always get us through.'

Meredith smiles. 'Yes, I'm headed for the Andersons' place, up from the Mangapurua Landing.'

'Well, I never – we'll be neighbours. Reg and Mrs Anderson live just up the track a bit from our farm. I'm Mrs Bettjeman.' She beams and shakes Meredith's hand up and down. 'Come and sit with me, dearie, so I can get to know you a wee bit. What brings you up this way?' Nancy Bettjeman leads Meredith to a seat on the deck.

Meredith speaks briefly of her aunt's death and steers the conversation away. 'How long have you been up there?'

Mrs Bettjeman sighs. 'It's a few years now. I met my Fred and married him in wartime. Me, a nursing sister and Fred wounded at Gallipoli. What was I thinking, to fall for him in the hospital? But there you are.' Mrs Bettjeman laughs. 'I do go on a bit.'

Meredith nods her head for Mrs Bettjeman to continue. It suits her best to sit and listen to this talkative little woman.

'Quite a story. We married and with our wee daughter, May, on the way Fred went back to fight in France. He got typhoid and they shipped him back here. Quarantined he was, we weren't even allowed to see him before his boat sailed. Nothing must do. I packed up the baby and followed.'

Mrs Bettjeman crosses her arms and settles into her seat. 'Well, dearie, Fred was set on getting himself a wee sheep station and me never ridden a horse before. Life is never dull up here.' Mrs Bettjeman points to the passing river. 'I remember my first trip up this river, just like you will, dear. Itching to get to our new farm and catch up with Fred on his soldier's settlement block. At first he came up here with just an axe, a camp oven and a piece of canvas to string up. Me and wee May had to stay down south with Fred's family while he built us a hut to live in. As soon as he sent us the word, up we came on the steamer, just like today, everything new and different.'

Meredith looks around the deck of the steamer and the muddy river beyond. Yes, everything is new and different. 'And the valley – what's it like?'

Mrs Bettjeman laughs. 'Not really what I was expecting. Me – a city girl. Fred met us at the landing. We had to walk up in those days straight after the war, and cross the creek on this terrible wire cage, truly frightening and then a whole line of pack horses waiting for us on the other side.' Mrs Bettjeman pats Meredith's arm. 'You'll be pleased to know at least some things have improved. We have a swing bridge now and the horses can come right down to the landing to meet the boat.'

Mrs Bettjeman pauses and shakes her head. 'Well, lassie, if I wasn't already scared enough. Fred's brother took May in front on his horse and Fred led my horse with me up in a saddle for the very first time. Scared nearly to death I was, trying not to look down at the creek way below. I hope you're not scared of heights, dear? The track is better now. Back then, just a goat track with sheer drop-offs down the side into the creek. Would you know it, one of the pack horses rolled off the track in front of us. I thought it was my wee May gone over the side. But lucky for us it was just a horse we lost that day. We did retrieve my luggage though. My silver Tilley lantern, all the way from Scotland, still has a dent in the side to tell the story. You need to be a strong lass in country like this. There's nothing certain about living up here.'

Meredith nods and finds herself relating the longer version of the demise of Aunt Gwyneth to Mrs Bettjeman. The stick banging on the wall, the pillows, the unfortunate sliding down the bed, the final silence.

'So tell me, dearie, is there a young man in this story?'

Meredith pauses. She seldom speaks of Peter. 'Yes, there was, but he died in the war.'

Mrs Bettjeman tuts. 'Are you still keening for him?'

Meredith nods and wipes her nose. She looks down at her hands, knotting her handkerchief around her fingers until the tips tingle and the colour changes to a dull red blue.

'Yes, I still keen for him but it's like he never existed.'

Mrs Bettjeman helps Meredith unwind the handkerchief and hands her another, which is pressed flat and smells of lavender. 'How did it happen, dearie?'

'We were sweethearts. He wrote to me whenever he could, first from Gallipoli and then from France. Always gay letters, full of bravado about his mates and his plans, the things we would do together after the war when he got home.' Meredith raises her eyes to the steep bush-clad hills gliding by the steamer. 'This is the sort of place he hoped to farm after the war.'

Mrs Bettjeman nods and looks at the hills. 'All the Kiwi boys I nursed were the same, keening for a quiet hillside, a dog at his heel and a woman at home with a wee fire lit.'

Meredith starts to crumple Mrs Bettjeman's smooth clean handkerchief in her fist. 'The letters stopped. He was buried in a trench for three days, then shell shocked in hospital. They sent him back to the trenches.' Meredith drops the handkerchief on the deck where oil is sitting on water in a puddle under their seat. She reaches down. The handkerchief is wet and one corner is stained black.

She doesn't tell Mrs Bettjeman about his last letter – the writing wobbly and smudged. Not like him, not his usual strong hand. The letter had said that thinking of her was the only thing keeping him alive in the mud. But even she wasn't enough. Meredith balls up the black, stained handkerchief. One day he'd just put down his gun and walked away from the trenches. They'd put him in jail for a year. Every day Meredith had looked for a letter, but he'd never written again. It was the Allies who shot him, not the enemy. A deserter they called him. No honour, no name on the cenotaph in the place up north where he was raised. No nothing, his family too embarrassed now to even mention his name – just like he never existed.

Meredith wipes at the tear that slides to the dimple in her cheek. Black oil is left marking the spot. She glances up at Mrs Bettjeman. 'He died.'

Mrs Bettjeman folds her arms around Meredith.

'It's like I'm the only one who still believes in him. If I stop loving him, he's gone forever.' Meredith stuffs the handkerchief into her mouth to stop the howl that is halfway up her throat and buries her wet face into Mrs Bettjeman's offered shoulder.

Mrs Bettjeman holds Meredith and pats her on the back, easing the sobs upward and out of her shaking frame. 'You will never stop loving him, dear, but you will move on.'

They rock together on the seat. When the sobs subside, Mrs Bettjeman eases Meredith away, pushes the wisps of hair back behind her ears and extracts the sodden handkerchief from Meredith's mouth.

Mrs Bettjeman rubs the black oil streaks off Meredith's face. 'That's better, dearie. Let me tell you the story of my sister. Her Australian sweetheart was killed on the very last day of the war. It was a terrible thing. But she was brave like you and travelled out here from Scotland to help me with the wee ones and guess what? She settled down with our neighbour, Herb Bolton, right next door to me and Fred. She has a family of her own now. She and Herb and two kids. She's just like you, dearie; she'll never forget her fallen soldier. But life goes on, dear.' Mrs Bettjeman tucks the sorry handkerchief away in her bag and brings out peppermints for them both to suck on.

# Four

# BEANSTALK

Did Jane despise him or maybe, underneath, she cared? Those were the questions that consumed Beanstalk at 3.00am. Not the first time a patient had kept him awake at night, but never like this. The textbooks said that it was commonplace for a patient to fall in love with her doctor. Transference could be usefully employed to therapeutic advantage. But what of the doctor; could the process work in reverse?

He knew he had been a constant source of gossip to the single nurses as they walked the grounds in their white starched uniforms and red capes. Their bright painted mouths reminded him of a row of sparrows, sitting on the guttering, waiting for the next thrown crust. A bachelor doctor was a piece of bread worth fighting over but none of the sparrows caught his eye.

Feverish in his attempt to help Jane, he gave up attending the balls at the Nurses Home, preferring instead to pour over his books. At least he now knew that Jane had insight, and acute observational skills. Her poetry showed that she knew what was going on around her. She even knew his nickname that was used widely by the staff. Of course, it was expected that the patients would address him as Dr Bean, but in this circumstance he was lenient. It seemed that already Jane knew him better than he expected a patient ever would. After all, his friends referred to him as Beanstalk, a name that had stuck since his childhood days. So, he had not reprimanded her. Instead, like a young fool, he had remonstrated with her.

'Please Jane, write in sentences, write what you are thinking, write

for me how you feel, write about your past, your future, write anything.
Dear Jane, please write, anything at all, just for me.'

## Hanging Out Eggshells

Another line of washing hung to dry
Lick your doctor's lips and peg us out
Wire made taut then lifted off the ground
Gunshot gossip cracking in the wind
Riding high our entrails breaking free
Strung up patients cracking in the breeze

Observe me hang my eggshells – fragile things
Each line I write for you – a garbled clue
Pass the pegs – but dare not touch my hand
Egg yolk dripping rotten from my pen
We both inhale – but neither smell the stink
My nose destroyed – and yours too trained to think

You watch me take my fragments from the wire
Writing words – supposed to set me free
Your hope – the wind will one day blow me clean
A sweetened cloth laid fragrant in the sun
But eggshells crack – and I must save each piece
My hope box claims them safe beyond your reach

# Five

# Kate

At breakfast, Ian is standing in the door frame of the kitchen. He has not made me a coffee. His arms are folded. This is not a good sign.

As much as he never likes to be reminded, there are brief moments when I see Ian's father standing there. Just like the day we'd gone with Ginny to sign the foster papers so Ian would never have to go home to his old man again.

Ian's father had been standing in the lawyer's office, tall and formidable, his purple turkey neck tipping over the top of his buttoned-up white shirt. I'd watched his neck tipping over the collar all the way around like a hard-crusted edge on a muffin when you overfill the tin. Ian clung to Ginny's hand and hid his face under her cardigan while I stared at his father's tie in front of the bulging top button. The tie was knotted casually, unaware of its peril. The swollen dam behind the button could boil over at any moment, taking the unsuspecting tie in its wake when the crater lake let go.

Ginny had brushed it away when I had asked her why Mr Dunn was always angry. 'Poor man, never the same after Korea.'

'What happened?'

'I'll tell you when you're older.' She'd shooed me out the door to feed the chooks.

I shake away the thought of Mr Dunn and motion Ian to the couch. Why is he angry with me?

Ian chooses to stand. 'What's all this made-up crap about Eric?'

I drop to the couch and quickly revise the yarn I'd spun for Ursula. It could be the truth. I wince now to think of the things I had said to her.

But typical, she wouldn't leave it be. Bloody Ursula, it's her fault I had to invent the whole sorry little thing.

It's not my fault – sometimes when I close my eyes a warrior woman is there, making it all better than it ever can be. She says things that just come out of my mouth. Things that are not exatly true. What had my warrior woman said to Ursula? It had started out as nearly truthful.

*My friend had wanted me to go with her to a party at the doctor's residence. Intent on catching herself a house surgeon but only wanting someone to walk across the threshold with. And me, intent on leaving from the moment we arrived, out of place, shrunk back against the wall beside the door. My ex-friend and the car keys had joined the throng of pretty things that circled the doctors like moths around self-assured lanterns. Me, I was marooned behind the pushed-back door. I watched the laughter, the banter, the too-loud music, the heads inclining, the touch, the dance, and the stairs leading up to the bedrooms above.*

Ursula likes my 'poor me' stories to end badly, but things never end badly for my warrior woman, when she is wearing a sword and riding high.

*Ouch, a yank on my flowing dark hair. I looked down into molten brown eyes and white smiling teeth. A perfectly formed but tiny man reached up and took my hand. Without a word he led me onto the dance floor and my, could he dance. Later we took a breather and only found one seat. It seemed only natural that he sat across my long awkward knees that were now comfortably hidden beneath his attention. His name was Eric Heng: Cambodian, a delicious chocolate gold.*

But it gets worse. I double wince at the next bit but bloody Ursula had it coming. I just gave her what she wanted to hear. All those times baiting me on the couch, it served her right for poking around in my business, always wanting to know about the Eric thing. So I put her off the scent, white butterflies and all. I just said the things I knew she'd hate to hear.

*I stood for him in the middle of his room and raised my arms above my head. Eric's soft hands moved over me. His tongue explored the bony prominences and hollows as my clothes were peeled away. His hands were everywhere but teasing, refusing to touch the places that matter. Finally he reached for my nipples, lifting them upward off my chest. Rolling them between his fingers as he led me around the room. My eyes were closed. I followed him. He told me I could trust him. I believed Eric. He steered me backward. I felt the bed behind my thighs. He lowered my nipples down. My naked body lay itself back, rocking, waiting, wanting this. Afterwards we lay, legs tangled, bellies touching, breathing together but taking turns, the white belly taking air and expanding forward, the brown belly giving space and then taking the space back as the white belly's breath was gone.*

I could see Ursula didn't believe me so I'd laid it on some more.

*Eric so different from the fumblings of raw-handed farm boys. Rodney from up the road, his first kiss so far down my throat that I'd wanted to gag on the bench seat of his Holden, parked outside the local hall down at the port.*

Ian shows me the formal little message he has taken from Eric's secretary, asking that I rearrange my missed medical appointment with Dr Heng to a time later in the week. Ian's face is flushed, his father's red neck is shouting at me. 'Get out of here with your tired little lies.'

'How dare you.' Bile rises in my throat. I leap to my feet. My words explode in his face. 'How dare you judge me when your whole life's a pathetic lie?' The warrior woman goes for the jugular. 'Ursula parades around here, but no, it's insipid little Ian who goes out into the real world week after week, covering up your big fat lie.'

An angry growl comes from deep in Ian's chest. His neck is mottled purple now. He lunges forward to grab hold of my arm.

I twist away, snatch up my helmet and run. Bloody Ursula; it's all her fault.

Tears blur my vision. The road to Piha winds up amongst shining bush. Too fast I tip backwards and forwards into each curve and cut across blind corners into the path of cars that don't choose to come at that moment.

There's a lookout at the top. I pull in, cut the motor and watch the sea driving endless lines of white caps towards Lion Rock. The lion is not concerned. He divides the waves fairly to the north and south. He's looking out to sea and doesn't bother to watch as each wave hits its head on the beach behind him and disintegrates. There's nothing for me down there. I turn my bike and plunge back down the road into the thick, green bush. I can't go back to our flat. I'm riding on the correct side of the road now. My bike takes me home to the farm.

*ooOOoo*

At West Hills the door is wide open but there's no one in the house. The agitator is threshing around its bowl of dirty water with the last of the men's shearing pants. Other women have moved onto automatic machines, but not Ginny. How would she get three loads out of the same water when the tanks are low in the summer if she had an automatic?

I head down the path to the clothesline where Ginny is hanging out the second load. She's pegging up a tea towel with a picture of a geyser exploding at Rotorua. I pick up a work shirt and hang it up by its tail end. Ginny reaches for the throw that she uses to keep the flies off food in the kitchen. Bang – just like that, she's straight into it.

'Can we talk about this Kingseat thing? John wanted me to wait until you asked, but what if you never do?' She hangs the throw and reaches for a pair of cotton underpants that need new elastic.

I turn away from her and pick up a pair of jeans that are cut off at the knees.

Ginny is looking at me to see if I'm putting my fingers in my ears yet. 'I know you already know. Isn't it normal to want to find out about your birth family?'

'Yes, let's pretend I'm normal.' I draw in my shuddering breath, drape my huge hands over the washing line and look down at Ginny. I hold her gaze for a moment, willing a white cabbage butterfly to pass between us. It's worked other times; we seldom talk about my visits to Eric or the medication I'm supposed to take to help me get to the end of each school term without exploding or taking to my bed with the curtains pulled. I take another breath and pitch for Pollyanna and the glad game we used to play.

'So…you want to tell me that my real mother worked at Kingseat Hospital. It's okay, I know that she was some sort of nurse there.' I turn away from her and pick up a towel that is fraying at one end, hoping she'll back off. But not Ginny.

'It's time we stopped hanging out eggshells.' Ginny spins the line around. 'Your mother didn't work there.'

I'm putting my fingers in my ears and I'm starting to hum. Ginny pulls my fingers away and sits me down on the wooden seat under the peach tree.

'So my mother was a nutter then, as if I didn't already know that?' I scowl at Ginny. There – it's done. The unsaid finally spoken. I look up into the branches where bees are buzzing in the open flowers.

'And Dr Heng – you might want to talk to Eric about this too.'

'Piss on Eric. So you think I'm a nutter too?'

Ginny wipes away a tear. 'You're perfect.' She pulls my head around and makes me look into her eyes. 'You're not a nutter and don't swear.'

'Freak, Mum. What if I turn out to be a monster?'

Ginny pauses for a moment and puts her wash-wrinkled hand on my ponytail, tugging it gently as she always does when she wants me to stop and listen. 'Don't call it a nuthouse. It's a psychiatric hospital and people go there for lots of reasons. We both know you're not a monster.' Ginny gives me a watery smile. 'I've often thought about your birth mother, every milestone in the Plunket book. I still feel sad she never got to meet the woman you grew to be.'

'What about my real father then? Did you ever wonder what sort of creep would get a nutty girl pregnant?'

Ginny doesn't speak for a moment. She stands and gives the rotary line another push. 'Don't judge. Sometimes life just puts us in the wrong place and things happen.' She picks up the old cane washing basket and we head back inside for the last load.

Ginny fishes out the shearing pants from the washing machine tub with a wooden stick and pokes them through the wringer. I pull them out the other side and push each pair under the cold rinse. Ginny leans over the machine, switches off the agitator and we both listen as the constant swish of water dies to a dull hum. I flip the wringer around and fish the first pair of trousers up out of the rinsing tub and watch them disappear through the wringer and down into the cane basket in a wet, flattened heap.

I take a deep breath. 'What happened that day at Kingseat, the day you picked me up?'

Ginny launches into her story. It sounds as if she's rehearsed it a thousand times in her head and now it spills over in a breathless rush.

'The doctor said I wasn't to have any more children after Luke. We didn't talk about it in those days. I suppose I got depressed. I really wanted a little girl. John agreed that we should adopt, so I put our names down.' She pauses and stares for a moment towards the western hills. 'I remember the day they rang to say they had a baby girl that needed a home with a farming family. I remember leaving the washing in the machine and running over to the woolshed to tell John. He had to let the unshorn sheep go so we could drive up to Kingseat to get you.'

She can see I'm clenching my fists to stop my fingers moving up to block my ears. I nod for her to continue. She gabbles on. 'We drove to Kingseat Hospital. I remember those big palms all the way down the long drive and those tall brick buildings standing all around. Right at the end of the drive was the reception building. One of the patients was standing on the lawn with a hose, watering the grass in the rain. Funny what you remember. It was raining hard and him standing there, the rain running down off his wet hair and he's spraying water all over the place.'

'Frick, the loony watering the lawn.'

Ginny stops and leans over the back of the machine to flick on the water pump to empty the bowl. I pull the plug and let the tub water go. Ginny removes the agitator blade and swishes the last of the dirty water out of the bowl, then uses a hose to swill some fresh water around while the pump screams a high-pitched wail. Job done, she silences the pump, picks up the last basket of washing and we head back out to the line.

We both begin to hang out the dripping work pants.

I speak through gritted teeth. 'What fricken happened next?'

'We parked the car and went into the reception. A woman at the desk, she rang out for us. I heard her saying into the phone, 'Can Beanstalk please come to reception?' I always remember that. Weird, isn't it?' Ginny reaches into her apron for more pegs. 'This man walks in and introduces himself as Dr Jack Bean. I kept wondering if he was Jack in the Beanstalk. You know, in uncertain moments you have to hold your breath in case you laugh hysterically at the wrong thing. It was a psychiatric hospital, after all.'

I grab the pegs she's holding out and pull the last pair of trousers out of the washing basket. 'Fudge, Mum, get on with it. What next?'

'What next? It's a long time ago.' She bends to pick up some pegs that have dropped on the grass under the clothesline.

'What next, Mum?'

Ginny squints at the western hills again and shudders. 'I remember John and I being led down a corridor with shut doors on both sides.

They showed us into this dreary little room. I remember looking around while we waited. There was a big lock on the door, grey walls and a high looming ceiling, nothing on the walls except layers of chipped paint and a high window we couldn't see out of. That man Dr Bean, had all these big keys hanging off his belt. It gave me the heebie jeebies. I couldn't concentrate on what he was saying to John.'

'What next?'

'Well, we signed the papers and there you were, all wrapped up in a hospital blanket. You had a shock of white blonde hair, big green eyes and the longest blonde eyelashes I'd ever seen on a baby. So alert and looking at me. I just sat there and gazed down and you just stared straight back up. It was like I had been waiting for you all my life.'

Ginny picks up the empty basket and squeezes my arm. 'You were good for me. No more pills, I came right after that.'

'And that's it?'

'Well, fairly much. While I was fussing with you, that man Jack Bean, turns out he was the doctor looking after your birth mother. He told John that you were from a farming family where there had been a house burnt to the ground. We weren't told any names of course, but my friend Mary from nursing days helped us work it out. She lived down Wanganui way and she remembered reading about the incident in her local paper. A funeral at Jerusalem for a woman, some terrible fire, and her daughter, Jane, put into the hospital. We figured out that must have been your grandmother. Her name was Meredith, so that's why we called you Kate Meredith Whyte.'

Ginny drops the basket and plaits my ponytail through her fingers just the way she did when I was little.

'So why Kate *Meredith* Whyte? Why not Kate *Jane* Whyte?' I'm wrenching my hair out of her reach and spin around to glare down at my little mother. 'Why didn't you name me after Jane the nutter?

Ginny hands me the washing basket and turns her back to walk to the house. 'We just liked the name Meredith better. It seemed too sad somehow to call you Jane. You know, plain Jane. John liked Meredith best. We thought you might want to know all this one day. We've been waiting for you to ask. It's not that we didn't want you to know, it's just that we wanted you to be ready.'

Am I ready? Am I ready for this? Will I ever be ready for this? I'm reaching to put my fingers into my ears; my mouth is forming an oval shape.

Ginny turns back and reaches for my elbow, I twist out of her grasp. 'Why would I want to find a mother who vetoed herself off my birth certificate and left my father's name blank.'

Ginny stares at me for a moment and holds me while we both cry. Then she steadies herself as farming folk do and takes a big breath. 'Come inside. I want to show you something.' She dumps the basket in the washhouse and strides on down the passage to the best sitting room that we hardly ever use. I follow her over to the mantelpiece.

'Did I tell you, I saw a kōtuku in the winter? I rode out to the back paddock to open the gate and help John turn a mob of hoggets through. You know the bit where it drops down to the estuary?' Ginny picks up a framed photo off the mantelpiece: a family photo with all the Whytes standing in a neat, tight, brown-headed row and me at fifteen, albino blonde and towering above them all. In the photo I'm scowling at the camera, chin tucked down between my drooping shoulders.

Ginny smiles at the photo and rubs the dust off it. 'I know you hate this photo, but the kōtuku reminded me of you. The Whytes are here like a row of whio ducks dabbling around on our own little creek and you are a kōtuku, a splendid white heron that hasn't found its proper lagoon yet.' Ginny gives it a final polish with the sleeve of her cardigan and puts the photo carefully back in its place. 'One day you will be magnificent, mark my words you will.'

I put my fingers in my throat and pretend to gag.

She turns away. It's time to get the lunch on. The men will be in at twelve on the dot. Ginny heats yesterday's bacon bone soup and adds more water, a leek from the garden and another handful of pearl barley to make it go further. I put the cloth on the table, cut bread, open sardines, and make tea in the big brown pot.

John scrubs his hands in the washhouse tub, lathering the soap up to his elbows and then washes the lanolin away. 'Can you give us a hand after lunch? We need a wool girl who can sweep, keep the sheep up to us in the shed and take a mob away.'

I nod.

He rubs his forearms on a towel and smiles. 'We'll kick this crutching business into touch in a couple of days if you can help us out.'

And the magnificent kōtuku gets on with it. The hum of the shearing plant, the bang of the waddy stick on the grating and the tin wall of the shed, the yap of the young huntaway. Any noise; it all helps. I sweep and pick up the dags with two wooden planks off the side of an apple box, shiny green now with lanolin and shit. Over and over I pick up the dags, a mindless hot job repeated again and again to yet another song on the radio shouted out over the roar of the machines between ad jingles. I sweep in time and even start to mouth the words. 'Trust British Paints...'

Sweat drips off the singlets and bare shoulders of the shearers who stagger, still hunched, into the catching pen to pull out the next old ewe. The pen gate glances off the body of each sheep and slams shut. Each fat ewe is tipped up, legs parted, pink tits uppermost, then a fist into the side of the gut to hitch her leg enough for the shearer to carve away the sloppy green dags from around her tail. Over and over, the ritual is done, the mob is crutched.

*Harr lay lu yar.* Kingseat is pushed back to where it can be contained inside a small kernel at the back of my skull. Same thing next day. I'm keen to help. Up early for another big muster, a long day in the shed, the crutching cut out and the sheep taken away. A celebration, everyone showered up, beers on the deck while Ginny adds butter and mashes potatoes for the topping on the shepherd's pie.

The phone on the wall rings three shorts. Ginny runs to answer.

She listens without speaking. 'She's right here. I'll put her on.' Ginny gestures, her hand over the receiver. 'It's the hospital.'

I take the phone from Ginny; the smile is gone from her face. I know it's about Ursula. I listen and hold in my sobs until they hang up and it's just the beeping that I hear. I turn to Ginny. 'It's all my fault.'

Ginny puts her arms around me.

'She went to work as Ursula instead of Ian.' I sob against Ginny's apron. 'Some mongrels were waiting for her in the carpark on her way home. Ursula is asking for me.'

Ginny raises my face and wipes away the tears. 'Shall I come too?'

I shake my head. 'Best it's just me. We had words.'

Ten minutes later the whio ducks line the deck and watch as the kōtuku's taillight snakes away down the driveway. Back on the tar-seal I wind the bike up. The white line flickers and then blurs, cutting a line across each corner, but tonight I must stay on my own side of the road. Ursula needs me.

# Six

# Beanstalk

Embarrassing to admit, with him being a doctor, but Beanstalk hadn't noticed the tight drum forming until the nurses mentioned it. After he was told, he had berated himself. How dumb could he have been? But he was not used to watching for the gentle swell of breasts and the belly button beginning to protrude. Not so obvious under loose hospital garb but obvious enough when it was pointed out to him by the nurses and he found himself drawn to look closely, more often than he should. He may have been a doctor, a psychiatrist by training, used to looking out for the highs and lows of order within disorder, but he'd always been a bachelor, unused to the vagaries of women who don't act like patients. Beanstalk was shocked at his need to look often, shocked at the pleasure he took, watching this developing bud.

The adoption was prearranged. The next of kin, a Mrs Dougherty, replied to his letter and sent back the signed form. Mrs Dougherty vetoed the mother's details and said she didn't know who the father was. The space on the form would be left blank. The social worker met with Beanstalk and together they agreed that a farming family would be best for the baby. Was this ever discussed with Jane? Why hadn't Beanstalk talked about this with Jane on a quiet day out on the tidal creek? He never did, and it haunts him still.

The nurses called the midwife when it was Jane's time. They fully sedated her in anticipation. The baby was gone before she came around and all this was never spoken of with Jane. Was it best practice back then, never to consult the patient? Beanstalk still thinks about these things at

3.00am when he stares up at the ceiling of his bach.

The pregnancy never discussed. He had wondered at the time, did she even understand she was carrying a child? Him, a grown man, unable to discuss a flower growing to full bloom within a silent woman.

After the baby had gone, he talked to her of other things, but never of the tiny blonde-headed baby girl, who was carried away in a battered carrycot by a kind farming couple. Beanstalk lay there awake at night and cursed the coward in him still.

Beanstalk resumed walking and rowing Jane on the tidal creek. He would hold Jane's hand but it wasn't the same. He'd made another mistake and after that the water was only ever muddy brown. Jane seemed to want to goad him now. He was reminded of his mistake ever after when he looked at the green eyes behind the monster mask. And he, still desperate. 'Please, Jane, how can I please you?'

No response.

Beanstalk became desperate for Jane to resume writing and, of course, she did. But her next poem still wrenches at his head and his heart. She'd handed Beanstalk the notebook and watched as he read. Afterwards, he stood there as mute as she was, couldn't look her in the eye. There were no words he could say to comfort her.

Over the years his thoughts had often returned to the moment he'd first read this poem. He'd never found the right words – just a share of her deep aching for what could never be.

## Stolen Treasure

Stretch marks on my belly
Tattooed on white parchment
My fingers run blind to find
The lines that intersect
But the treasure is gone
Stolen from this tomb

Only the mummy remains
Embalmed in blood-stained rags
The cord has rotted away

Stretch marks on my belly
Telling tales of the cross
I carry on my shoulder
A bridge from nowhere
To somewhere out there
Nothing remains
But the mummy left behind
I wear a death mask
The bridge will rot away

Stretch marks on my belly
Cold fingers tap Morse
Searching for my treasure
A bloodied red ruby
Fool's gold winking hope
But all that shines is gone
New wounds leak from old scars
Angry blisters that can't heal
This mummy is rotting away

# Seven

# Meredith

The *Wairere* noses into Jerusalem. A black-clad nun stands on the landing surrounded by a mix of dark- and fair-skinned children, dressed alike in smocks and aprons. Small hands reach up, all eager to be the one to carry the mail bag and stores that are handed down from the steamer. Meredith can make out the buildings of the marae and the church set on a ledge with hills rising up behind. The steeple faces the river like a pair of praying hands clasped together with fingertips facing skyward. The convent is tucked in alongside, a simple barn-shaped building, two stories high. Below the convent is an orchard, heavy with summer fruit, wooden props in place to stop the branches on the peach trees breaking.

Mrs Bettjeman stands at the rail. She waves a greeting to the nun and speaks to Meredith of Sister Mary Aubert, the plucky little nun who had first ridden her pony up the native tracks before even Hatrick had boats on the river. Mother Aubert had settled in Jerusalem and established a convent and a mission school. Once Mr Hatrick started bringing tourists up the river, the little nun made money for her community selling medicinal potions and cherries from the convent orchard. Mother Aubert was long dead and gone now, but her work continued on in this quiet place.

The nun gathers up the children and her parcels. They wave to Meredith as the paddle steamer pulls away.

Finally, a turn in the river and there up ahead on the right bank is Pipiriki House, a handsome wooden building, tall and very broad, squatting above the river. Meredith can see folk standing along the balcony that wraps around the upper storey.

A young Adonis with laughing white teeth is flexing a glorious brown torso under his unbuttoned shirt and rolled-up sleeves. He stands astride the flat deck dray catching the suitcases one by one as they are thrown down from the riverboat.

Meredith catches her breath and watches the late afternoon sun drip down off the young man's breast bone onto hard muscle as he turns backward and forward with the luggage. The glistening beads lodge in the line of black hair that shows below his belly button. His pants are drawn in to sit on his hips with plaited twine. She looks away.

The old mare attached to the dray is unmoved by this scene. She waits with statue patience, one foot tipped up showing her unshod foot. She will wake, when needed, to pull the loaded dray of luggage up to the hotel.

The passengers step down off the steamer. Meredith stands wide-gaited for a moment until her feet adjust to the land. She joins Mrs Bettjeman and the passengers who laugh and joke as they walk up the track that zig-zags up from the silted river bank, under the rowan trees heavy with red berries. The last of the sun is on their backs before it dips down over the hills on the far side of the river.

Mrs Bettjeman puffs up the hill. 'This hotel is not what it was a few years ago but at least they do cook a good mutton stew and the sheets on the bed are clean. Such fun to have electric lights, lass, and hot water at your whim for a good wee bath. We don't have these things up our valley.'

Meredith lies in bed that night listening to a morepork and the distant singing from the Maori quarters. Maybe this river is already creeping into her blood. She says good night to Peter and pulls the crisp white sheets up over both of their heads.

*ooOOoo*

At 5:00am the *Ongarue* is puffing and ready to go. Meredith watches Pipiriki slip away downstream into the river mist. There's a new crew. Mrs Bettjeman introduces Meredith to Jumbo the deckhand. His deep voice reverberates off the steep rock walls of the river overhung with flax and toitoi as he sings above the throb of the engine. Bush-clad cliffs hang above the river on both sides now, forming a narrow green corridor with the water gushing towards the smaller steamer which takes on the upper reaches of the river.

At the bottom of some rapids a Māori boy fishes out the wire rope that is floating there ready to winch the boat up. In other places he leaps off the side with the end of a wire rope unwinding in his grasp as he splashes up the river, sometimes running over rocks, sometimes swimming to attach his end to a steel peg driven hard into the cliff at the top of the rapids. The winch engages and the little boat is pulled up over the white, broken water.

Paranui is the next stop. The smoke and smells of the native village waft down as the mail bags, cream cans and supplies are endlessly tossed on and off, more keening and singing as the boat pulls away.

Around another corner stands a solitary farmer on a small muddy outcrop. Rough and unshaven, he licks his chapped lips ready to catch his mail bag and a full bottle of whisky flying end for end over the water divide as the boat pulls away. They watch him take the cap off the bottle and raise it to his mouth with a trembling hand.

'Poor sod.' Mrs Bettjeman shakes her head. She explains to Meredith how Hatrick's boats are only licensed to sell grog once their boats are moving on the river. A lonely man who needs a drink never misses the catch of a full bottle tossed from the moving riverboat.

Jumbo pours out hot drinks, a mug of the blackest tea Meredith has ever seen, topped up with a generous dollop of condensed milk. She warms her hands on the dented enamel mug and watches the wet, shining bush slip past her. Peter is everywhere here.

Mid-morning, Mrs Bettjeman is nudging her as they come around the last bend before their valley. The Mangapurua Landing is just a slab of grey papa rock on the righthand bank of the river. The Māori boys leap ashore and place a plank across to the landing. They hold each end of a long mānuka stick to serve as a handrail. Meredith feels like the queen as she walks down the plank to the landing. She is not used to the careful attention of handsome men. Her leather suitcase comes hurtling after her to be caught and placed at her feet. Then more stores and luggage, several men helping catch the parcels. Meredith searches their faces. This one must be Fred Bettjeman gathering up Mrs Bettjeman's shopping, and this one must be Reg. Meredith steps forward to shake the warm, calloused hand of a lanky farmer with a ready smile.

'Nice to meet you, Miss Innes.' Reg picks up Meredith's suitcase, perches it on his shoulder and they set off up the rock.

Meredith waves to Mrs Bettjeman, says a quick hello to Fred and hurries up the pathway off the riverbank after Reg's long-legged farmer's gait.

'My Agnes is looking forward to having you. It's pretty lonely for her up here.' Reg's steady uphill cadence is not broken to puff or rest; this man is hardened to uphill walking under a load.

Meredith can only nod her head and concentrate on her breath.

'Meet Ginger. Do you ride? She's a quiet thing.' Reg links his hands and Meredith is legged up onto the chestnut mare's broad back. He turns to his own mount when he sees that she is comfortable on a horse.

Meredith's feet slide easily into the stirrups. Just like putting on an old coat and finding something you thought you'd lost still inside the pocket. Meredith pats Ginger's solid neck. She hasn't been on a horse since 1918. The flu epidemic had come to the farm that year. Meredith had slowly burnt the pillows and buried first her only brother, then her mother and her father as well. When it was over, the farm owner had wanted her gone at once. He'd paid her a small sum for their horses and burnt the rest of the family's effects once Meredith had left with the same small suitcase that Reg is now swinging up onto his horse.

Aunt Gwyneth was sympathetic, 'but just for a few months, until you find your feet.' But of course, Aunt Gwyneth had taken to her bed and Meredith had stayed, fourteen long years of plumping pillows.

Reg balances her suitcase across his saddle and Meredith and Ginger plod along behind him up through bush and past an abandoned farm, the fences falling over and the native bush claiming back the front paddock.

'The Morgans' old place. They've pulled the plug.' Reg indicates a small pathway leading away from the main track. 'Lots of places like that up here now. Hope you've a good head for heights.'

He clatters his own horse, Paddy, over a rough swing bridge built from hand-split timbers and held together with wire ropes each made from twisted number eight. The bridge sways and shudders under the weight of man and horse. Far below Meredith can see a bush-clad stream sliding under the bridge. Ginger follows across with an easy gait.

As they ride, Reg gives Meredith a run-down on the settlers. Phil Bennett's place is on the right: a well-maintained cottage and outbuildings behind a fence of close nailed palings. There is smoke in the chimney.

Following the creek, Reg rides out onto a narrow ribbon of pathway across the centre of a huge, papa rock cliff face with a vertical drop from the pathway down to the creek way below. He pulls up and points to the rocky outcrop below them on the opposite side.

'Welcome to Battleship Bluff. See the bow of the boat down there?' Reg pivots in his saddle to point out how the river turns sharply around a rough rocky outcrop of papa far below them on the other bank. Yes, from above it does look like the bow of a sleek, grey battleship. Reg cartwheels his arms across the vista. 'We even have our own scenic attractions but no tourists to enjoy them, unless we count you.' He laughs as they continue on up the track.

Next is the Mowats' place. Reg tells her about his friend Pat Mowat who lives here with his mother and sister Mary in this small shingle-fronted cottage. There is movement of the curtains and a hand waves from the kitchen window. Then further on, more derelict homesteads.

'Funny outfit this. Here we're moving in just as most of the folk are leaving. Nine settlers gone in the last year. It's not like we've scared them off. Just Depression times, no money in wool. Poor buggers can't pay the lease and the stores won't give them any more tick. Some folk just pack their traps and call it quits. It's a bit different for me and Agnes. We only came up here last year. We had nothing when we came, so you could say we have nothing much to lose.'

They ride on past more bluffs, with slips and drop-offs creating sheer walls of white-grey papa rock with a settler's homestead here and there carved out on the flats between the bluffs, high above the creek. He points out the Bettjemans' place on the right, the house with multiple additions and the garden shipshape. The brick chimney is puffing her welcome. Then a school house that the settlers have converted from an abandoned hut where the Testers used to live.

A small girl with brilliant red hair waves out as they pass the next farm. Reg tips his hat and they ride on. 'That youngest McDonald lass is a corker kid. Just started school with our Myra. Four girls in the family and no sons. Her older sisters work on the farm doing all the jobs you'd expect from young blokes. Some folk don't agree with it, but up here, what can you do? If I was Hugh McDonald, I'd be the same. They're all great girls.'

They wind on up the hill and get to the Andersons' place. Reg reins Paddy in and points out the boundaries of his leased block. 'Abandoned when we got here, we've worked like billy-o. No stock to start with, just took some grazers for Pat Mowat and I got some work with the road gang. We saved and scraped together five pounds to ride out to Raetihi and buy a hundred head of sheep. I drove them home, a motley bunch, but up here they need to be hardy. I got a couple of old rams off Fred Bettjeman and hey presto, now we're in the sheep business. We're doing okay.'

Meredith looks down and sees a makeshift wooden hut with new shingles showing on a recent lean-to addition. Could this be Agnes? A lean woman is running up the hill to meet them, a toddler in her arms and two older children trailing behind. The children hang back and watch from a safe distance as their mother hugs Meredith.

Agnes holds her for a moment at arm's length and takes a good look. 'Not bad for a woman who has spent all these years chained to her aunt's deathbed. We'll get some sunshine into those peaky cheeks, won't we, Myra?'

Five-year-old Myra nods. She reaches out for Meredith's hand and leads her down to the house. Young John also nods a greeting. He is seven and manfully takes the suitcase from Reg. Agnes follows along with Michael squirming in her arms.

'Righty-ho, see you later.' Reg whistles for his dogs and is gone up the hill.

'And this is your room.' Myra leads Meredith into the small wooden hut that is out the back door and a few steps down the outhouse pathway lined with verbena. Agnes has been working her green fingers and already young rose cuttings were getting away in the small garden by the door. Inside the whare, it's dark with no windows. The only light comes from the open door. Meredith can make out a bed in the corner, built with a timber frame and a jute wool sack stapled across under the kapok mattress. By the bed is a butter box with a candle placed on top. Reg has built a set of open shelves and Agnes has made a curtain to pull across the front out of a flour sack stencilled with bright yellow daffodils and red roses. On the floor a wool sack has been opened out for a mat and also stencilled right around the edge to match the curtain.

Myra points to the curtain and the mat. 'I helped Mum do that with a potato and I fixed up the flowers for you as well.'

'Thank you.' Meredith picks up the jar and smiles as she sniffs the honeysuckle. No one had ever thought to pick her flowers before.

Myra grins and watches as Meredith opens her leather case and puts her few clothes up onto the shelf behind the curtain. She makes up the bed with her new sheets and places her books by the bed, a Bible, the photo album and her only childhood book that Meredith's mother ever read to her, so long ago.

Myra pounces on the book and turns the pages to see the illustrations. Meredith sits down beside her and together they look at the pictures. There are the Darling children: Wendy, John and Michael, flying around the nursery and here the Lost Boys in Neverland are building a house for the Wendy bird. The menacing Hook with his crew on the Jolly Roger and of course the marvellous Peter Pan himself.

Myra looks up with shining eyes. 'Can I be Wendy? My brothers are John and Michael already. Can you read this book to us, please, please?'

Meredith looks down into the big eyes of the small girl; she pulls her close and feels the warmth of her excitement. 'Of course, I will read it to you.' She clears her throat to begin the story of Peter Pan and Wendy.

*ooOOoo*

It's still dark when Meredith hears Reg whistle to his dogs as he heads out to the horse paddock. She sets her door ajar so she can see, dresses quickly in a cotton smock and runs across to Agnes' house. A bucket of milk is on the table, still warm from the cow. Agnes dishes up plates of porridge from a blackened camp oven, which she has lifted off the fire.

'The teapot's hot. How's that bed?' Agnes dips some milk off the top of the bucket onto the porridge and hands a plate to Meredith.

'Slept like a top. Must be something in the air up here?'

Agnes grins. 'That's the secret; there's not much in the air up here. At least it gives us space to think: pure and simple clean air and hard work.'

Meredith nods her head and takes up a spoon and digs into her porridge.

'Rise and shine.' Agnes pulls the curtain back from the doorway to the children's bedroom. The tousled heads of John and Myra emerge and they're soon up at the table eating porridge while Agnes bustles about cutting yesterday's loaf and slicing cold meat for school lunches. Then she's mixing potato yeast into flour to start rising a new loaf in the biggest camp oven, which is warming by the fire.

Myra catches Meredith's eye. 'Can we read some more of *Peter Pan* now, please, please?'

'Away with you, girl. It's time to get to school. Get a move on.' Agnes stamps her foot. 'Now, the pair of you.'

The barefooted children stuff the sandwiches wrapped in a *Weekly News* sheet into their school satchels and head for the door. 'Bye, Mum.

Bye, Miss Innes. Can we call you Meredith?' The door slams shut and they listen as the laughter of the running children fades away.

Agnes sighs and pours herself a cup of tea. 'Let's sit and have a proper cup before we do the washing up.' She hangs a kerosene tin of water on a hook over the fire to heat.

Meredith joins Agnes. They sit on the front step and look down the valley, watching the steep sides emerge from the morning mist. The hill opposite is ragged with burnt stumps and newly planted grass between the slips, which run off the face of ridges, scarring deeply into new gullies.

'Reg did that paddock.' Agnes points proudly. 'Got a decent burn on, good strike with the grass seed. Now we just need to keep the wild pigs off. Damn pigs can root a paddock over in two shakes. Up here we get sick of eating pork but if we stopped killing pigs, we'd be done for.'

Meredith nods. She looks across at the raw hillside, scoured with slips and fresh rooting, just a slight tinge of green in patches amongst the burnt stumps. Its ugliness makes her shudder.

Michael calls from his cot and the water for the dishes is hot. They both go back inside and the work begins.

The days meld together as Meredith settles into the rhythm of the place. Monday is for washing: hauling kerosene tins of water up from the creek to hang over an outdoor fire in a frame that Reg has built out the back. Scrubbing each load in the tin bath, then into the kerosene tin to bubble over the fire, bobbing the clothes under with a long stick before fishing each item out. The buckets of wet washing are then lugged back to the bench, pushed and pulled through the hand wringer and finally hung out onto the clothesline. It's a long one-wire affair, held up in the middle with a prop stick cut from a tawa pole, tall enough to stop the sheets dragging in the mud.

Tuesday is a day for cooking: always the daily bread but cakes and pikelets as well and jam to make, stirring the biggest pot over the fire, not stopping for a second, sugar and plums too precious to let the bottom burn, red hot cheeks and sweat pouring down her front, stirring until

Meredith's arms ache, testing the set of the jam in a saucer until it forms a skin on top, tipping the scalding jam out into beer bottles, which have been cut down into jars with a hot wire, brown paper pasted on top, the sparkling jewels put up on the shelf as a measure of their work.

Wednesday in the garden: hoeing up the rows of potatoes, crumbling off the dirt and stowing them in a hessian sack in the corner of Meredith's hut. There is cutting and storing pumpkins, picking the last of the runner beans, preparing the ground now for winter cabbage, sowing more silverbeet seed, planting cuttings, collecting seed for next summer's flowers and always weeds to pull. Softening the stark wooden house, making it homely, Meredith tills a small patch in front of her whare and sows the handful of Flanders poppies she has brought with her to the valley.

Thursday is for sewing and mending on the old treadle: patching ripped trousers, cutting down Reg's worn out shirt for John, unpicking an old woollen skirt to make winter overalls for Michael. Meredith cuts out a dress for Myra from a clean flour sack and begins to draw up smocking threads ready to embroider a front panel to sew in below the yoke. Agnes writes letters in anticipation of the mailman coming by the next day. Meredith writes no letters. She can't think of anyone out there in the wider world who would care enough to write back.

Friday, they clean the house from top to bottom: hanging out the mats to beat on the clothesline, more cooking, more gardening, nappies to deal with every day, stirring up the mutton fat and caustic soda in a kerosene tin over the fire to make soap.

Saturday there is more cooking and towards evening the wooden bathtub is filled. First children, and then the adults each take their turn. There is a clean set of clothes for everyone. Meredith doesn't join in this ritual. She lugs a kerosene tin of hot water, the tin bath and a small billy-can out to her whare. She strips naked and steps into the small tin bath, first soaping up and then tipping over a billy full of water that is cooling fast and makes her shiver.

Sunday, even Reg stays home for most of the day. A day to rest, to read, and take the kids for a swim down in the creek. Reg sits in a huge wooden seat he has made under the peach tree. He smokes a pipe and takes a sample of Agnes' fine Luisa plum wine. The weeks go by.

In the evening, Myra and John beat a path to Meredith's whare after dinner to hear her read from *Peter Pan*. Agnes comes too and brings out her knitting. They perch together on Meredith's bed with the book on their laps.

'Did you know I've met Captain Hook?' Myra turns her big eyes from Meredith to her mother.

Agnes frowns at Myra. 'Nonsense, child.'

'But what about Mr Stanley?'

'Now, Myra, stop this wild talk. Mr Stanley never made the rank of captain in the war and he certainly isn't Captain Hook now.'

'I know, Mum, but he does have a hook.'

'Rubbish, girl. The poor man had half his hand blown off in the war. It's hardly a hook: just his thumb and first finger gone. He still has three good fingers.'

'But his fingers do curl around a bit like a hook and he's scary just like Captain Hook.'

'Codswallop, girl. Time for you two kids to be getting back to the house.'

Agnes shoos Myra and John out the door and then turns back to Meredith. 'Now there's a thought. We do have a dance coming up at the Bettjemans' homestead and I must introduce you to Mr Stanley. While he does have a hand that looks a bit like a hook, that hardly qualifies him as scary.' Agnes rubs her hands together. 'Now there's a man who could do with a good wife.'

That night Meredith wakes with a start, disturbed by the ticking of the crocodile. Peter is there in the shadows but where is Hook? She opens her arms to Peter and pulls him in close. It's just a morepork and maybe a kiwi out there in the dark, breaking the silence in the valley.

*ooOOoo*

Meredith has already ironed her best white shirt. She sits on a chair at the kitchen table, her mouth full of pins. The day of the dance has arrived. Agnes stands on top of the table wearing her new party dress, unpicked and remodelled from an old-fashioned garment with a floor-length taffeta skirt. There's just the bottom left to sew. Meredith holds a wooden spoon against the hem line in place of a measuring stick and tugs at the fabric as Agnes turns around to make a final check that the pins are evenly placed.

Reg puts his head around the door and runs his eye over the new calf-length dress with wide lapels and a pencil-shaped skirt. He winks at Agnes. 'That's my girl. You still scrub up well, for an old thing.'

'Huh.' Agnes sweeps her new dress out of Meredith's grasp and twirls around for him to see. 'Off with you, but remember to come home to milk that cow – don't start on that beer barrel too early.' She turns back to Meredith. 'Men.' She's laughing and shaking her head as Reg closes the door.

He's heading down to the Bettjemans' place to help sweep out the woolshed, move the press and polish up the dance floor. Then the men will put up punga fronds as decoration and set up a convenience over the grating. Just a kerosene tin with both ends cut out stood on end in a catching pen, with a wobbly toilet seat on top.

Meredith doesn't reply; her mouth is still full of pins. 'Stand up straight.' She motions to Agnes and then sits down to hand sew the hem. Then it's back to the baking. There's still sandwiches to make and a bucket of cream to whip. Meredith puts on her apron and stirs up the fire. There will be two suppers: one at eleven and then another at three in the morning.

'Our dances always go all night.' Agnes tips a chocolate cake out of the camp oven. 'It's not safe to ride home around the bluffs until it gets light, so everyone stays till daybreak.'

*ooOOoo*

First supper is done and cleared away. By midnight the dancing is in full swing. The beer barrel is set up in a catching pen and doled out to the men sparingly between dances. Most of the children have gone to sleep, draped over their mothers' knees and then carried and laid out on clean wool sacks and coats in the 'dressing room', just another area of the pens roped off with tarpaulins.

The accordion is running hot. Reg plays lilting waltzes and Pat Mowat livens it up a bit with a four-step, foxtrot and then a rousing one-step.

Earlier in the evening, Myra and her young friend, Muriel McDonald, had taken turns dancing with whichever father wasn't playing the accordion but now both girls are fast asleep.

Hugh McDonald is settling in now with some more Scottish square dance sets. Pat Mowat called the moves: 'Line up, face the press, swing your partners, basket weave, promenade two by two, swing your partners, line up and face the beer barrel.'[1]

Meredith does not dance. She stands by the wall, just outside the cast of the kerosene lamp.

Agnes catches her hand and pulls her forward. 'Come on you. It's everyone in for the Gay Gordons.'

Meredith takes her place with the other women on the outside of the circle. 'Promenade forward, promenade back, swing your partner, promenade forward, step away, step forward to meet your new partner, swing your partner.'

Each new man steps up. Some of the men press the small of her back, pulling her breasts in hard against their chest, holding her close, bustling through the moves. Others are smooth and gentlemanly, maintaining a modest six inches between her chin and their chest. Others are a little

---

1 Agnes Anderson's recollection of the square dance call at woolshed dances in the Mangapurua Valley. See Arthur Bates, *A Pictorial History of the Wanganui River* (2nd ed.) (Wanganui: Wanganui Newspapers Ltd, 1986).

drunk and energetic, listing in the turns as they spin Meredith around against their counterweight. Young boys reach up and dance at arm's length.

And this must be James Stanley. A bearded man offers his hook. Meredith's hand fits neatly into the space where his thumb and first finger once were. The scar is soft under her fingers but the hook made up of the outside three fingers is gripping her hand firmly in the turns and around they go. He doesn't hold her close. He doesn't meet her eye either. As he lets Meredith go, he is staring into the space over her right shoulder. He is tall and trim, wide-set shoulders, a good head of hair flowing down over his collar, not recently cut. He offers his hook to the next woman in the circle, old Mrs Mowat. He swings her carefully around as a gentleman should.

How would Peter have danced with Mrs Mowat? Definitely like a gentleman. Meredith retires again to the wall when the music stops.

At the last supper Agnes pushes Meredith forward. 'Mr Stanley, have you met my friend, Miss Innes?'

His head inclines forward and piercing eyes search Meredith's face. What is he looking for? His eyes flick away.

'Obviously we have danced but no, we haven't met.' The hook and his good hand reach out to grasp both of Meredith's hands. 'I'm James Stanley.' His head inclines again but he doesn't smile.

At 5.00am, for the last hour before daylight, everyone settles around on the wool bales and a few kitchen chairs for a singalong, while the accordion plays on. As it gets light, hands are linked, and the strains of *Auld Lang Syne* join the dawn chorus as the birds outside start up for the new day.

Children still sleeping are lifted up onto horses or into traps. Best clothes are stuffed into saddlebags and *Auld Lang Syne* is sung again as the settlers plod out onto the track. James Stanley turns his horse left down the track. Meredith turns right up the valley and rides Ginger home to the Andersons' place.

*ooOOoo*

*Dear Miss Innes,*

*It was my pleasure to make your acquaintance at our recent dance. I understand from Reg that you are a single woman without encumbrances. It is my wish to get to know you further with a view to possible marriage. Reg has suggested that I would come to dinner on Saturday next. I look forward to this occasion.*

*Yours sincerely,*
*James Stanley*

*ooOOoo*

*Dear Miss Innes,*

*At dinner, while I spoke almost exclusively to Reg, I did however have time to observe you and approved of your sober habits and pleasing ways. I look forward to seeing you again. Mrs Anderson, as you know, has issued me with a further invitation to dinner. I look forward to this occasion. If the weather is not inclement, I also look forward to walking out with you for a ½ mile on my way home.*

*Yours sincerely,*
*James Stanley*

*ooOOoo*

Agnes has cooked the wild roast pork to perfection, the potatoes are crisp and there is even apple sauce and gravy with jam roly-poly for afters. Meredith hushes the children and clears away the dishes while Reg and

James talk about breeding sheep. The hook is mesmerising as it moves around above the table. Myra watches its every move.

Meredith raises her finger to her lips to quiet Myra's urgent eyes and bursting question as the hook circles above the little girl's head. 'Shush, later, I will tell you later.'

As James puts on his hat, he is still talking to Reg. Agnes waves for Meredith to get her coat. 'Meredith will walk with you, Mr Stanley?'

James Stanley starts, and turns to Agnes. 'As you think, Mrs Anderson. Am I to settle this thing?'

Meredith returns with her coat to see Agnes nodding and smiling at James Stanley.

'Hurry Meredith, Mr Stanley is waiting.' Agnes pushes her out the door as James strides over to untie his horse.

They walk in silence, the horse between them. Meredith tries to think of something to say. 'What's the name of your horse, Mr Stanley?'

James Stanley shrugs. 'I don't usually name things.' They walk on in silence.

Foxgloves along the edges of the bank are flowering. The bells tip over in bright colours, mostly pinks and purples, gayer than Meredith is feeling. She doesn't mention them. What else can they talk about? She reaches up to pat the horse and startles as Mr Stanley speaks.

'Reg tells me you had a sweetheart in Armentières. I was in the trenches there as well.'

Meredith stops walking and stares at James across the horse's snorting, tossing nose. 'You knew Peter? You were there?'

James Stanley shakes his head, staring out over the valley. He watches a kāhu gliding in the distance; the large harrier hawk is doing slow circles. 'No, I'm not saying I knew him. I never met your Peter, but of course I knew of boys just like him. We were all the same. All of us in the same muddy mess.'

Meredith steps across in front of the horse to James, gripping his arm with both her hands. The horse tries to buffet her away. 'Please, please, tell me what you know?'

James Stanley stares across the valley. His eyes are following the hawk. 'It's like this,' he breathes out heavily. 'Four years of war, first Gallipoli and then the Western Front wearing him thin, even before the Minenwerfer got him. Those mortars mess you up: ears ringing, can't think, nerves shot to pieces, every movement your heart thumps, every noise you jump real bad, head throbs bad, skin gone bad, laying there in the mud waiting to die. Covered in pieces of your cobber who just did.' James turns to look at Meredith. 'He just walked away from it all, didn't he?'

'Yes.' Meredith turns to rub the horse's nose and hides her face in the soft short hairs where the neck meets the shoulder, away from James' gaze. 'He just walked away. It was his allies that caught him, called him a coward, put him in prison, broke him some more and shot him dead.'

James Stanley watches the kāhu plummet downwards after some prey that they can't see from where they stand.

'Your Peter, the likes of him, he was no coward. At least he had the guts to walk away. The cowards were the ones who didn't have the guts to do that.' He glances down at his left hand and rubs the hook with his good hand. 'Come on, girl.' He clicks the reins and the horse starts to walk.

Meredith stumbles as the horse moves off and then hurries to catch up to the man and his beast.

James looks over at Meredith and then straight ahead. 'Mrs Anderson tells me you are looking for a husband. You could do worse than me.'

Meredith glances at his profile. It tells her nothing of his thoughts. She nods.

'So it's settled then. Reg said he'd help me build another room onto my hut down at Jack Ward's old place. It'll take us a few weeks to get it shipshape, so shall we say Saturday five weeks from now? There's a registry office out at Raetihi.'

Meredith nods again. They walk on in silence, the horse with no name filling the space between them. At the first bluff, Meredith turns back and walks home alone. Tears fall down her face.

# Eight

# Beanstalk

He was left with the question: could writing set Jane free? The boat trips no longer held the same magic. It seemed to Beanstalk the lost baby had become an ever-present block, even worse than Jane's muteness or her refusal to communicate. He read with fervour on the subject of Lowell and his confessionals, wrought women writers much like Jane herself. He shared with her the work of Plath, Sexton, and, of course, New Zealand's very own Janet Frame, avoiding a lobotomy at Seacliff Lunatic Asylum after the publication of her first book and moving forward to acclaim and a writerly life.

Beanstalk told Jane about these patients, how they had been encouraged to write their way to wellness and had published books along the way. He read to her from Sylvia's recent volume *Ariel* as they walked together on the Kingseat lawns with the coarseness of kikuyu in summer, a far cry from the well-clipped grass of Boston or London.

Or did he pride himself on being another Dr Martin Orne to the celebrated Anne Sexton? How he had shuddered ten years later when he had read of Anne's very public death. Dressed in her mother's fur coat with a glass of vodka in her hand, she had closed the garage and started the car. At least he had spared Jane that. At least she hadn't died with a scathing literary review in her wallet. Nothing was ever published or scrutinised by the public eye.

Was Jane listening to the poems he had read to her? Did she take anything in? In her own way, Jane had let him know. What a fool he had been to single out Sylvia. A poet who had died in her own kitchen with her children sleeping in a room nearby.

## Choking on Sylvia

You feed me pages of *Ariel*
I spit out the dead woman's words

Plath, Plath, Plath

You say it beats wires on my head
Or a lobotomy that steals perception
Permanent deflection, unwanted connection
Willing me instead, to write…what?
Mummydaddysisterbrothers, uncovered lovers?
You salivate…anticipation
I scribble back…indignation
Sylvia seeps through my blocked door
I smell her gas oven and spit back the fumes

Plath, Plath, Plath

# Nine

# Kate

At Khyber Pass I pause under the roar of overhead traffic, turn right, left and then up over the apex of the ridge. Atop the gates of the Domain, a naked man is on the point of balance, throwing something invisible into the sky. He indicates a leafy place to park between two oaks where only a motorbike can fit.

The ward clerk smiles at my enquiry and doesn't need to consult her list when I ask for Ian. 'Third room on the right.'

Three rooms along, I scan the names on the door. Someone had crossed out *Ian* and scrawled *Ursula* across the name plate in what looks to be red lipstick; there is laughter in the room.

'Hello, darling.' Ursula spies me and waves from the bed. 'I'm over here.'

The top of Ian's shaved head is just visible above the heads of the student nurses who are gathered around his bed.

'Just in time – I am about to demonstrate my new Turkish bubble pipe to these lovely ladies.' Ursula pulls up her hospital pyjama shirt to reveal the tubing that comes out the side of her ribs into the bottle by the bed. 'Now, let's see if we can make the bottle burp. There you go, ladies.'

There is a round of applause and the students move on to the next bed. Ursula lies back against the pillows. I survey the damage. The left eye is half closed but cleverly disguised by bold blue, green and purple strokes across both eyelids and heavily applied eyeliner. The bright red lips are also slightly bulging on the left but no broken teeth.

Ursula smiles. 'Don't worry, darling, I'm fine now. I get to go home tomorrow if this lung stays up. Thank God they didn't take my handbag. Still have my make-up kit. Makes me feel so much better. Can you go home and get a few things for me? A nightie, so I can get out of these ugly pyjamas.'

I sit down on the bed. 'Which wig will I bring?'

Ursula folds her arms across her chest. 'No wigs. No more Ian. I'm going to grow my hair out.' Ursula runs her hand across the stubble on her scalp and tosses her head as if she already has a shoulder-length mane of hair. 'Watch out, Kate.' Ursula grins up at me and puckers her over-red lips. 'There'll be no stopping Ursula once she has her own hair to let down.'

*ooOOoo*

Back at the flat Ursula cuts off her plastic hospital tag and makes us both a coffee with the percolator on the stove.

I pick up the heart-shaped shortbread Ursula has placed on my saucer. She is watching me as I crush it into small pieces and pretends not to notice as I drop the crumbs back onto the saucer.

'Are you going to press charges?' I ask.

Ursula shakes her head and braces the side of her ribs as she laughs out loud. 'No. Whoever needs a bunch of stuffy policemen involved? But I will get even.' Ursula carries her coffee over to me and sits down on the couch. She stretches out and crosses her legs. 'Revenge, it's all about revenge. It's always the victor that gets to write the history down, who gets the final word. The audience believes what the winner wants them to remember once the job is done. It was the victors who dropped the bomb on Hiroshima and no one cares to remember how many people got melted.'

I can see a plan is coming, an Ursula-style plan. I sink further down into the couch.

'We're going to need the Whyte Force. Tell them to bring some lengths of dog chain and fencing wire.' Ursula starts ticking things off her fingers. 'Pliers, duct tape, stockings, a black felt tip pen, waterproof of course.' Ursula stabs her hand in the air. 'And let's not forget the television *Six O'Clock News* team.' She winks at me and gathers up the coffee cups.

I set out to phone around the Whyte Force, all four of my brothers.

People wonder why we're such a tight bunch. It's Ginny's fault. The first Whyte Force manoeuvre was a frog march. She'd spent all day on the floor helping Ian cut out and sew his first dress and there we were, Ursula and I pimped and ready for the rugby do down at the port.

Four reluctant tousle-headed Whyte boys stood before their fierce little mother.

'Rural folk look after their own, and don't you forget it. Whytes are Whytes.' Ginny strode up and down the line. 'Ursula is a Whyte. Look out for her and Kate at the dance and bring them both home safe.'

John rattled his newspaper for good effect and made sure the station wagon was full of petrol.

We drove in silence to the hall. There was a big crowd so we parked way down the end on a verge. No one spoke as we walked back towards the hall. Light was spewing out and a tape deck blaring. We stepped through the main door and the music stopped. Everyone looked at Ursula and a titter started around the room.

'Play *Dancing Queen*,' someone shouted. More tittering, tapes clicked in and out of the machine, then the whirr of a rewind and the song started.

Not just anyone could be that girl. Ursula mouthed the words; she gave a whoop and grabbed my brother Luke. They were first up on the dance floor, and my how she could dance. By the chorus, the rest of the Whyte boys had dragged partners onto the floor. Rodney from down the road had stumbled out of the corner and given me his bashful hand and by the next chorus everybody was up. At supper the girls were crowding around admiring Ursula's dress.

Ginny was waiting up when we got home to hear how the rugby boys had carried Ursula on their shoulders for a lap of the hall at the end of the night. Family is family.

The joke is on the city folk who live behind their locked doors thinking they're the open-minded ones.

ooOOoo

At 5.30am, I lock the door of the flat, swing my leg over my motorbike and hold it steady while Ursula climbs onto the back. 'We aren't exactly going to blend in, are we?'

Ursula settles her bright pink leathers onto the pillion seat, flips down the foot pegs and puts her arms around my waist. 'Who said anything about blending in? What we need here is a stand-out performance.'

The Whyte Force is waiting on the side street lined up in their farm utes. As we pass by, they pull out behind us and join the convoy. Ursula stands up and raises her hand above her head, jumping about on the pegs, waving the convoy forward. I concentrate on keeping the bike steady. Up Dominion Road we go, past the brightly-painted Asian food signs, plain-faced company buildings and the few remaining villas, some of them grand homes before the road became a four-lane corridor. Then up onto Symonds Street, we turn left and roll down over the motorway, already starting to build with the traffic of the day. Then on past the old Grafton Bridge with concrete arches curving up and away from the gravestones, which are tucked underneath us in the bushy gully beside the road. Ursula waves us on down towards the university. Leafy plane trees form a tunnel between the tall buildings. Still silent, it's too early for students to be about. At the second stone church we turn left and left again past the clock tower. There is Albert Park on our right, a formal affair, laid out in concentric rings of civic pride pimped with rows of petunias. Queen Victoria still reigns at the top end, facing off with the band rotunda down below. Dead centre is the fountain.

Ursula waves the utes on down the street while we park my bike and stare at the fountain. It's a black cast-iron affair. Four cherubs each ride a dolphin and blow an arc of water out of their conch shells high up into the air. Above the cherubs is the figure of a woman. She holds a conch shell on her shoulder, which cascades more water back down into the circular pond below. Wrought iron park benches look on from all sides.

The Whyte boys park their utes and take up their station inside the public toilets, which are down the hill beyond the Moreton Bay fig tree. Ursula and I sit on my bike and wait. We don't take off our helmets, bumping heads to talk.

'Perfect.' Ursula laughs through her raised visor. 'This couldn't be more perfect. Look at that. Here they come already. Right on time.' She pulls down her visor and lowers her voice to a whisper. 'Just one little memo – that's all it took to get them out of bed early.'

Three business suits stride past us down the footpath; the largest of three disappears into the toilet, the remaining two loiter outside. Several minutes tick by. After a consultation between the two, the second one strides into the toilet.

'Two down, one to go.' Ursula is already punching the air.

I grab her arm to hush her and indicate for her to watch as the third man is striding up and down now. The road remains quiet. He walks to the doorway of the toilet and calls out. After one final look about, he too steps into the toilet.

'Yes. Got the lot.'

Two of the Whyte boys frog march the first man up the hill. He is stripped to his underwear and has duct tape over his mouth. The Whyte boys have slipped a fishnet stocking over his head and prod him along. The man's fat sedentary belly wobbles uncertainly as he is marched towards the fountain.

'How easy was that?' Ursula laughs and punches both her fists above her head. She leads the way.

We both climb into the fountain between the dolphin-riding cherubs and chain the first man in place. A crowd of early morning commuters is already gathering.

'Good morning, darling. So pleased that you spared the time to join in our little protest. After all, it's for such a good cause.' Ursula winds the chain tightly around his hands while I tie off the ends with fencing wire, twist it extra tight with the pliers and cut off the sharp ends so no one gets hurt. Soon all three men are in place, facing outwards, lashed to the centrepiece of the fountain. They give up struggling and bow their heads.

From her pocket, Ursula takes out a thick, black felt tip pen and in big letters writes one word across each of their fat bellies in waterproof ink: *No Drift Nets*.

'Don't worry, duckies, your clothes won't get wet. We'll just leave them here for you, nicely folded on this park bench. So good to see you boys doing something constructive with your spare time. Have fun. The media will be here soon. Make sure you show your best side for the camera, won't you, darlings. I really appreciate you turning up this morning. Have a whale of a time now, won't you. It's such swimming fun to have you all here.'

Students and workers are gathering around the fountain. I drag her back to the motorbike and we are just riding away as a TV news station wagon pulls up.

### Saying No to Drift Nets – One Stomach at a Time

*Today three brave men put their stomachs where their mouths usually are. They took part in an art installation protest in Albert Park in aid of the Greenpeace No Drift Nets campaign. The men arranged to have themselves lashed to the Albert Park fountain, baring their stomachs for the cause.*

*The three men, whose identity was masked by fishnet stockings don't want to be named. We do know they work for an IT company located nearby. Their manager arrived at lunchtime to dismantle the installation. He said he was proud of his workers and the publicity they had achieved for the No Drift Nets campaign. A large crowd had gathered at the Albert Park fountain by that time. Greenpeace were not aware of the protest, but are delighted with the response. Their spokeswoman says it's great to see ordinary citizens supporting this campaign. 'We will be visiting the company to thank these men. We are hoping to take this successful installation to other town centres.' Greenpeace will use photos of the installation as part of a poster campaign, which will be sponsored by their IT company.*

*In parliament the PM said, 'New Zealanders are embracing this matter and our government will be supporting the worldwide ban on high-sea large-scale drift nets.'*

*The Near Truth*


*ooOOoo*


Back at the flat I sit upright on a kitchen chair.

Ursula is making me coffee before she starts on dinner. She looks at me strangely. 'What happened to the Neanderthal woman who always slouches on the couch?'

I glance down at my shoulders which aren't in their usual forward hunch, it does feel a bit strange. I look across at Ursula. 'Maybe it's time the Neanderthal woman suffered the same fate as Ian – dead, gone, kaput. Maybe it's time to stop sitting on the couch.'

Ursula whips the cream with a fierce right arm. She doesn't say anything.

I tell her about visiting Ginny. About my birth mother, Jane, and my grandmother Meredith. Somehow, I feel more grown up. I look around our dingy flat as if I've never been here before. Maybe this is true. The walls have been painted in purple by a previous tenant and the calendar is on the wrong date. I rip two pages off to bring it up to the right month and stop in front of the new Greenpeace poster that Ursula has hung on the wall. The fat tummies with the water dripping off give it a certain pregnancy.

Ursula glances up from the stove. 'This *No Drift Nets* thing has spread like a virus, darling. I see those posters everywhere: shop windows, brick walls, the works.'

'How's your boss about it?'

Ursula is shaking sugar crystals onto the top of my special coffee, carefully creating a pattern.

'Philosophical.' She hands me the coffee. 'He says it will take time to blow over. He wants me to work from home for a while or take some leave. But he wants Ursula to come back. Isn't that sweet of him?'

'Is that what you want?'

Ursula tosses her head, which has already sprouted a short, strong crop of hair. 'I'm still deciding what I want. I've got options.'

Our eyes meet. I look down at my coffee and stir in the sugar question mark she has embossed into the whipped cream.

'The boss says there's a place for me on the marketing team. He thinks conservation could be a fresh new advertising lever for selling his IT solutions. How funny would that be?' Ursula raises her spoon. 'But I'm not making any promises to the boss. Maybe I go away for a while? Maybe I'll just disappear? Would that worry you?'

Was I listening to her? Probably not. I clap my hands down on the kitchen table and fix Ursula with a steady look. 'We're going on a quest.'

Ursula's eyebrows shoot up. 'A quest. Hmm, are you sure about this?'

I look her in the eye. 'Sure, I'm sure. We're going to Jerusalem to find my grandmother.'

'Go girl.' Ursula grabs my hands and twirls me around the room until we are too dizzy to stand up.

# Ten

# Beanstalk

Why had he shared Plath with Jane? The suicidal images in Jane's poems became worrisome, and not something he could share with his colleagues. What would they make of her personal references to him? Besides, he was her muse. He did not want to share her. More importantly, he did not want to lose access to her care. An easy thing for the superintendent to switch him to another dreary caseload and let someone else polish his shining star.

So he stood by and watched as Jane unpicked and parodied the poets he had fed to her. He forgave her any charge of plagiarism – after all her poems were only for him to read and she a poor provincial girl, trying to make sense of a world far removed and a baby taken.

**Ariel in Outer Space**

There is no Pegasus to spur me away from this place
Black red berries aplenty you encourage me to gorge
My face, your eyes a glitter on water beyond a muddy tide
The sun is distant here, no cauldron within my reach
To arrest my already scalded skin
This Godiva has nothing left to peel away
My child's cries went unheard by this mother
Melted down these dreary grey walls then fell away
With the thirteenth layer of flaky paint

# Eleven

# Meredith

'Giggling just like a pair of school girls.' Reg shakes his head but his eyes are smiling. 'Keep an eye on that wife of mine in the big smoke.' He'd ridden the four miles up the valley with Meredith and Agnes to put them on the mail bus to Raetihi. Now he sits up on his horse, holding Ginger, ready for his return trip after the bus has gone.

Meredith nods and waves back at Reg as she climbs up onto the bus. Agnes is blocking the aisle as she stops to shake the driver's hand. This is her first trip to town in nearly a year. She makes her way down to the back of the bus, greeting the other passengers as she goes, raising her voice above the roar of an engine that can't be trusted to settle to an idle.

Teddy Johnson has swapped over the mail bags and stands alongside Reg to wave them off. He shouts up through the window of the bus to Agnes, 'No kicking your heels up like at Bettjemans' woolshed. Come home safe, the pair of you.'

The bus lurches off and Meredith is flung down into the back seat next to Agnes. They wave to Reg and Teddy and then settle in for the five-hour trip. The bus, an old thing converted from a truck, has no floor near the front and next to no brakes except the crash gearbox and reverse in emergencies. It coughs and roars, lumbering over the hill, and squeezes close to the bank around the sheer edges of drop-offs.

Swaying around a corner, the bus pulls up at a new slip that spreads across the road. The driver leads the way and the men all climb out to help clear a path for the bus. The cruel papa rock is newly exposed right above them where a tree and its meagre supply of topsoil have given up and just slipped clean away. Meredith and Agnes climb down and help as well to push a whole tree off the narrow ledge where the road runs around a bluff. Roots and all, they watch it crash and smash its way down to the creek below. The men get busy on a couple of shovels and soon they clamber back and the bus is on its way again.

Finally, they arrive at Raetihi, a long street lined with shops, banks, hotels, and proper electric street lights. The bus lumbers to a stop outside the depot. Agnes pulls out her long list and they set off immediately.

Agnes hurries along the footpath towards the large store. 'Let's start in Wilson and Co. We have an account here,' she whispers as they step into the cool, dark space and the bell dings behind them. 'They're standing us tick until we get some wool off the backs of our motley sheep, God willing.'

Agnes' list is long: elastic, wooden pegs, new boot laces for Reg, molasses as a treat for the children, a new bridle bit, a buckle piece for the pack saddle, more fencing wire and dried fruit for a wedding cake.

At the haberdashery they rub each fabric between thumb and fingers and crumple the edge to check for creasing. They settle on well-weighted, plain white cotton – something that Meredith can dye later and still wear as a useful dress. They choose a pattern for a loose-fitting style with a belt tie.

'That way you can still wear it when you're expecting.' Agnes rubs her tummy.

Meredith nods and smiles at the shopkeeper who measures out the four yards of smooth white fabric.

'You girls sewing up a wedding frock, then?' She draws out and cuts off a short length of lace. 'This will be pretty on the neck line. My compliments to you, dear, for a long and happy marriage.'

They thank the shop lady and hunt out a pot of blue/grey to dye the dress afterwards.

The afternoon is gone. The shops are closing their doors. Time to head along the street to the boarding house.

'This is the life.' Agnes stretches back in the chair while the staff place cups of tea and their meals on the table. 'Electric lights, a hot bath and someone else on the cooking. I've just died and gone to heaven.'

'But only for one night,' Meredith reminds her. Their bus is leaving town again at six the following morning. They tuck into the shepherd's pie with a large side of steaming vegetables and eat until they can't face another forkful.

'About James Stanley.' Meredith looks across at Agnes. 'I don't know a thing about the man. I don't even know where he's from.'

Agnes nods. 'He's alright. Mrs Bettjeman told me that Jack Ward went down to Wanganui a few years back and met up with him at the RSA, same regiment. The story goes that Mr Stanley was at a loose end so he came up here with Jack. When Jack walked off his land, Mr Stanley stayed on and built himself a bit of a house next to Jack's old whare. He does roadwork when the council is paying, helps out other farmers, does a bit of extra work for Fred Bettjeman and runs a few head of stock for himself on some abandoned land further down the valley. He's just squatting up here, never took a lease, but he's okay. He keeps to himself fairly much. We see him at the dances, always polite, not much to say to the ladies.' Agnes pauses and looks across at Meredith, who is stirring her tea. 'You'll be alright with him.'

The next day Reg is there to meet the mail bus and help them pack down all the parcels. 'Gosh, have you got a kitchen sink in there?'

'I only wish.' Agnes climbs up into the saddle and pulls Meredith up behind her onto Ginger's broad back. 'Now wouldn't that be a fine thing if we did have a kitchen sink with running water. Life really would be a dream.'

*ooOOoo*

The days speed by. The dress is cut and the lace is set in place around the neckline. Agnes looks up from rinsing the washing. 'Shall we take a trip to see your new house? Reg is working down there today. We can throw this lot on the line and pack up Michael in two shakes.'

Meredith catches Ginger and they're off down the valley with Michael perched up front. It's a glorious warm day without a breath of wind. The steep bush-clad hills echo back the distant sound of wood being chopped and a farmer bellowing at his dogs. Meredith smiles; this valley is starting to feel like home. The birds of the valley are enjoying the day. Quail are seen on the edges of the track, wax eyes and fantails flit about and fat wood pigeons are after the kōnini berries.

The little house sits alone on a wide flat above the creek between two bluffs.

'Nice bit of land this. Your garden will come up well here.'

They stop to look at the house and circle once around the yard before sliding off Ginger's broad back. The house is made from shingles with two proper windows, good iron on the roof and a well-repaired cooking chimney. Jack Ward's original whare, drunk and crooked on its wooden piles, still stands out the back. There is a path to the outhouse but no garden except for Mr Stanley's vegetable patch, just silverbeet and a line of carrots.

Reg is up a ladder nailing the wooden shingles he has cut onto the wall of the new room. He waves and climbs down as they arrive. 'Not a bad little abode for a bride, don't you think? This new lean-to will have a bench and I'm going to make you a wooden wash tub and there's an extra bunkroom in here for when the kids come along.' He smiles. 'Before you know it, you'll be begging me to come down and build another extension on the place when your family is bursting at the seams.'

Meredith holds her breath and steps inside. The main room is spare but at least it's clean and newly swept. Just a kitchen table and two easy chairs made from axe handles and wool sacks. There's the usual array of blackened pots on the hearth, a food cupboard and a meat safe with the mesh secure. Meredith doesn't dare to look into the bedroom. She has started a double quilt, piecing together bright material scraps into hexagonal shapes.

Agnes twirls around in the kitchen and throws her arms in the air. 'One day we'll all have Orion stoves with a little hot water tap and a copper for the washing just like Mrs Bettjeman and Mrs Mowat.'

Reg catches hold of Agnes. 'One day, old girl, but don't go holding your breath now.' He catches Agnes by the waist as she whirls past him.

Meredith walks outside. She watches James Stanley wielding the hammer with his strong right hand. He steadies the next nail; the first hit bends it sideways. Meredith sees the set of his face as he re-laces the nail between the remaining three fingers on his hook hand. This time it holds steady long enough for the first hammer strike. She looks away, not wanting to be caught watching.

He continues to work as if she isn't even there.

Agnes comes around the corner. 'Come down off that ladder and have a civil word with your betrothed.' She laughs and nudges Meredith with her elbow. 'You're both safe. I'm here as a chaperone.'

James Stanley shows no sign he has heard. He finishes nailing the board and then comes down the ladder. He takes off his hat and nods to Agnes; his eyes flick to Meredith then look away. 'Greetings, ladies.' Stanley looks down at the hat, which is swirling around in his hands and then places it back on his head, pulling the sides well down.

'Come on Meredith,' Agnes nudges her again, 'spill the beans. What do you think of this new improved mansion?'

'Very nice.' Meredith glances up at Mr Stanley. 'It will do me very well.'

Mr Stanley grimaces and turns to Reg who is coming around the corner. 'I'm going to need another handful of nails to finish this side wall.' No one speaks.

Agnes and Meredith climb back up onto Ginger. Reg is throwing Michael in the air in somersaults and the small boy shrieks with laughter. Reg passes Michael on up to Agnes for the ride back up the valley. 'Thank you for coming, fair maidens,' he cries as they make ready to ride away.

Mr Stanley touches his hat as they ride past his ladder but says nothing.

On the track back up the valley, Agnes kicks Ginger and they trot for a while. Michael is bouncing and squealing with delight, clutching Ginger's mane.

'This will be you in a couple of years' time. That spare room filled with little squealers like this one.' Agnes slows to a walk. 'Don't you think that Mr Stanley is quite dashing in that silent, manly sort of way? I know he doesn't say much, but if it wasn't for my Reg and a house full of kids, I could quite fancy him myself.'

'No, I don't think he's dashing.' Meredith's head bumps forward against Agnes' shoulder. 'But perhaps that's for the best. If I don't love Mr Stanley it means I can keep on loving my Peter. I will be a good wife to Mr Stanley, but I'll never love the man.'

Agnes says nothing. She flicks the reins and Ginger walks on into the cooling autumn air. Even Michael is quiet now, rocked to sleep on Ginger's neck, encircled in the strong arms of Agnes.

*ooOOoo*

'It's the day, it's the day, it's the very, very day,' sings Myra as she watches Meredith putting on her new white dress. She claps her hands, and helps to brush Meredith's long hair until it shines like the black keys on the piano accordion. Together, they roll it up and secure it with a pin. 'I'll never call you Mrs Hook,' she whispers to Meredith. 'That's a promise. If you come for dinner can we still read *Peter Pan*?'

Meredith pats the excited head, which is bobbing up and down on her bed. 'Yes, of course I will still read to you. In fact, you will be reading to me before much longer.'

'Yes,' breathes Myra, 'I'm nearly up to books without pictures.' She skips outside to pick the last of the autumn roses and wraps the stems of the three that she can find with brown paper. 'So you don't get pricked,' she tells Meredith proudly as she hands them to her. They stand at the door. Meredith is ready to go.

'Well my, doesn't that slouch hat suit Mr Stanley?' Agnes screws her eyes against the sun, watching the horseman's progress up the valley.

Mr Stanley stops in front of them but doesn't dismount. He says nothing, nodding to Agnes and Meredith in turn. He pulls his horse in sharply. The horse with no name stamps on the spot and tosses her head against the reins.

Reg rides up from the paddock leading Ginger.

'Can I come up with you, Dad, to see them off at the mail bus, please, please?' Myra jumps up and down tugging on Reg's stirrup. 'Please, Dad, pretty please?'

Reg puts down his long strong arm and lifts Myra up behind him. 'Just this once. Are you big enough to ride Ginger home by yourself, while I lead Mr Stanley's horse?'

Myra is delighted.

From the doorway Agnes waves as she reaches down to stop Michael from crawling out into the mud. 'Go well. I'll have your supper ready here tomorrow night. The Bettjemans are coming over as well. Mrs Mowat sends her love.'

Reg kicks his horse. 'Come on, let's get going. That woman of mine can talk the leg off a chair, given half a chance. If we don't get away soon we'll miss the mail bus.'

'Don't forget to tuck in that old lace hanky I gave you and the blue brooch on the garter and…' Agnes is still shouting last minute instructions as they trot around the corner and away up the track.

The mail bus pulls out. Meredith stands and waves to Myra out the side window. She holds up the bouquet of roses for Myra to see and the small girl blows her a kiss as they disappear around the first corner. Meredith sits down in the seat alongside Mr Stanley. She stoops her head and breathes in the homely scent of the roses, taking longer than she needs, not sure what to say now they are alone. She glances across at Mr Stanley who is staring straight ahead. He has both hands atop his knees and sits rigid to ensure that the jolting of the bus doesn't allow their shoulders to touch. Meredith says nothing. She sniffs the roses again and looks out across the aisle at the steep-sided bush on the opposite bank of the creek and tries to keep her thigh back from the centre line of the seat. What would Peter think? What would Peter make of her marrying Mr Stanley? She tries to conjure up a picture of Peter in her head, but the brow is too heavy. It's not Peter that she sees. The unsmiling silhouette of Mr Stanley is getting in the way.

'Off to tie the knot? You're a lucky man, Mr Stanley.' The bus driver smiles at Meredith. 'To think you found this lovely young lady way back there amongst that wild bush. The registry office is just around the first corner on your right.'

Meredith smiles and nods to the driver. She climbs down off the bus clutching her leather suitcase and the bunch of roses, which are starting to wilt. They make their way along the street. Side by side, each carrying a bag, they look straight ahead, neither speaking. As they turn the corner, Meredith lets Mr Stanley take the lead. She catches the door of the registry office as it closes after him.

'Just write your full names here.' The man stabs his index finger down on the page. He retrieves the pen from behind his ear, dips the nib into the ink, and holds the pen out towards James Stanley. Meredith watches as the nib pauses in mid-air then drops a big fat blot of blue ink onto the page.

'Sorry.' The man blots the page and re-dips the pen. Again he holds it out. Again the nib pauses, the blue ink forming another blob. Meredith stares at the nib.

James Stanley does not reach for the pen. He motions for Meredith to take it. 'Not one much for reading or writing,' he mumbles. 'You do it.'

The blue ink is wobbling. Meredith stands rigid, unable to lift her hand to the pen, so…who wrote…those letters… Mr Stanley doesn't … then who wrote…?

The man waves the pen at her. 'Come on, lass, we can't dally about here. No time for nerves.' He places the pen in her hand and guides it over the correct place and applies the blob just before it falls into the first letter of J…ames, leaving her to finish the Hilton Stanley. He points to the next space and slowly Meredith writes her full name, her surname

Innes for the last time. The pen is running out of ink now, scratching deeply into the paper on the final letters.

Another dip and they both sign. James holds the pen in a clumsy hand and signs a quick squiggle. The little man rushes out to get the lady in the front office to witness something that she has not seen. Meredith stares down at the empty desk in front of them both.

The man returns, flourishing the document. 'All done,' he says and smiles. 'The groom may kiss the bride.' He looks from one to the other; neither Meredith nor James move. They are statues, their arms bolted to their sides.

*ooOOoo*

It's the same boarding house where Agnes and Meredith had stayed on their shopping trip. They are shown up the stairs to their room by the housekeeper who throws open the door. The room is large and gloomy. Meredith stands in the centre, unsure where to put her suitcase. There's no vase for the flowers. Trying not to look at the double bed, which is leering out of the shadowy recess against the far wall, she moves to the window and lays the flowers down on the narrow ledge. Outside the town is going on as if nothing has happened. Meredith is stunned to see a woman and her daughter laughing as they cross the street. The sun is shining down on the pair. Meredith watches as the mother takes her daughter's hand and they move away, disappearing from her view. They walk together with steps perfectly matched.

'Have you been with a man before?' James Stanley is standing by the door next to his carpet bag, which has dropped by his feet.

Meredith looks away and shakes her head. 'Peter and I were sweethearts but we were waiting for marriage. I was young, not even sixteen.'

'I'll get some whisky,' he says. 'We'll both be better for it.' The door bangs shut behind him. His hurried feet are fading down the stairs. His carpet bag is lying where he has left it by the door. The sides of the bag curve inward like the stomach of a starving beast with nothing inside.

Stock-still in the room, Meredith thinks of Peter. Yes, she can see him now – how he had looked at her, his last kiss and whispered words. Her body that would have melted if he hadn't pulled himself back. 'No,' he'd said, 'I need something to come home for.' He had patted her and held her at a distance, unable to trust himself up close, not wanting to break his word.

'Peter.' Meredith whispers his name and sinks down in the chair in front of the mirror. She lowers her head into her hands. The street noise penetrates only a little into this gloomy room where there is not even a clock ticking.

*ooOOoo*

The room is getting dark. It must be well past dinner time. Meredith feels the hollowness that tells her it is a long time since breakfast. She hasn't eaten or taken any water since porridge with Myra a world ago, back in the valley. She needs the bathroom and creeps along the hall. She drinks water from the tap, which runs cold over her hands. Back to the empty, darkening room, she sits again in the chair at the mirror. She lets her hair out, as is her habit at night time, letting it fall away down, reaching nearly to her waist. She brushes it absently through her cold, hungry fingers, too tired to think beyond each soothing stroke. Her face is in shadow now, grey and unfamiliar in the mirror.

There are steps and a stumble outside the door. Meredith freezes as the door bursts open and bangs back against the wall. It's James. He stands for a moment. The light from the hallway frames his swaying figure as he catches himself on the door surround. In the mirror Meredith can see his face is red, his tie is gone and the front of his shirt is dirty and ripped. His head is swinging backward and forward. He steps forward and trips on his carpet bag, which flies across the room from the end of his boot. He staggers towards the double bed in the alcove. Meredith's eyes follow as he slaps his hand heavily down on the bed.

'Where are you, girl?' He turns in the half-light, swaying on his feet. 'Speak up. Where are you? Mouse got your tongue then?' He steps forward and when he sees Meredith's face in the mirror his head snaps back with a jerk.

'It's you.' James Stanley lets out a strangled wail. 'It's you, you whore.' He staggers forward and grabs Meredith by her long hair, pulling her backwards towards him off the chair. 'Monique,' he cries. 'Monique, won't you ever leave me alone? Your pretty French ways. I'll teach you, Monique. I'll teach you again for lying to me and being with every other soldier.'

Meredith drops to the floor and claws with her hands, digging her fingernails into the rough wooden floor, trying to get away from him towards the window. The hook entwines in Meredith's hair and jerks her back towards him like a dog on a short lead. She is on her knees. Her hands scrabble at the bare, undressed floorboards but she makes no progress.

James Stanley draws out the sheath knife he wears on his belt. He tugs on her hair and Meredith falls flat, face downward on the floor. He is towering over her now.

'I'll teach you, Monique, I'll teach you for your dirty whoring ways. I loved you Monique,' he sobs as he jerks Meredith's head backward off the floor, snapping her neck back. He is hacking her long hair off hard in against her skull; her face is falling forward, her nose is smacking hard down onto the floor. Meredith lies still.

'I loved you, you stupid whore. I still love you. I didn't mean to, Monique, I didn't mean to.'

James Stanley flips Meredith over, grabs her throat and presses down. 'I didn't mean to, Monique, but I couldn't stop...' James' head is back, his mouth is open, and another high-pitched animal wail. He is staring down at Meredith.

Meredith feels her breathing stop. She stares up into his wild eyes as her head is lifted up and shaken backward and forward. Both hands encircle her throat; the hook is digging further into her windpipe. In slow time, she watches his eyebrows rise up and his mouth drop open forming yet another wretched howl as his brain finally wades through the whisky.

'Meredith.' He lets go. Her head drops back to the floor. Clunk. 'Meredith.' He sways on his feet. 'Meredith.' He drops beside her, pulls her up to sitting. 'Meredith, forgive me.' He is cradling her, using his white shirt to stem the flow from her bleeding nose. His sobbing head falls for a moment forward onto her chest; he is willing her to breathe. 'Please forgive me, Meredith. Bad dreams. I thought you were someone else. I won't touch you again, Meredith, I promise. You are safe, you're safe with me.' James Stanley stands up slowly and backs out the door. 'I won't touch you again, ever, I promise, never.' James Stanley runs back down the stairs leaving the door banging wide open.

*ooOOoo*

Next day on the mail bus Meredith wears her hat pulled down with her remaining hair tucked up inside. Her shirt dress is buttoned up to cover the bruises on her neck. Her nose is swollen and her eyes are turning black. The hat scoops forward, the brim providing useful shadow. The bus snorts and puffs up the hills on its way back to the valley. Mr and Mrs Stanley sit side by side in silence. The driver observes their faces in the rear-view mirror. Birds of a feather he decides. He has never seen such a grim-faced pair.

Reg meets them at the end of the mail run. The Stanleys decline Agnes' kind offer to stay for supper. They choose instead to ride straight home. Meredith will need his help to dig out the wooden splinters that are festering underneath her fingernails. James Stanley will do this for her, holding the needle in a firm but gentle hand.

# Twelve

# Beanstalk

Night after night he had lain awake. The ceiling of his meagre room became monotonous in the small hours. Damn that girl, why should he lie awake at night worrying about the mental health of a small monster, ugly as sin with green whirlpools for eyes that gave nothing away, behind angry lids that could never close? And nor would Beanstalk's eyes close. Up at his desk again at that ungodly hour he leafed through the literature. Maybe it was depression; maybe a surgical or electrical solution would be best. Yet the thought of taking up a knife or placing electrodes on such a disfigured head made him shudder. There had to be a simpler solution.

Focus, that was what he needed – a new focus. The poets had been a mistake. Clearly he had been a fool to introduce Plath, with such a well-publicised ending, but he must be forgiven for introducing Jane to the work of Sexton. Back then the princess of the psychotherapy world was still alive and heralded for what she was achieving as a poet. Hindsight now was a bitter pill. If he'd known then what lay ahead for Anne Sexton, dressed in her mother's fur coat with the car set to idle in a dark closed space, he would have thought better than to press those books onto poor burnt Jane.

Damn the poets. Beanstalk leafed through the article he was reading. What really was Jane's complaint? Had anyone sought a diagnosis beyond burns so repulsive that no one could look upon her, a refusal to communicate except in her poems and, so it seemed, no other place to go? Her general health was robust, her life expectancy potentially normal

if the risk of suicide could be curtailed. What of her family? He resolved
to discuss the matter with Jane. Well, hardly a discussion – a soliloquy
on his part while Jane stared at the wall. He had received no reply to the
letter he sent to Mrs Dougherty.

## Cup This Fragile Form

Cup this fragile form in your hands
Feel the bloody weight
Of those gone before
Brevity quickens the loins of longevity

Drink deeply while you can
Weep tears into earthly scars
Let nothing erode
Except the inevitable hills

Mighty cliffs thrust upward to sky
Then fall away like ashes in the river
Peaches wrinkle the cheeks of the edges
Ancient ledgers written in silt

Keep the accounts clean
Count only the infinite stars
Like families falling
Looming larger than the shape of words

Sculpt our land with scrapings
From beneath my nails
Hasten to leave your mark
But leave no lasting prints

Cup this fragile form in your hands
Families broken
Eggshell scars on empty arms
The land is slipping away

# Thirteen

# Kate

John Whyte agrees to loan Ursula a bike for the trip. He scratches his head. 'You'll have to ride hard if you're going to keep up with our Kate… but when I coached the Under Fifteens, wasn't there a young winger who could ride a bike on its back wheel the full length of the rugby pitch?'

Ursula grins at John. 'Surely not.'

Just as we're about to leave, Ginny runs out with a tin of Anzac biscuits. I bungee them into my pack on the back rack and give my mother a hug.

'Give my love to Meredith,' Ginny whispers.

The goodbyes are over, the bikes are warm and we're off. Ursula scours a full 360 in the shingle in front of the shed and rides down the driveway on the back wheel just for John's benefit.

Heading south, she tucks in behind me. I can see her in my mirror. She's taking my line on the corners. We're travelling in unison, past the dairy flat lands and then on up into rolling country where sheep and beef cattle graze between the scrub and rush bushes.

At Te Kuiti we pull in for petrol. The service attendant is trying not to look at Ursula's leathers. Ursula sits astride the bike, holding it upright, thrusting her pink chest forward, blocking his view of the fuel tank. The attendant fumbles to undo the cap on the tank between her long legs. I sigh and go in to pay the bill. Bloody Ursula.

At Awakino, in the fish and chip shop, the young boy serving has a fat round face. 'What'll it be?'

The newspaper parcel slides across the counter, the shop door dings us gone. I hold the parcel warm between my knees as we ride on down to the Tasman Sea and park the bikes. Spinifex is bowling on the sand. We squat down in the lee of the bikes to watch a lone surfer paddling and ducking waves. Further out he goes, though we never see him catch a decent one. Each wave lifts him up and rolls past, despite his flailing arms and legs. The surfer overlooked by an ocean that is going about its business. Each time he is left behind, rising and falling, held in place like driftwood on the surface of the sea. I wonder, at what point will he give up? We take turns throwing chips to the squalling seagulls. Their red beaks and insistent open mouths are more immediate in our view.

Back on the bikes, the coast is on my right handlebar. Up ahead, a mighty mountain stands alone on the seaward edge, as if on the water. We pull up to a lookout. Mt Taranaki, usually so shy and hiding behind cloud, is sleek today, the top white with snow above the black and white dots of grazing dairy cows on the green lower slopes.

I tell Ursula the legend of Taranaki's tiff. The womanly mountain named Pihanga, flaunting her flanks of green bush to both Taranaki and Tongariro up on the Central Plateau. Then a terrible fight between the two tall mountains when Pihanga chose Tongariro. It was Mt Taranaki who waded off to the western edge of the island, leaving a deep gouge where the Whanganui River formed in his jilted wake. The river still runs away from the triumphant Tongariro to the Tasman Sea where Taranaki now stands alone on the western-most point.

Ursula climbs up on the saddle of her bike and faces south into the cold wind that blows off the mountain. She balances there a moment then raises both arms with palms outstretched. 'Taranaki, you fool, why didn't you stay put? If you really loved her you should have stayed and fought to the bitter end.'

I watch as Ursula jumps down from her bike and turns her face away from me to put on her helmet. I wonder if the surfer is still out there with the waves passing him by.

We ride the tar-seal hard all the way to Wanganui. It's a sleepy town, camped along both sides of a slow river not far from its white frothing mouth. We ride out onto the breakwater and watch the collision of white water on rock and the brown river spewing out. We crisscross over the three bridges to get our bearings and find ourselves a motel with imitation Spanish arches plastered over the previous era. I look at the ugly swirls and wonder what will be tacked on next to cover the folly of yet another spent fashion. This place will do. I indicate left and Ursula follows. We pull up in front of the reception and take off our helmets.

The woman behind the fake flowers on the counter has her head down. She doesn't look up as we walk in.

Ursula strides in ahead of me. 'Do you have a room for two?' Ursula waits for a reply.

We both stand there while the woman behind the desk runs her finger down the near-empty booking sheet. Her head is bent forward to show her real hair colour where it parts down the centre of her head: a dying grey mouse separates the two halves of office lady red.

'Yes, sir, is that for a twin or a double?'

We say nothing. The woman looks up. We watch the redness spreading upward from the wrinkled crevice that runs skew-whiff from the centre of her bosom. She is looking at me standing a full head taller than Ursula. 'Sorry, sir, I mean, miss.' Redness is now burning her cheeks as well.

I lower my voice a couple of octaves. 'Sorry, I didn't hear you clearly. What did you say?'

'Just asking if you want a twin or a double,' she squeaks. Even her forehead is now engulfed in flames.

I turn to Ursula who is kicking me in the shins and continue in my low tone. 'What will it be, darling, shall we take the double?' We both flee the office, falling about giggling over the baggage tied onto the back sides of our bikes. Of course, it's a joke. Ursula knows it's a joke.

We dump our gear and head out to find some food. A footpath takes us along the bank of the river towards town. There are formal grassed gardens with proud soldiers guarding dishonoured monuments and a pond that is now filled with concrete. Across the road, there's a jetty with a restored riverboat tied to the dock. Further along the wharf, the main street runs up the gully perpendicular to the river. Victoria Avenue has old shops dressed over with hanging baskets. Bright flowers, designed to avert the eyes of shoppers from the cracks and craggy necks of old buildings that peer out over the footpath awnings.

We order pizza and a liquor store sells us a bottle in a brown paper bag and throwaway glasses. We return to the river.

At the dock, the *Waimarie* is newly painted, the work of gnarled hands, volunteers who hold the history of the river close in their tightly-fisted paint brushes. Stripped back bare then further layers added. *Waimarie* is one of Hatrick's old steamers, recovered from the river mud and restored. A seagull watches us from the roof of the riverboat. The captain's wheel is covered with dark canvas. The boat is silent today; there are no tourists around for a gentle ride over the lower reaches where the river runs brown silt, like the history, down the drain and out to sea.

A few steps away there's an old corrugated wharf building, converted now into a workshop, a museum of sorts with a blackboard out front that gives the time for the next sailing. It says only Saturdays at this time of year, and only if there is enough demand. The building is locked shut but the information centre is nearby. We put our hands either side of our faces to peer through the windows and view photos on the walls that tell the history. Steamboats are plying this black and white river with sepia fogging the edges. Mr Hatrick's portrait dominates. He lounges back in a large chair with broad arms. His pipe sits comfortably below his walrus moustache. Hatrick is looking directly at the camera. He feels no need to smile; his fortune made, his place in history is secure.

Ursula collects the pizza and we sit down on the wharf next to the riverboat. We drink the wine and throw the edges of pizza to the seagull that scoffs each piece and then returns to his vantage point on the riverboat. We don't talk much.

'Best get going?' Ursula stands up, the last of the pizza crust in her hand. She picks up the rubbish and the empty bottle. 'It'll be a big day for you tomorrow.'

'Maybe I've changed my mind.' I slump further down against the wall. 'Maybe we go on down to Palmy North instead, through the gorge and just ride up the East Coast route?' I pull my ponytail hard across my face until my scalp stings.

Ursula stands above me, her face hard. 'Maybe you should just ride straight home and blubber on lover-boy Eric's shoulder.' She turns away to eye the bird, which is intent on the last piece of pizza that she holds in her hand. 'Maybe I should have been born a seagull,' she continues in a sing-song voice. 'Bright red lips without the need for constant painting; a voice that demands attention; an ever-changing crowd to perform for; plenty of food and no bills to pay.'

I shrug my shoulders. 'Whatever.'

Ursula hurls away the last of the pizza. 'No bastard of a father to answer to, no beatings in dark alleys, no despair, no living in a body that betrayed me at birth. And best of all, no pathetic friend called Kate. All the opportunities in the world, but too unsure to even bother to understand what she has.'

'A uterus maybe?' I put my fingers in my mouth and pretend to gag.

Ursula turns to me. 'You make me sick.' She strides off down the pathway that follows the river back to our motel.

I run after her and spin her around. 'Seagulls make me sick, living on the scraps that no one else wants.'

There are tears in Ursula's eyes. She tries to pull free. I haul her around to face me again. 'Or was Ian the seagull, all those years he stayed at our place, scavenging for titbits of leftover love?'

Ursula shakes herself free. She runs ahead back to the motel and slams the sliding door in my face. I wrench it open again, jarring the glass in its frame. Ursula is on the bed and tears are running down her cheeks. I'm towering over her. I hate myself more than usual. We shouldn't be doing this to each other. Tears cloud my eyes. Too much wine, I can't stop, it's not my fault. Where's Ian who always helps me calm down, pats away my paranoia, makes me feel better, signals when to put my fingers in my ears, never judging me?

I pull Ursula up off the bed. 'I hate you. Give him back to me… give him back.' I'm tearing the earrings from her ears, drumming my fists on her chest, ripping away the necklace, the blouse, the fancy bra, the fake boobs, tearing at the padding on her hips, ripping off the frilled underwear and there is Ian at last.

We both look down and see that Ian is standing up to Ursula. We are fighting and scratching each other's faces, we are kissing each other's faces. Did I make love with Ian or Ursula? Neither of us knows. We are now both covered in Ursula's lipstick and Ian's semen. We pull the quilt up over both of our heads and hold each other as we weep.

It's all Ursula's fault. I tell her I still love Eric. I take the warmest quilt and move out onto the couch.

*ooOOoo*

Helmet jammed on my head, glasses on, visor up, I fire up my bike and wait for Ursula to pay our bill. Visor down, without looking back, we ride out the gate. Right over the next town bridge, left onto Anzac Avenue, past the respectable homes that face the river and then take the left fork up River Road. The river holds my left hand around the bluffs and fallen rock. Standing up, I ride hard. There's nothing in my mirror. Ursula has pulled back. It's the narrow road, the speed, the sheer drop off the side that forces me to concentrate or I'll kill myself. This calms me down. I stop at a tall papa cutting and Ursula soon pulls up beside me. We don't talk. I reach down and pick up a piece of the fallen rock and rub the fossil shell between my thumb and fingers. We both watch it disintegrate. The soft, grey mudstone is falling apart in my hands. I rub the last of it off my gloves and pull away from Ursula.

We stop again where a tourist finger-board points out what remains of a water-run flour mill. The signboard tells of times when optimistic missionaries and enterprising Māori grew wheat in fields where gorse and mānuka now stand. Neither of us speaks.

*ooOOoo*

At Jerusalem the mailbox says *Sisters of Compassion*. We turn up the hill and stop the bikes in the carpark, which has a sign: *Visitors are welcome*. We shake our heads free of the helmets. Up above by the convent, a small figure is waving and calling to us; we are welcome to ride on up. Is this a nun dressed in track pants, running shoes and a big, warm jersey? We tuck our elbows through our helmets and ride on up the drive, past the spread of an old walnut tree, to park by the abandoned school room where the vice is still attached to the child-sized woodwork bench. The sister stands with the weeds she has been pulling at her feet. She takes off her gardening gloves and draws me into her sweet, sweet, smile. She nods her head at my question and points on up past the church, past the little house where the sisters now live. She tells me where to find the gate, which leads to the graveyard. One famous, others forgotten.

A small, unmarked bush path trodden by recent feet takes us up around the side of a hill beneath punga and then out onto someone's front lawn. There's no one home. We sidle past the square white house, which sits like a sentinel with two push-up windows that watch us go by. Between two young tōtara, I turn right and there is Hemi. *James Keir Baxter. 1926–1972.* His headstone, a river boulder painted white, sits on open ground. There's no concrete hemming his body in. The grave is decorated as a child would arrange trappings around the resting place of a beloved pet. An uneven necklace of river stones is placed around the edge of where his body must lie. Inside this border is a sprinkle of green weeds, a couple of concrete blocks and other leftover flotsam from previous visitors, all creating small points of brightness beneath the tōtara tree.

I bow my head and whisper his high-country words back to him. Not today, Hemi. I am not about to surrender my angry heart to the sky – it remains crouched in my chest. I take my cirrus red face further down the hill.

A path seldom trodden moves on to more graves in another clearing. *Meredith Margaret Stanley (née Innes). Died tragically 1965, the beloved mother of Jane Wendy Stanley.* The grave is well kept, with a jar of flowers only recently dead. Alongside there is an older grave. A plain grey-black concrete slab, the grass is trimmed around the edges. *James Hilton Stanley. Died tragically 1942, the beloved husband of Meredith.*

My breath is shaky. These two people belong to me. I sit down between the graves and place a hand on each of the warm slabs, connecting my grandfather and my grandmother together with my long arms and beating heart. I wait, willing something, anything to pass from my hands to theirs or from them, my grandparents, to me.

Another sister appears. She has a kind face and smiles as if in recognition as she walks across the uncut lawn towards us.

Ursula plonks herself down on the grave of James Stanley, and whispers to me as we watch the old nun picking her way towards us. 'Meet Kate, the unsure daughter of the tragic Jane, who is the daughter of the deceased Meredith.'

'Fuck off, Ursula.' My words are said through gritted teeth as I smile and stand up to greet the nun who takes both my hands in hers. Hands that are soft and warm, she doesn't let go. She is pressing carefully around my hurt.

'So pleased to meet you.' The nun smiles. 'Will you join us for a cup of tea, dear?' I walk alongside the nun back down the hill to the old convent building. Ursula follows along behind, a cringing dog, recently kicked.

The saucer is warm on my lap. The room is plain. There are chairs drawn back against the walls, a simple wooden cross on the wall and a Madonna gazing upwards from the mantelpiece. Sunlight is glancing down through high west-facing windows, making dust from the past come to life. Ursula chooses a chair behind my line of sight and declines the tea.

The older nun marvels at who I am. 'It was before my time, dear, but I do remember the sisters telling me the story of your grandfather, James Stanley. He was drowned in the 1942 flood, washed down from the Mangapurua Valley, his body found right here close to Jerusalem. Not a common thing for us to bury a settler but he came to us, in need of burial after the waters receded.'

The nun pauses and looks up at the Madonna. Is she thinking, as I am, about his bloated dead body? I nod, encouraging her to continue.

'It was trying times during the war.' The little nun pours more tea. 'Did you know, Kate, your mother, Jane, was born here?' I shake my head, not trusting myself to speak. The cup rattles on the saucer. The little nun continues. 'Your grandmother, Meredith, must have stayed on here after the funeral. She had nowhere to go, poor thing, and she was expecting a child. I'll just get a cloth, dear.'

I stare down at my shaking hands, still not trusting myself to speak.

'That's better.' The sister mops the tea off my lap and the trickle that has made it down onto the carpet. 'Now, where was I? Ah yes, your mother Jane. The old sisters always spoke fondly of little Jane. I have a picture of her here somewhere.' The nun opens a tall wooden cupboard with glass doors and lifts down an album. 'I remember which one she was because the sisters always spoke of her hair. A golden unruly mop. Here's the one.'

I squint at the faded black and white photo. The children, about twenty of them, all bunched in together. They are well-brushed and dressed in old fashioned pinafores and aprons. Several nuns are holding young babies, older children holding the hands of the little ones.

'This is Jane.' The nun points to a sturdy toddler in the front row with a mass of wild hair and a defiant smile. The small child has scrunched up the front of her skirt and apron with both hands. The hem line is riding up crookedly above her baby-fat knees. Jane is looking straight at the camera. She is refusing to hold anyone's hand.

I hand the album back. 'Do you have any pictures of my grandmother?'

The nun shakes her head. 'By all accounts your grandmother was quite unusual. She wore men's trousers and spent her time hunting pigs with dogs and a sheath knife. They used to say her old dog could hold any pig and she would borrow extra dogs from the marae. The sisters always spoke well of your grandmother. She kept the whole convent fed on wild pork, as well as cooking and cleaning the place. They were sad to see her go. Meredith and little Jane had become part of our family here at the convent. But everything changes.' The nun reaches for my empty tea cup and pours more tea.

'So, when did they leave here?' I am concentrating on my breathing. I'm winning; the refilled cup is not rattling.

The old nun glances down at the photo. 'I would say not long after this picture was taken. After the war finished maybe, they went to live up at Whangamomona. I did meet them once. Mr Dougherty brought Meredith and little Jane back up here to see her father's grave. She must have been about ten. I remember her bouncing curls. I gave her a peach for the journey home. You should have seen her face – it lit up as if I had given her something really precious.'

The nun lifts her eyes back up to the Madonna. 'And of course, I do remember your grandmother's funeral, her choice to come back and be buried here alongside James Stanley. Another exception.' The old nun sighs, touching her fingertip to her forehead, then her heart and bows to complete the sign with a light touch . 'Another tragedy, Kate, your grandmother taken in a house fire. You know he still comes to tend the grave.'

'This man, you know his name?'

'Oh yes, dear. Of course, we know him well.' She smiles. 'Toby Dougherty. He still comes all the way from Whangamomona to tidy the graves. He always stops in and has a cup of tea with us and brings us fresh mutton from his farm. Such a lovely man, tall and strong.' She looks me up and down for a moment.

I concentrate on holding onto the cup. It's rattling on the saucer again. I clamp my large hand down over the delicate flowery rim. 'What about Jane – did you get to meet Jane again?'

The nun pats my shoulder and takes the cup. 'No dear, she was in the fire as well, badly burnt, poor girl. At the funeral they said she was still in the hospital. We prayed for her soul. They said she mightn't pull through.'

The nun bustles back to the glass-fronted bookcase. 'Are you going on up the valley, dear? I have a book here for you.' She presses a Bible into my hands.

The nun directs me to the church. It's Ursula's choice not to come. Sunlight slants in from the west. It's warm and quiet. I slip into the very back pew. Next to me on the wall a wāhine Madonna is holding the baby Christ. He is plump, brown and well-loved.

In the convent, there are narrow beds and cots in the nursery room where the children used to sleep. They are made up with cotton sheets. The children are gone, but the nuns still tuck the edges in with love beneath the well-washed candlewick and rent the place to passing strangers in need of quiet repose. On the wall I read the poem that Baxter had written for a departing sister. A chook is calling out to the world to say she has just laid an egg, which is hidden somewhere in the long grass of the orchard. Fruit is hanging all around. The sun is shining on the freshly-weeded roses. The peaches in the orchard and the figs in the front paddock next to the walnut tree will be ripe soon and groan on the trees just as Baxter describes in his poem. The nuns have stripped away the old man's beard.

Back at the bikes, I undo my pack and slip the Bible into the side pocket.

Ursula is beside me with her hands on her hips. 'So, darling, the trail runs hot. Are we off to Whangamomona to hunt out the mysterious Mr Dougherty?' Ursula pulls the helmet down over her head.

'Don't "darling" me.' My hands clench the straps of my own helmet, which I wrench down onto my head. 'Go home, Ursula. I'm not going to Whangamomona. I'm not even sure that I want to find Toby Dougherty.'

'So the tragic Kate is still unsure. Why is that a surprise to me?' She shrugs her shoulders. 'We could just go to Palmy North instead. I could even pretend to be Ian and namby-pamby you like he always did. Oh sorry, I forgot. Isn't that Eric's new role in life?'

'Piss off, Ursula.' The anger inside my heart bursts in a pus-filled mess. 'And take that fucked-up little coward, Ian, with you.'

'Your wish is my command, darling.' Ursula steps forward and bumps her helmet hard against my chin piece. 'But just be careful what you wish for.'

Her bike disappears at speed back down River Road.

I kick my bike twice before it fires. Up the River Road, it starts to rain. Tears fall down both sides of my visor. I continue alone.

# Fourteen

# Beanstalk

He pored over her most recent poem. Nature again. First it was birds on the estuary, then her baby, then his unfortunate poetry experiment and now back to the landscape. But which fragile landscape? Somewhere down in the hills of Whangamomona where she came from, perhaps? Beanstalk had a moment of reflection; Jane was a natural reader, possibly a voracious childhood reader.

He strode into the day room with resolve and sure enough she was back reading that well-thumbed Enid Blyton rubbish. He winced at this backward step from real poetry to tacky children's fables but shrugged and took a trip into Papakura and brought back every Enid Blyton book he could lay his hands on. With rising excitement, he watched her brush through the titles and seize just the one book, which she cradled to her chest.

**First Book Without Pictures**

Far away a tree still grows enchanted wood
Never blighted, just Enid and me
Riding the slippery dip
Watching Fanny and Dick
Gorging on Google Buns

Silky feeds me gold
Pop Biscuits exploding
Honey runs down my chin
I catch the sticky drops with my fingers
Lick them clean

And then, what a peculiar thing
Slish slosh, Dame Washalot empties her tub
oft suds drip through me as I read
Washing me away from beneath my eiderdown
Even the soap tastes delicious

I climb further up the enchanted tree
And there is dear old Moonface
Crying out for me to stop
I climb faster, never pausing
Gobbling everything up, right to the top

Which magic land will be in the clouds today
The land of topsy-turvy or is it make-believe?
Just beware if the cloud moves on
We can never leave, happy ever after
With Moonface in a book without pictures

# Fifteen

# Meredith

Meredith is doing the washing the day that Agnes and Myra ride down the valley to visit the new bride. Hot water heating in the chimney fireplace, the washtub set up in the lean-to ready for rinsing, she's working on a stain that won't budge from her white shirt.

'Meredith! Your hair!' Agnes takes in the short blunt cut that Meredith has straightened as best she can with the scissors and no mirror. She slides down off Ginger and stares at Meredith.

'I like it.' Myra claps her hands. 'Just like the fashion models wear on the "Ladies' Page" in the *Weekly News*. Mum, can I have my hair like that?'

Agnes swots at Myra. 'You'll want a fancy new dress next. Not to mention high heels and a matching handbag.'

Meredith smiles and pats Myra on the head. 'You'll be a lady soon enough. How's your reading?'

Myra looks around. 'Where's *Peter Pan*? I'm sure I can read him by myself now. I'm up to books without pictures.'

Meredith smiles her delight and waves Myra towards the bedroom. 'Peter's always on the shelf by my bed.'

Myra settles herself with the book on Meredith's bed.

Agnes looks about the room and glances into the bedroom where Myra is curled up under the eiderdown. 'Your new quilt looks lovely on the bed.' She takes in the hundreds of dancing hexagons on the completed quilt, the only colour in the house. There's no new furniture, no pictures on the walls. She gestures outside. 'Let's hang out this washing.'

Once out of earshot of the reading child, Meredith knows the inquisition will start. She pegs up a pair of trousers.

'So how is it with Mr Stanley?' Agnes hangs up a double sheet.

Meredith hangs a cotton shift. She doesn't reply.

'Spill the beans, girl – how are you two getting on?' Agnes hangs up a black singlet.

Meredith hangs up a dish cloth that is showing signs of wear. 'Why don't you write to Mr Stanley and ask him yourself? Maybe he'll write you back one of his formal little notes just like in my courting days.'

Agnes colours a little. She hangs up a white towel and steers the conversation to other things.

Once the last of the washing is pegged, Meredith puts her prop under the line, pushing the washing up to where it can catch the breeze. They walk around the house, inspecting Meredith's new garden. Agnes has brought cuttings of her roses, petunia seedlings and some verbena cuttings as well. They pass the whare. The door is open. Agnes sees the makeshift bed: a woolpack pulled up hastily before first light with a horse cover over the top for warmth. There are no sheets.

*ooOOoo*

Chop, chop, on the chopping block. James Stanley cuts up meat for his dogs; it's getting dark and he'll soon be in. Meredith stirs up the embers and hangs the stew back on the hook to warm. She ladles hot water into a basin and takes it out to the lean-to. Mr Stanley likes to wash before he comes inside.

James Stanley stands in the doorway. His face, neck and bulging forearms are dripping wet. He takes the towel that Meredith has left for him on a chair by the door and stands in front of the fire to dry himself down.

The house is swept clean, everything in its place, bread ready for tomorrow.

James doesn't look at Meredith. They sit at either end of the little table to eat their meal. Stew with dumplings on top. The lumpy white dumplings are flecked green with parsley; Meredith always makes them this way. James Stanley carefully dissects the dumplings, moving each tiny piece of parsley neatly to one side of his plate. He holds his fork the correct way up with the curve uppermost.

The fork is clamped down against his palm with the three remaining fingers on his hook hand holding it firm. Not a word passes between them. After the meal, he places his cutlery together in the centre of the plate and is gone out the door to the whare. He will be up again at first light.

In the mornings, Meredith rises before he does. She stirs the porridge and makes cold mutton or pork sandwiches for him to take up the hill. James doesn't look at Meredith. He sits to eat his porridge and then he's gone.

On Saturday he takes the tin bath and a kerosene tin of water to the whare. On Sunday he hunts for pigs and brings the best carcass home on his horse. On Monday morning he leaves his dirty washing by the door of the lean-to. There is no variation.

Meredith sits on the step with her cup of tea and watches him ride away. Does she love him? No, but then she knew she never would.

Does she hate him? No, she doesn't hate him. Sometimes she sees his pain, which touches her own. She understands James Stanley; he's a better man than a lot.

Does she fear him? No, she trusts him completely. Their hands never meet, not even an accidental brush on the teapot handle.

Nothing given, nothing expected, but food, a roof, a cold bed, a place to be. Meredith busies herself with the dishes, weeds her garden, and straightens the house. Other women are busy with babies. The empty day stretches ahead.

*ooOOoo*

Chop, chop, on the chopping block. Meredith puts the wild pork roast in the camp oven back on the hook to heat and stirs up the fire. She carries out the water to the lean-to. In the corner she has laid down a sack. The bitch looks up with baleful eyes, willing Meredith not to come near her new litter.

Meredith waits for James.

He steps into the lean-to and glances down. 'So she's whelped, has she?' He grabs the sack out from under the old bitch and starts picking up the new born puppies. The bitch cowers out of reach of his boot.

'Mr Stanley, please.' Meredith grasps a handful of his rough coat. 'Can I just keep one?'

'Why?' He stands there, the wriggling sack in his hand. He's frowning down at her. There's a fierce line that furrows his eyes deeper in and his eyebrows touch together.

Meredith concentrates on his chin, which is solid and reasonable. 'A companion. I'd like a companion, please.' Meredith can see the furrow deepening and the head is about to start shaking from side to side. 'I'm here alone all day. Swaggers or road men call. Sometimes I'm afraid.'

James' eyes widen. He's looking at her now.

'And I want to get out and work with you on the farm.'

The furrow disappears. James slowly puts down the sack. 'You'd have to train the pup, and know what to do if the dog bales a pig or gets caught in a fence.'

Meredith nods.

'You'd have to wear trousers with a belt for a sheath knife and know how to use it. I can't be all the time looking after you out there.'

Meredith nods again.

He shrugs gruffly. 'Take your pick. You're probably better to choose us another bitch.' He holds the sack open.

Meredith reaches in and draws out a black pup with tan markings about the face and a white slash across its chest. She turns it over – a bitch. Meredith looks up at James and holds on tight to the warm wriggling body.

He nods and walks out to the creek with the remaining pups in the sack.

Meredith finds another sack. She lays it down for the old bitch to lie on. 'I'll call you Spark.' She hugs the warm little body and returns the puppy to its mother.

The bitch looks up at Meredith then settles on the sack. She sniffs at Spark and lets the one remaining pup latch back onto a swollen teat.

James drops the wet, unmoving sack beside the lean-to and looks down at the suckling pup. 'Only one week on the bitch mind, then it's up to you to feed the pup. I'll need the old bitch back up the hill.'

James washes his arms and face and strolls into the house. He eats his dinner in silence and then stands ready to head out to the whare. He reaches for the door and pauses for a moment without looking at Meredith. 'You can grow your hair back if you want to.'

The door shuts behind him.

*ooOOoo*

A heart attack is when a blood vessel blocks and a small piece of the heart withers and dies. The rest of the heart is weakened but carries on in the meantime around the dead canker that lies blackened and unmoving somewhere in its depths. Again and again their road blocks when the bluffs fall away, sometimes staying shut for a whole winter. Another family leaves, and then another. Just a whisper, no big farewells, another unmoving part in the valley.

Agnes starts up a Women's Institute. 'You must come along, Meredith. All the other ladies are making the effort. We need to beat this thing and have some fun together.'

Meredith nods yes and rides away down the road, Spark always at her heels. She knows she will never go to the institute. Whenever there's a woolshed party or summer tennis at the Bettjemans' place, the Stanleys never quite get there either. The district knows that the Stanleys keep to themselves. Some folk just prefer it that way.

The Women's Institute collects pennies, their goal to raise funds for a community hall, which will never be built. No one thinks to build a church. The valley is like a platoon at war where religious differences are set aside. No one denomination rules another. No one thinks to build a shrine to thank God for what he has given them here in this valley. Good folk read the Bible around a family table and a vicar is found for baptisms, but there's never a regular Sunday service.

Christmases come and go. The newspaper is full of advertisements for fancy new electrical appliances, but nothing changes in the valley – the power is never put on and who could afford those fancy appliances anyway? They are lucky to have a phone, the line put in by the local men. It loops from one hand-cut post to the next for those who choose to subscribe. The Stanleys never do.

Bridge builders come. The news ripples down the valley. They are planning to replace the old swing bridge with one that cars can drive across. The plan is for a solid concrete structure overarching next to the old swing bridge down the river end of the valley. The master plan that brought Fred Bettjeman to this valley all those years ago is finally being enacted. Nancy told Meredith that it had been a clincher for Fred when he signed up a lease on their farm. It was going to be a main road one day, right up their valley.

Huh, one day had taken a while. They had said it was to be a grand highway, all the way from Stratford to Raetihi. A sister bridge on the Whangamomona side had been approved as well, somewhere north of the river. Both bridges designed in permanent materials, concrete, made to last. The final master stroke was to be the joining link, a bridge over the wide, lazy Whanganui River. Fancy, after all these years, the project was to start.

The road down the valley is widened to get the trucks down to the bridge site so the timber for the boxing can be brought over the hill from Raetihi. Meredith pulls to the side on her horse, Holly, and watches the progress.

Word goes around that one of the trucks is over the bank. Meredith rides down to see the wheels facing upward way below in the creek.

Winter washes out the road again and takes away the boxing for the buttress they have built. The trucks stop for a whole year. The pulse of the valley is a hesitant ribbon that cannot hold a regular beat. More settlers are leaving.

*ooOOoo*

Meredith has grass seed to collect from the landing. She saddles Holly, calls Spark and sets out to meet the riverboat. Spring has finally come and once again the road has been cleared enough for trucks to crawl down to the swing bridge end of the valley. Meredith stops to look at the eight by two plank they have laid across one of the washouts to run the outside wheels of the trucks across the sheer drop to the creek. Holly sticks close to the bank and they continue.

Just before the swing bridge there's a camp of tents and a woman is busy in a makeshift kitchen. Meredith waves out and dismounts to take a closer at the progress. She stops on the swing bridge to watch two men who are working atop the centre of a precarious wooden arch built from a patchwork of timber in two pieces, which have just been connected together across the deep ravine downstream from where she stands.

A young man joins her on the bridge. He is carrying a Brownie box camera, which he nestles into his elbow as he nods and tips his hat. 'Dave Sandford. Meeting the boat, are you?'

Meredith nods and gasps as she notes the lean frame, square chin and Peter's clear blue eyes. The moment passes. This boy is barely out of his teens and Peter's been dead all these years. She covers her confusion by calling Spark to her side before she looks up at the boy again. 'You're helping with the bridge then?'

Dave nods. 'That's my old man and his apprectice out there on the boxing – just heading across to take a picture.' He follows Meredith across the swing bridge and walks with her to the best vantage point on the downstream side of the track. He whistles out to the two men who stop work and stand upright for a moment on the centre of the arch high above the creek.

Meredith watches Dave's young, strong hands adjust the camera and click the shutter. 'Quite some bridge,' she says.

Dave grins. 'This is just the boxing. Soon we can start mixing concrete. Just like an eggshell, it's the arch shape that gives a bridge like this its strength.'

Meredith stares up at the flimsy wooden arch pieced together 130 feet above the creek. 'Strong enough to drive a truck over?'

'You bet, and built to last. It'll still be here when your granddaughter comes calling.'

Meredith flinches and turns away. She must hurry; the riverboat is due.

ooOOoo

Up on the hills, Meredith musters sheep with Spark running to her whistle. James is over the next ridge pushing his mob down as well. In the gully, the mob comes together and Meredith rides on ahead to turn them into the yards at the bottom. She counts the sheep as they run and leap past the gate. The tally is more than James had hoped for. He nods to her as she closes the gate. A job well done.

They work together in the shed. Meredith tips each sheep over in the catching pen, cuts away the foot rot, crutches, checks the teeth, inspects the udder, marks the rejects with raddle, then pulls each sheep out to James who hand shears the main fleece off and then pushes each naked sheep down the port hole.

At the end of the day, Meredith and Spark head back to the house to get the fire lit and the dinner on while James takes the stock away. She puts the pot of leftover stew on to heat and measures flour to make dumplings. They turn out plump and white. Meredith gave up growing parsley some years ago. It was a waste as they never seemed to use it in the cooking anymore. After dinner they talk about how they will muster the next block. James helps dry the dishes then heads out to the whare. There are sheets on the bed out there now and Meredith has made him a quilt but the bath water is never shared.

*ooOOoo*

Up on the hills, Meredith is mustering sheep down a difficult ridge. Spark hunts them out of the pig fern and Meredith flogs them on down the hill. James Stanley is in the next gully. She can hear his dogs and knows they're onto a pig. Spark's ears prick to the excited yap and then the high-pitched squealing. The dog looks up at her with expectant wet eyes and Meredith nods. Spark streaks away to join the hunt and Meredith follows. The noise is coming from a steep section of the creek. Meredith slips off Holly and scrambles down. She draws her sheath knife as Mr Stanley has taught her to do.

It's a boar, still young but well grown. Spark has latched onto his shoulder. The other dogs snap and growl at his black bristled face. Meredith can see the short tusks as the head flings backwards and forwards, trying to catch the soft underbelly of the dogs as they bark and nip at him. James Stanley has his knife ready. He moves in behind the distracted pig, intent on the back leg, which he must grab to flip the pig over while its attention is taken up front with the dogs.

Stanley grabs the leg and heaves the pig's hind quarters into the air, knee ready to drop down and pin the pig on its back, knife ready to stick its throat. The pig flips, the knee drops down, the hook hand reaches for the front leg but the threshing pig is struggling to right itself. The left hook hand slips off the front trotter and the pig struggles to get back over onto its feet. James Stanley drops his knife to wrestle the pig back down with his strong right hand. Too late – the tusks rip the length of Stanley's bulging right forearm like a knife cutting through a red fleshed plum.

Meredith is there. She catches a leg, flips the pig, her knee goes down and her knife cuts deep into the neck in just the right spot. The terrible squealing gets worse, filling her head entirely. The young boar's life blood spurts out and stings her eyes shut. She swallows the warm salty mess, which is hitting her face, her chin, her neck, running down under her clothes. Her hand is slippery on the knife. She must stick the pig again and hack around to get the wind pipe and enough blood vessels to finish the job. The squealing stops at last. The involuntary kicking of the trotter continues beneath her. Meredith climbs off the pig, rubs her eyes clear of blood and turns to see to Stanley. She rips her shirt and binds his arm. The blood stops pumping out but she has seen the severed ends of white sinew, his fingers unmoving.

James Stanley stares down, first at his limp right hand bandaged to the elbow in strips of Meredith's shirt and then he moves his gaze to his left hook hand, which is cradling the right. He jerks his head up and stares at Meredith. 'Why didn't you let the pig finish me? A clean death. You would have been free then.'

Meredith doesn't answer. She finishes cutting some meat from the loin of the pig and then helps him stand up. 'You are my husband, Mr Stanley.' She steers his elbow on the hook side. 'Best we get you home and up to Mrs Bettjeman to see if she can stitch this up.' James Stanley is leaning on her now. He needs whisky, badly.

# Sixteen

# Beanstalk

Who in the world was Moonface? He felt a sinister presence in this girl's past. Was Moonface the father of her child? As usual, whenever he made a gentle suggestion he drew a blank. Jane's stubbornness could be most irritating. Why would she not write answers to his questions in simple sentences, of which she had proved herself more than capable? Instead she just wrote poems at her whim. He worried that even this channel of communication might end. Like all facets of a psychiatric patient's existence he feared her poems would become repetitive, going over and over the same subject matter or peter out to nothing. He pondered how he could keep her moving forward. Were there other books from her past that could inspire her to write more broadly? He tried *The Jungle Book* and *Anne of Green Gables* but neither sparked her interest. He bought a beautiful volume of *Peter Pan* with glossy illustrations, but Jane had turned away and refused to even open the book, let alone touch it. Ungrateful tyrant, he'd thought, and yet at 3.00am he still puzzled over her. Jane had become a curse that Beanstalk was powerless to either shed or solve.

Who was this damn Moonface person who'd begun to pop up in her poems? What had he done to her? His only hope was that further poems would give him the answers he sought. Patience and time were his only allies in the darkest hours of the night and Jane wasn't going anywhere. Beanstalk consoled himself with this thought, but was she a fly caught in his trap, or was it the other way around? He sighed and tried to sleep.

## Reading With Moonface

I never did like *Peter Pan*
My mother knew him well
Every word by heart
It always made her cry

When she sat by the window
I would run to Moonface
He never cried
We would read together

Sat by the fire
*The Faraway Tree*
My first ever book
Without pictures

# Seventeen

# Kate

At Pipiriki the silt track down to the river is slipping away in places. I pull in and park my bike under rowan trees covered with bright red berries. Across the road is the museum, a small wooden house with top-storey gabled windows where a riverboat captain once lived. The museum is right next door to where the mighty Pipiriki Hotel once stood, burnt down years ago. Someone has tried to rebuild it but yet another dream has fallen by the wayside at Pipiriki. The roof is on but there's broken glass in the aluminium and a sign warning against trespassers. Vegetation tries to right the wrong and weeds are springing up. The partially finished building sits and moulders behind trees that have grown in front and now block the view where folk would once have stood and watched the paddle steamers coming up the river. I clamber over the tape and stand where the front steps should be. I can't even see the river.

In the museum there are pictures of the old paddle boats. They are long gone now. Jet boats have replaced them. Handsome V8s take tourists up the river for day trips and are pulled out of the river at the end of the day, parked up above the boat ramp at Pipiriki. Farmers use jet boats as well, tying up at lonely landings, where the river is still their only road.

I glance at the old pictures of the mighty Pipiriki House, a mass of balconies with women promenading in long skirts, people sitting and standing by the river, everybody waiting for the next steamboat. All gone now, the hotel burnt to the ground and the populous Māori village gone as well. There are just a few scattered houses dotted about with paddocks in between.

Today there are no tourists about, nor locals either. The river is deserted, just an empty boat trailer parked up behind a four-wheel drive with tyre marks where they have backed the jet boat down into the river over the grey silt.

I seek out the spry little woman who has let me into the museum. What does she know of the Mangapurua Valley?

She smiles and points up the river. 'Oh, you mean the Bridge to Nowhere? Quite the thing, jet boat trips, very historic. Are you wanting a boat trip?' She picks a book off the countertop and hands it to me. 'Arthur Bates has written about it all.'

*The Bridge to Nowhere.* I glance at the subtitle: *The Ill-fated Mangapurua Settlement.*

I point to the title. 'Sounds a bit grim.'

The little woman nods. 'Did you have a connection up there? We often get descendants of that valley passing through here.'

'My grandparents.' I pick up the book and flick to the pictures, black and white shots of pioneers standing by newly-built huts or astride their horses.

'That's nice, dear.' The little woman rustles about under the counter. 'I have a map here showing where the soldiers leased the land up there after the First World War. What was the surname?'

'Stanley.' I look in the index at the back of the book and run my eye down to 'S'.

The little woman pauses. 'Sorry, dear, there were no Stanleys up there.'

'What?' I pull my eyes away from the book and frown down at the little woman. 'You're wrong – my grandfather, James Stanley, was there with his wife Meredith in 1942. He must be one of those families.'

'I'm not wrong.' The little woman raises her chin. 'I know exactly which families were left there in 1942, which was just before the valley closed. It was the Bettjemans, McDonalds and Johnsons. No one else, dear.'

I slap the book back down on the counter. 'But the nuns found him drowned, washed up at Jerusalem. They told me he'd washed down from that valley in the 1942 flood. James Stanley must have been up there.'

The little woman stiffens. 'I'm not saying he wasn't there, dear, I'm just saying your family isn't in the history books. Just not original settlers.' She pauses for a moment and reaches to take my hand. 'There were squatters up there, dear – sad, desperate people who lived in the empty houses during the Depression times. No one wrote down their names.'

'So my family wasn't good enough for the history books?'

'The history gets written down by the ones who made it through,' she says, shaking her head. 'Maybe there was no one left in these parts to tell old Arthur Bates the tale of your family. Neighbours in these parts don't gossip about things that aren't their business – not in history books, anyway.' The little woman busies herself polishing the counter. She is looking down at her own anxious reflection in the glass rather than at me.

'So what do you know about my family that isn't in the history books?' I don't mean to clip my words. If Ursula was here, she would be kicking me under the table right now and saying something that would smooth it over for me.

'About your grandfather. What was his name again?' She doesn't look at me. She is buying time, polishing, polishing. Round and round goes the cloth.

'James Stanley. I'm just trying to piece it all together.' I try for a winning smile but it doesn't go quite right, more like a grimace that falls flat between us. Where the hell is Ursula when I need her?

The little woman misses nothing. 'I did hear a story of someone taking his last wool clip down to the landing on a sled during that flood time. After the 1942 flood they found the the sled upended and wedged into the creek downstream from Battleship Bluff, all the bales gone,' she glances at me, 'and the farmer was reported missing as well. Maybe that was your grandfather.'

'How come that story never made the history books?'

'No one wants to get history wrong, do they? Sometimes it's just safer not to include the parts where the details are a bit vague.'

'A bit vague?' I step closer to the counter, towering over the little lady. 'How do you mean vague?' I realise too late that Ursula would be kicking my shins doubly hard by now.

The little woman steps back from the counter and pauses. I can see she's trying to think what she should say next. Her mouth is clamped shut.

I lean forward into her indecision, bending over until our eyes are level. 'Wouldn't you want to know if it were your family?'

The little lady stops polishing and puts down the cloth. She speaks slowly. 'Well, it's nothing really, but they do say the young man who had been working for your grandfather left after the flood and took your grandmother with him.'

'A young man?' My hands are shaking; I put them behind my back. 'A young man, you say?'

'Yes, a young man who had come from Whangamomona, I believe. He was staying up there at the time of the 1942 flood.'

'Do you know his name?' I am whispering now. 'Please.'

The little woman turns to put the map away. 'No, dear, I don't know his name.'

'Toby Dougherty?' I whisper and watch the little lady startle as she closes the cupboard. I slap my fist down on the desk. 'And none of this made the history books?'

The little lady steps forward and folds her arms. 'What makes history is for a family to decide. Maybe it's your choice how their history should be told.'

After paying for the book, I stalk out the door. The little lady locks up behind me. There are no other tourists today. I walk down to the river and sit on a fallen log, covered in silt from the last flood, and begin to read what Mr Bates has to say about the ill-fated Mangapurua Valley.

*The Mangapurua is an increasingly popular 20 mile long valley branching off the Whanganui River 20 miles above Pipiriki in the most remote section of the Whanganui River valley.*

*One would think of this area as just another of the beautiful lonely valleys, which fall into the Whanganui River until the intriguing reminders of man's failed attempts to subdue the valley catch the eye. Such things as a drift of daffodils in the scrub, the skeleton of an apple tree, remnants of a house, remains of a chimney and above all the sudden shock sight of a massive concrete bridge across a deep gorge in a seemingly trackless patch of punga, brush and manuka catches one's imagination.*

*These are all that remain of a settlement that in 1917 moved into and cut down the virgin bush of this remote place. At one time, just under 40 returned servicemen, the majority of them married, called this valley home. They moved into the valley, which had been especially opened up for them by a grateful government as a reward for their military service during the 1914–18 World War.*

*The scheme was a complete and utter failure. One by one, the disillusioned settlers walked off their farms, abandoning their holdings to the erosion and the regenerating bush. By 1942 all but three farmers had left the valley and these last three were forced to leave when the Cabinet made the decision in 1943 that the treacherous access road would no longer be maintained. By 1944 every person had left the valley and all had departed virtually penniless despite giving their heart and soul to vainly attempting to subdue this seemingly promising valley. The valley was left deserted and forlorn.*[2]

*ooOOoo*

For the next couple of days, I take a cabin just along the road and curl

---

2  Arthur Bates, Introduction, *The Bridge to Nowhere: The Ill-fated Mangapurua Settlement* (Wanganui: Wanganui Newspapers Ltd. 1981), 7.

up with Arthur Bates' book to read more about the Mangapurua Valley. I read, I walk about, I think, I sit on the silt down by the river and read some bits over again. Tales of returned soldiers, some with broken bodies, and others with broken minds, most with no experience of farming, but all with high hopes of making it in this forsaken valley of God's own. Ex-soldiers walking in with a lease, a debt, a tent, an axe, a rifle and a camp oven. But their war wasn't over, just a new location and a new enemy. A company of returned soldiers at war against the slippery papa rock of the Mangapurua Valley. The prize they each sought: a sheep station to hand down to future generations. So much hope, so much grit, so much determination and hard work, a never-ending slog, not knowing that the odds were stacked so they could never win. In the end, they were losers, one and all. In the book there are warm-hearted stories of friendship, martyrdom, tenacity and resilient women who raised their children well and survived to move out of the valley and rebuild their lives again in other places. No mention of any Stanleys though. I throw Arthur Bates against the wall in disgust.

*CABINET*                                    *Date 30th April 1942*

*Present – Rt Hon. P. Fraser, Hon. W. Nash, Hon D.G. Sullivan*

*1.Flood damage, Ruatiti Riding, Waimarino County: recommendation by Public Works, State Advances and Land Departments that because of the excessive cost of repairs the road should not be further maintained. Treasury recommends the following action in relation to the settlers –*

*(a) Land Department and State Advances Corporation to notify all settlers that road will not be maintained further and that they will have to abandon properties; the notification to include advice of amount of remission of liabilities and other concessions.*

*(b) No promise of compensation is to be made, but each case will be considered on its merits following settlers' representations.*

*(c) Ex gratia payments limited to £250 to be made in necessitous cases to cover removal and other expenses. Payments to be made out of fund for similar grants in the case of 'Uneconomic Farms Amalgamation.'*[3]

*Approved*
*P. F.*
*4.5.42*

In 1943 the three final families were forced to move away. Only the wild pigs remained.

I ride out to Raetihi, through winding tracts of bush and then farmland, well fenced now, sheep content behind eight wires with no more native forest, just grass and rush bushes amongst the broken papa faces.

The man in the Four Square shop is helpful with food and points down the road to the farm supply store that will sell me a tarpaulin that I can use as a fly. He says it will be a nice time of year to be camping in the valley.

The lady behind the counter at the garage tells me to look out for Tom Mowat. 'He's a Raetihi local, but he'll be up there just now chasing pigs and trapping possums.'

My heart lurches. Mowat is a name from Bates' book. I look over the chewing gum on the counter at the lady who is passing my change. 'Would that Tom Mowat know anything about the valley?'

The lady nods her head. 'There isn't anything about the valley that Tom Mowat doesn't know. His folks used to live up there and he skives off every break we get from the shearing to head back into those hills.'

'Will he mind talking to me about the old people?'

---

3  Bates, *The Bridge to Nowhere*, 164.

The lady laughs. 'Get Tom started talking about that valley and you will have trouble shutting him up. The jet boat drivers complain that the folk who meet up with Tom are often late down to catch their ride out.'

'How do I find him?'

'That's easy done. He has a camp set up at the McDonalds' old homestead. Just watch out for a row of macrocarpa trees on your left as you go up the valley.' She grins as she hands me my change. 'He's been in there a few days so hit him up for some wild pork for your dinner and tell him it's time he was getting back here. Tell him we'll be starting back shearing lambs in a couple of days.'

*ooOOoo*

The driver ties up the steel-hulled jet boat and holds her steady against the slippery papa while the tourists scramble out onto the Mangapurua Landing.

'Right folks, walk this way to the famous Bridge to Nowhere.' The driver leads the way from the landing onto well-formed steps and a small tramping track that curves away up through the bush.

'This was the main route in and out of the valley in the early days for the first settlers who would come up here with all their worldly goods delivered by the steamers. Nature has a way of smoothing things over though.' The driver and his little party walk on in silence.

From the back of this motley crew, I watch a pair of puffing fat white cotton pants and clean sandshoes climbing up ahead, then a family with kids already asking, 'Are we there yet?' A couple of hunters are pulling ahead with a gun each and backpacks, and finally a young European couple who speak little English.

Twenty minutes up through the bush and there it is. We stop at a lookout to admire the eggshell arch and delicate vertical pillars that hold up each end of the bridge across a deep gut with a small creek, disappearing amongst the punga way below.

The jet boat driver gathers us around him. 'The guys who helped build this bridge ran a joinery factory down at Raetihi – that's why the form work is so good. It's a work of art if you ask me. Bill Sandford's crew did all the boxing timber and then poured the concrete. Not bad for men who built furniture and coffins for a living before they took up bridge building. All the concrete done in a hand-turned concrete mixer, tipped out by the bucketful and pulled out there on a wire to make that arch, rammed down into the boxing. All done by hand, no safety rails. It's a 39 metre drop down there to the creek. Anyone want that job?' The kids in the crowd shake their heads and set off running on up the path. We hear a whoop as they pop out from amongst the punga onto the narrow concrete bridge.

I walk on up and step out onto the bridge. Only wide enough for a single car, the sides are concrete and the top rail is solid and warm to my touch. All around me is dense, shining bush and birds singing. Fantails are flicking about us catching the insects we disturb in this silent place. At either end of the bridge the creek is camouflaged by overhanging bush but standing in the centre, I can see the water way below in the deep papa canyon. Upstream, still hanging, are the remains of the old swing bridge. Just one wire left now, strung across the creek with a few pieces of hand-cut timber yet to fall away. The lichen and rusted nails must be nearly ready to let go of these last wooden remnants.

The kids tear across the bridge and back. 'Is this all there is?' Disappointed, they slump down beside the jet boat driver who is getting out a thermos from his backpack. The kids perk up again when he pulls out a packet of biscuits. The tourists gather around the driver who pours tea from a thermos and hands it around and offers seconds on the biscuits.

He sees me looking at the old bridge. 'That one was built in 1919, pack horses only. This one,' he pats the concrete railing, 'went up in 1936. Only a handful of cars ever drove across. By then, the last few folk left in the top of the valley mainly used the road out to Raetihi. Occasionally the ladies would still take the riverboat to Wanganui rather than rough it on the road. A bit of a white elephant you could say – a fine new concrete bridge with nowhere to go.'

The hunters have gone on. The rest of the tourists have already left to straggle back down to the boat. The jet boat driver has put on his backpack, ready to follow them down. He gives me a wave as I shoulder my gear. We have agreed I will meet him back down at the landing on his trip up the following day.

I stand alone on the Bridge to Nowhere. The silence is broken only by a tiny fantail that joins me on the concrete railing. The small brown-headed piwakawaka dances and flits, tweet-a-tweet. She is showing me her fan, telling me a serious story that I can't quite understand. The sun is gone behind a cloud. I watch the fantail and wish that Ursula were here with me now. Bloody Ursula.

Arthur Bates sits on my shoulder reminding me of the stories that I have read in his book. This is the swing bridge that claimed the hand of Jack Ward's mate. Both men helping out the bridge builders when the hand was crushed between a block and tackle. They carried him out of the valley on a stretcher. Jack Ward's mate never returned.

Across the bridge and on up the valley I follow the foot track. Once a road wide enough for a truck, but now it peters out quickly to just a tramping track, in places only just wide enough for my feet single file and even then slipping away down the side of the cliff into the creek below, requiring me to tread with care.

I look out for the spot where Fred Bettjeman had fallen over the edge, down into the creek. Bates had said he was saved only by a soft landing on the empty kerosene cans he was carrying back up to his camp, a misstep in the dark on his way home up the valley after an evening drinking whisky with the settlers from down near the landing.

This must be the path that willing neighbours followed when they carried Mrs Bartrum's upright piano all the way up from the landing to her rough-hewn little house, and then all the way back down to the landing again when the Bartrum's farming venture hadn't worked out.

Not the first or last trip where neighbours would pitch in to help carry someone's broken dream or injured body out of this valley.

Around another corner and here is Battleship Bluff, just as Bates described it in his book. Way below me on my left, the creek takes a sharp turn around a grey papa bluff with a blunt frontage that could be likened to the prow of a battleship. Is this the bluff that my grandfather fell over? Did James Stanley really die here, swept away in a flood? I look over the edge at the twinkling creek way below. It's just an innocent trickle of water today. I kick a rock over the edge and watch it tumble and bounce until it finally hits the creek far below with the sound of a small bomb.

Here is another house site with mānuka growing back. Is this where Pat Mowat lived? Will I get to meet his son Tom Mowat further up the valley?

At Ward's Flat there's just an old barbed wire fence still standing, held up by hand-split native timber posts. No sign now of the house that Jack Ward built, before he went broke and walked away penniless. This flat area now returning to bush must have been the field where young returned soldiers once practised rugby before taking on the neighbouring valley.

Further on up, a chimney stands alone in a rough-grown field – all that's left of the Bettjemans' homestead. I look around to see if I can spot where their tennis court would have been and the site of the woolshed where all the district's local dances were held. Nothing to see now amongst the regrowth. I walk on.

Up ahead I spot the dark heads of a row of towering macrocarpa trees, which must mark the site where the McDonalds lived.

I stop by the old macrocarpa hedge, huge now. It would take more than three men to handspan their bases. I step off the track, and sure enough, here is a camp of sorts. I step closer; the fire is still warm. There's a dead pig with its bristles singed off hanging in the tree and possum skins stretched out on boards, hanging to dry under a makeshift roof. I step further forward. The place is built from rough-cut tawa poles with polythene tacked over them to keep out the rain. Old woven wire bedsteads and a couple of camp stretchers are huddled side by side taking up most of the space under the canopy. There is a proper chimney though. Rusted corrugated iron is standing up on end to take the smoke to the sky. The top side of an old Orion stove is suspended as a hot plate over the open fire, held up by four lengths of number eight wire hung from a stout tawa crossbar overhead. There is a blackened camp oven and a meat safe hanging in a nearby tree. A Tilley lantern hangs from the central pole.

I start at a noise behind me. A man is standing there, his beanie pulled down low. He carries a gun and a small dead pig aloft on his shoulder. His pig dogs stand on either side of him. The dogs are straining toward me but are not moving, just a low growl, intent on their boss' next command. They slink to lie down around the edges of the campsite at his signal. The man leans his gun against a tree and hooks the pig up by its back hock on an S hook that is hanging there. He wipes his bloodied hand on the back of his trousers.

'Tom Mowat,' he says as he extends his hand. 'What brings you to these parts?' His handshake is firm and at fifty he's wiry and lean. His face has weathered well with deep smile lines. A man still fit enough to bend all day to shear sheep or chase pigs and carry them out of steep-sided gullies.

I tell him about the lady at the garage and that the lamb shearing is due to start up next week.

He nods his head. 'That'll be Jean. She doesn't miss a turn.' Tom stirs the fire. 'You'll be sharing a chop with me?' He tips water out of a drench container into a kettle and puts it on the fire. Next, he pulls an axe out of the block next to the hanging carcass and cuts meat for his dogs, ties them up nearby and checks their water.

Watching all this I breathe easier. He is a man who looks after his animals before himself. Walking back with wood to stoke the fire, he pauses for a moment, washes his hands in a makeshift basin then lifts the lid on an apple box that also serves as a seat. He takes out a tin of cocoa, tips several heaped spoonsful into each enamel mug followed by sugar and pours water out of the steaming kettle. I settle with my hot drink on a round of firewood next to the apple box and watch as he peels potatoes with his sheath knife and lays thick pork chops directly on the stove top where they spit and hiss. I tell him my story about the Stanleys. He's not one to interrupt.

His food is good. We share Ginny's Anzac biscuits and drink more cocoa.

I pull out Arthur Bates' book and hand it to Tom. 'Jean tells me you're related to the Mowat family they talk about in here?'

'Yep, my Dad was Pat Mowat.' Tom turns the pages. 'Old Arthur put some of our family pictures in here somewhere.' He stops at a picture of a shingled house with a horse-pulled hay cutter standing in front. 'Yep, this is the one. Did you see the flat just after Battleship Bluff? That's where my folks lived.' I look at the picture of the dollhouse-sized cottage.

'So were you born in here?'

Tom smiles. 'No, do your sums girl, I'm not that old. I was born down in Wanganui, six years after Pat left the valley. My mother was a Whakahoro girl. She knew Dad for a couple of years while he was still living up here. He played the accordion at all the local dances so got to run his eye over all the young ladies. But they didn't marry straight away. You see, he lived up here with his mother and my Aunty Mary. Maybe my mother was too smart to be the third woman in a tiny backcountry hut. Imagine that, stuck here all winter with the road closed, no power on, just a tiny house and no room to swing a cat. I remember Aunty Mary used to talk about it. They were excited just to have a proper wood stove and a wind-up clock.' Tom stands up to stir the fire.

'So what happened to all the houses?'

'They say that our one was accidentally burnt down by pig hunters years ago now. Nothing left except the Orion stove sitting out on the flat. See, here's the picture.' Tom turns the pages of the book to a photo of an old rusting stove sitting alone in the bush. 'Even that's gone now. Folk have come in here and dragged relics away over the years, just like this bit.' He kicks the old piece of stove, which hangs above the fire. 'Other folk took out what they could when they left the place – posts, fencing wire – some even dismantled buildings, others just closed the door and walked away.' Tom reaches for more wood.

'You still come back here, though?'

'Yep, I still come back here.' Tom smiles at the fire. 'Watch out, this place gets in your blood. My grandmother came here for six weeks and ended up staying for thirteen years. My grandfather was a bank manager down in Wanganui – they would have been well-to-do in those days, but he died young. My grandma and my spinster aunt, Mary, just came up here for a holiday to see Pat and never left. Maybe I'm the same; contract shearing gives me time off between runs when the weather packs in. I've squatted in here for years, running cattle from the Quins' place down to Wards'.'

He stirs the fire with his boot. 'Used to muster a hundred weaner beef off each year until the Conservation Department finally chased me out. Now I just come back to hunt the pigs. I like the quiet of the place.' Tom turns to me. 'So what really brings you here, asking all these questions?'

I tell him what the nuns had said about James Stanley and the 1942 flood.

Tom shakes his head. 'My folks were well gone by then. My father, Pat, wasn't one to talk much about this place once he settled down in Wanganui but I did hear him say that they let some squatters take over our old place after they moved away.' He smiled up at me. 'Never know, could have been your family.'

He throws more wood on the fire and we both stare at the licking flames. One of the dogs stirs and barks at something out in the darkness, but is silenced by a curt word from Tom.

Tom stands and stretches. 'If your folks were here in the valley, they would have been good people. My father always said it was the people who made this place. You had to be a good sort to live up here. Folks just got on with things, helped their neighbours, battled on until they went broke and then took the fight someplace else. Started all over again.'

Tom offers me an old, rusted woven wire bed frame rather than pitching my fly. I roll into the sagging dip in the middle, curl up and listen to the morepork and the distant murmur of the creek deep in the papa gorge below.

For breakfast, more slabs of pork and Tom's camp-oven bread. We walk together further up the valley. Tom shows where the schoolhouse stood on the Testers' place — just a small hut — and where Reg and Agnes Anderson carved out an existence for a few short years during the Depression and then moved on.

No sign of any Stanleys here. We walked on up to the trig, looking out to Ruapehu and Tongariro to the east and west towards Mount Taranaki who stands alone. I try not to think of Ursula. Tom points out where the deep brown Whanganui River runs connecting the slopes of the inland mountains to the sea, just an imagined line that is hard to make out in the dark forest land below us. I think about utu and bloody Ursula. It's time I was getting home.

Walking back down, Tom's dogs are suddenly alert and sniffing. They slip away into the bush. Silence. Tom holds up a finger and we listen: first a loud *woof, woof,* down to our left in a steep-sided gully and then silence with just the occasional *woof.* Tom smiles. 'Have you ever stuck a pig? My dogs are holders. When they bail a pig they bark for me to come, then they latch on and hold. They must have latched onto a big fella. They haven't got much voice left to bark.'

I can hear a pig squealing and no barking.

'Come on, those dogs need our help.' Tom jog trots off in the direction of the noise. I follow him down off the side of the track, plunging through the bush, pushing down into the scrub country, scrambling over fallen limbs and rocks, jumping across the bottom of small guts where water runs between silent pools. We reach the bottom of the main gulley and start clambering up the high-sided creek.

*Woof, woof.*

'Damn, watch out. My dogs have lost their hold – must be a big one.'

There's a surging and crashing up ahead. The dogs are barking and taking turns to clutch at the rear-end of a large boar, which is being driven down the narrow gut towards us. Tom has unslung his 303; he stands his ground. The black bulk of the pig is heading straight for us, huge head and wide tusks. Tom takes aim and a bullet rips. The pig drops at Tom's feet.

I try to make it look casual as I climb back down the tree I was scaling moments before. 'Great shot.'

Tom grins and gets out his sheath to begin gutting. 'Not bad. I'd say this guy could weigh in at 150 pounds.' He pulls out the steel to sharpen his knife. 'Sorry, I was hoping to show you how to stick a pig, but sometimes a rifle comes in handy if you need to take a quick shot. Best to do it straight up the snouter – drops them fast.'

Tom guts the pig and, using a pair of old dog collars, he straps each hind leg to the front leg on the same side. 'Best way to carry a heavy brute like this one.' He tests the two carry handles he has made and slides his arms through, lifting the pig up onto his back like an oversized tramping pack. I take his gun and follow the scary-looking black hunchback up through the bush and then back down the track towards his camp. The pig's head is sitting forward above Tom's head; the pig's tail hangs almost down to his knees. I can't see his Stubbies shorts. His buttocks and shoulders are lost against the underbelly of the gutted pig. I can just see his boots tramping along underneath the carcass. His careful footsteps take us back to camp where he drops the heavy load and then winches the carcass up into a tree.

Tom fills my pack with plastic bags of wild pork. I think of Ursula swooning over possible recipes. It's time I was getting back to meet the jet boat.

'See ya,' Tom shakes my hand. He glances up to see how far the sun has moved across the sky, gauging whether there's still time to go after another pig. 'I hope you find your family. Go well.' He's gone back up the track with his dogs running behind him.

Back down the valley, the bush is pushing in on me. The scars on the hills are filling now with mānuka, but nothing grows on the faces of grey papa rock. There are fresh slips on the track. This land never stops slipping away.

At Jack Ward's place and then again on Mowat's Flat, I stop and kick around where their houses must have stood. There's nothing to show me if the Stanleys ever lived here – not a clue amongst the purple foxgloves and the green bush pressing in. Just a bloody dead end. I walk back down over Battleship Bluff, my eyes on the track ahead. I think of the little lady polishing her counter. Maybe it's better not to know what happened here. The sun has gone now and I stop to put on my raincoat. A scrub bush hangs across the track and slaps against my face; its wetness runs down my neck. I want to be gone from this dreary place. I don't belong and there's nothing here for me. Veto. My footsteps ring hollow as I run across the concrete bridge and on down the track to the river.

At the landing, I catch my breath and watch the brown river, forever running away to the sea from this silent green cathedral. It's the end of the Anzacs. I eat the last biscuit while I wait for the jet boat and watch the water moving past me, never running clean. The story of my life. Foolish to come to this God forsaken place where the bush has claimed back so many broken dreams. Veto.

I think instead about Ursula: Ursula telling me what to wear, Ursula making me feel pretty for the first time in my life, Ursula kicking her high heels under the couch, rubbing her sore feet and then going down to the showroom to find an even higher pair. Ursula in our kitchen cooking me eggs, feeding me home-made vegetable soup just the way Ginny taught her, making coffee with cream and sprinkling her little messages on top. Ursula nursing me when I got really sick, kneeling beside me in the toilet, holding my forehead and keeping my hair out of the way while I vomited over and over. Ursula putting a bandage on my hand and sorting out with the landlord the window I broke with an angry fist.

Ursula ringing the school when she knew I couldn't get out of bed. Or was that Ian? Bloody Ian. It's time to go home.

The jet boat is coming, first a distant drone and now a final growl as the driver pushes the nose up onto the landing and shuts off the V8. The final rev sends a bow wave up the rock to meet me. I clamber over the windscreen and settle in by the driver. I'm the only passenger this trip. The boat reverses off the rock, clunks into forward gear and we're off, leaving an arc of droplets as the boat makes a tight turn out onto the river and heads down with the current. We pull up our hoods and hunch into the spitting rain, which is stinging our faces. In the rapids, the driver aims directly at the rocks, pulling around them at the last minute as he's trained to do for the tourists. I don't give him the pleasure of a response. He pulls up in a quiet spot to show me the drop scene, an optical illusion where the hills look like they fall down to the edge of a lake rather than a river. The same scene used in Hatrick's old tourist brochures with a picture of a young Māori girl in her dugout canoe in front of the sheer bush-clad cliffs. Here's a steel pipe, securely hammered into a mighty rock wall, used by the old steamers to haul themselves up the rapids. He tells me about the Māori boys who ran the wire ropes. We press on down.

The driver pulls up again at the top of a long 'S' shaped rapid, the Ngaporo. He gazes at the rapid and explains how the riverboat *Ohura*, overloaded with penned cattle, was being shipped down the river. The cattle had spooked to one side and the steamer had rolled over with two crewman lost. I look for fantails. There are no piwakawaka today.

The driver floors the accelerator. The motor responds, bringing us up to plane on the surface. More droplets sting our faces as we speed the last few kilometres back to the road head. The driver pulls his boat out of the river at Pipiriki onto its trailer. I pack up my bike.

It's raining again. On the road my wet weather gear and gloves are no defence against the westerly, which is hammering my left shoulder. I pass a stock truck, taking the worst of the water thrown up by its wheels and the smell of effluent stays with me, smudged green across my visor by my gloved hand, until more rain has washed it away. The seam on my wet weather gear is leaking at the crotch. I stand on the pegs to ease my stiffening legs and then sit back down on my wet seat and press on, hunching my shoulders against the wind. Hands gripping tight, ready to fight my bike when the wind pushes us across the white line at an oncoming truck when I pop out from the end of a line of trees. Then fighting the wind between shelter belts, riding the 40° angle to stay upright. Mount Taranaki is nowhere to be seen.

At Te Kuiti, I stop to fuel my bike. The same attendant who fawned over Ursula's fuel cap doesn't notice me. Today he stays inside hunched behind the counter. I fill my own tank and hurry in to pay. My fingers are so cold I have trouble undoing my helmet or putting the change into my wallet. Time to buy a hot meat pie. After the first bite I slip my numb fingertips in turn into the filling to warm up beneath the pie crust, licking the gravy from underneath my nails before the wet gloves go back on.

At Pirongia, the mountain is shrouded and silent. By Taupiri the rain has gone and this mountain is struggling out of the river mist. A black-clad group are carrying a coffin up the steepest part in the rain. I'm coming Ursula. I watch my speed and stick to my own side of the road, taking no risks today. I keep my eyes on the gap ahead.

*ooOOoo*

Back at the flat, I park my bike and open the showroom door. All is quiet. Perhaps Ursula isn't here. I brush past the rainbow of dresses and carry my load on up the stairs. The door that leads to our flat is shut with a note taped there: a white envelope with my name written in Ursula's large round letters with her favourite purple ink. I unstick the note and shove it inside my helmet. It will keep for later. The important thing first – I must talk to her.

No one is about. I tiptoe inside. The flat is as we usually leave it, tidy, everything where it should be. I drop my helmet and all my wet gear by the door then unpack the wild pork from Tom Mowat, a gift for Ursula. She'll love the story that goes with the food and the coarse black hairs that still stick to the pink meat in places. I put the parcels in the fridge. There's no cream. Bloody Ursula. How's she going to make my special coffee at breakfast?

Maybe she's sleeping. I tap the door open to Ian's room. It's dim with the curtains drawn shut. There is someone lying on the bed but it isn't Ursula.

My brain is on a train in a tunnel. My vision is closing in and travelling at a thousand miles an hour but I am standing still. I scream his name but it just hits the walls and carries on forever and ever, there is no end to the tunnel and no sides for the sound to bounce back from. Now, forever, never, there is no way back.

Lying on top of the neatly made bed is the form of a man. He's dressed in a black suit, narrow tie, hair newly cut, neatly short. His hands are folded across his chest, eyes closed. His face is ghastly white. I slam the door shut and crumple to the floor.

'111, Police – he's dead.' I collapse on the floor again and howl. But the voice on the phone is still there repeating the questions over and over. What's my name? What's his name? Where am I? 'His name was Ian Dunn.' I howl again at the past tense and then calm myself enough to answer as they ask for our address.

It takes forever for them to come. I stand in the middle of the road as the sirens get louder. I wipe the tears out of my eyes and watch the ambulance and then the police car pull in.

The ambulance officers carry their equipment up the stairs. The police car parks half on the footpath and leaves its lights going. 'Are you Kate Whyte?'

I nod and motion the officer and his partner up our stairs. A crowd is gathering on the footpath. I make to close the door but it is wrested out of my hands.

'Hello, darling. Why are the cops here?'

'Ursula.' I stare at her dumbly. 'Ian's not dead?'

She barges past me up the stairs. 'There's a mistake, sir. My flatmate gets excitable. I was just making a Guy Fawkes style of dummy for a big party we're planning. No one is dead here. Just a sacking dummy stuffed with wool and a death mask. Rather lifelike, don't you think? Would you like a coffee before you go?'

The ambulance guys decline but the policemen say yes and sit down to do their paperwork.

I grit my teeth and sign off my mistake. They compliment Ursula on the quality of the mask she has made and wink at me as they leave. I slam the door after they have gone and run back up the stairs to face her.

The train is coming out of the tunnel; I'm screaming at Ursula. Reaching, grabbing, hitting, spitting. She fends me off. We stand with the table between us. My fists are clenched.

'I love you, Kate.' Ursula wipes her tears and spoilt mascara across her cheek.

'And I love Ian.' There, the words are out.

Ursula raises her head, a comedy clown face with makeup smudged across the features of a handsome man. 'Ian is dead.'

'What about Wanganui?' I slouch down on the couch and reach for my ponytail.

Ursula comes to sit beside me and tries to take my hand. I wrench it back and push her away. 'Piss off, Ursula.'

She lands on all fours on the floor and then rises again, unsteady, onto her heels. At the door she turns. 'Did you ever stop to think how this thing messes with my head, a thousand times worse than yours?' Mascara is streaming down, merging with her face paint and lipstick. 'You know nothing about what it's like to be me. Made like a man with all the usual animal tendencies but in my mind and soul always a girl and now, a woman.'

'Fuck you, Ursula.' I turn away from her. 'Where does that leave me?'

'With all my heart,' she whispers, 'I wish I knew.'

She is gone down the stairs and out the door, leaving me howling and hitting the couch. Do I even understand what has been going on between us all these years?

When my sobs are spent I see it, Ursula's note lying on the floor where it has dropped out of my helmet. I rip it open. A card, an invitation, gold edges, curly writing, purple, just the way Ursula likes it. An invitation to attend Ian's funeral. RSVP to Ursula who is rising like a pop-up phoenix off the card. I crumple the invitation in my fist.

# Eighteen

# Beanstalk

But still the progress was slow, Beanstalk thought as he mulled over Jane's poems. The subject matter was still nature, the local surrounds and still Moonface in the poems. Beanstalk concluded it must have been Moonface who had entangled Jane in a web of some sort but he made no progress towards understanding what had occurred prior to Jane's arrival at Kingseat.

Back to the literature. Should he start ECT? Surely not yet. He cast back through Jane's poems and read again her image of hanging out eggshells, remnants of her past, like washing hung on a line and then safely stored away from him in a hope box. A place that she would choose, to keep her eggshell fragments *'safe beyond my reach'*. Maybe if he could create a place that she could keep her poems safely from him, maybe then she would start to write about her past. Beanstalk had bought a small weatherproof box, made from wood with brass corners and lined with metal. A small receptacle designed for precious things but plain in outward appearance.

At his next weekly review, he placed it on the desk in front of Jane and offered for her to take a look. Inside the little box he had placed the feather and his notebook in which she usually wrote in his presence, each poem pre-prepared and ready to be written down by Jane in an explosive rush as if bursting to escape from her.

He explained the hope box was hers to take away, but didn't explain that it was also his to find and easily monitored in a rambling hospital that had difficulty holding a secret, or so he thought. He chortled at his own daring as Jane carried away her new possession and the pencil he had provided for her.

It took him time to find her next poem, longer than he'd thought, but of course eventually he'd found the box hidden in a nook tucked up under a stairway. Old Ernie, the cleaner, became the one he relied on each time to find the box. No words spoken, but Ernie would lean on his mop and indicate with a casual thumb where he should look next.

One thing that Beanstalk had learned over the years working in institutions: there is always an Ernie the cleaner, mopping more than the floors.

And that's the way it became, a game of hiders and seekers – but he never could be certain who was the spider and who the droplet.

**Droplets Falling**

At dawn a spider catches droplets in my web
Embedded in my head I hang them out to dry

At night a droplet catches spiders in my head
Embedded in his web I try to catch the moon

By day an oarsman catches crabs, droplets slip away
Spreading murky rings on muddied water

An axe has felled the faraway tree and burnt the pieces
I look for Moonface in the droplets but he's never there

# Nineteen

# Meredith

The road is wet. Meredith waves out to Pat Mowat as he slushes past in his old car, always the optimist heading out to Raetihi in weather like this. It's the mailman who brings the news.

'Luckily Pat went over the bank below the McDonalds' place or we'd never have found him in time, just tyre marks going clean over the edge. Busted pelvis. They say he'll be in hospital in Raetihi for six months, laid out on a rack. Reg has hauled his car back up onto the track. If anyone can fix his car, Reg will be the one.'

The road on down the valley is rough with new slips. Meredith rides down to visit old Mrs Mowat and Pat's sister Mary. She sees how close to the edge Pat's wheel marks went in places. He could easily have tipped over a bigger cliff than the one that finally got him.

Mrs Mowat lays a crocheted cloth and makes the tea. She cuts slices off the Belgian square. 'To think we came up here just to stay with Pat for a short while to straighten out his house.' She glances around the tidy little kitchen with soup bubbling on the Orion stove. Her smile slides from Meredith to Mary. 'Maybe we are just slow straighteners, or maybe this place just gets under your skin. It's hard to conceive of leaving.' She wipes a tear. 'That's until something like this – Pat in the hospital and no one to muster the sheep.'

Meredith whistles Spark and sets off up Mowat's Ridge to bring their sheep down to the yards. She cuts the wood, brings them wild pork, docks their new lambs' tails and cuts off the purses with a sharpened sheath knife. The place is shipshape when Pat finally gets home to his battered car, which has been resurrected by Reg Anderson.

Mrs Mowat hugs Meredith. 'I won't forget this. Country kindness is the very best kind.'

There is always fresh baking left in the mailbox for Meredith whenever the Mowats are passing.

ooOOoo

Myra reaches up for the parcel that Meredith carries. 'Ooh, did you make something for Baby Jo?' Myra undoes the string and carefully draws back the creased brown paper, which has been used many times before. She lifts out a dainty cream Viyella gown for her baby sister.

Agnes is breastfeeding the bonny three-month-old baby. She lays Jo in her lap and takes the gown from Myra to look at the fine smocking below the little yoke and the pink rosebuds embroidered on the Peter Pan collar. 'It's beautiful.' Agnes glances up at Meredith's grim face and her rough, red, farmer-like hands. 'It's so fine. This needlework must have taken you ages.'

When Meredith doesn't reply, Agnes holds the pause and glances down at Baby Jo. The children that Meredith will never have hover between them both.

Agnes lifts the baby to her shoulder to bring up the wind and then hands Jo to Meredith. 'Did you hear how this little minx arrived? I still had two weeks to go. I was getting ready to head down and put my feet up in Wanganui for a few days before she was born, but fat chance of that. There I was in the middle of making a chocolate cake so the troops here would have something to eat while I was away. Silly me, thinking it was just a call of nature – slipped on the path on my way back up from the outhouse and it was all go. I scribbled a note and sent little Michael off to find Reg, where he was working down on Jerry's Bluff. Reg came galloping home just in time to heave the mattress off the woven-wire bed and Mrs Bettjeman wasn't too far behind.'

Myra interrupts her mother. 'You forgot to say that Dad jumped on his horse and left Mike behind to walk home.'

Agnes raises her eyebrows to Meredith. 'Yes, young Mike made it there and back. Not bad going for a five year old.' Agnes hitches herself up off the couch and nods to Baby Jo. 'Healthiest one we ever had. Reg says it must be the good air up here, not to mention the beautiful job he did tying off the cord with a length of cotton pulled off the old treadle.'

Meredith nods her head but doesn't speak. She has no story to compete.

Baby Jo is settling to sleep, sucking her thumb with tiny perfect fingernails cupping her small chin.

Agnes comes back with a pile of nappies that need folding. 'Did you go down to the opening of the new concrete bridge? I hear they cut a ribbon and Bill Sandford drove across and back.'

Meredith shakes her head, not taking her eyes off the baby in her lap.

The clean nappies are stiff, with peg marks at the corners. Agnes flattens and folds them one after another. 'But what nonsense, with the last bit of road down to the river not open yet, and with Phil Bennett leaving there's hardly anyone down that end to use the thing. Such a waste. Money would have been better spent sorting out the slips and potholes up this end.'

The baby starts to squirm. Agnes reaches for Jo to burp her again, catching the spill of sour milk in a nappy on her shoulder and then hands her back to Meredith. 'How is Mr Stanley's hand? I hear from Mrs Bettjeman it's slow to heal up.'

Meredith buries her face in the warm milky smell of Jo. 'Yes, his hand is slow. Mrs Bettjeman wanted him to go down to Wanganui to see if they could fix the tendons but he wouldn't go. It never came properly right, then the whole thing got infected.'

'Did you try a poultice of tea leaves and comfrey to draw out the pus?'

Meredith nods. 'It still pains him, but whisky helps.'

'Whisky helps, my foot.' Agnes frowns at Meredith. 'Whisky helps a man to an early grave.'

Meredith shrugs her shoulders.

'And you're doing all the farm work?'

Meredith looks out the window and doesn't answer.

'How are you getting by for money, let alone you buying whisky for him? I worry for you now that Mr Stanley can't do extra work on the roads.'

'We're getting by. A few pounds for our wool this coming summer and I have my pig snouts smoking in the chimney. I'll cash them in on my next trip to Raetihi.'

'Whisky will be costing you more than the government bounty on a few pig snouts.' Agnes shakes her head. 'Pig hunting, sheep work, cooking and cleaning and you still find the time for this as well.' She holds up the small embroidered dress and shakes her head again. 'I don't understand how you keep going, or get by for money.'

'I did get a helping hand when my aunt died.'

'And you're spending your inheritance ordering in whisky for that old coot?'

Meredith shrugs. 'The whisky helps.' She turns to Myra. 'How's your reading coming on, a big nine-year-old girl now?'

Myra beams and nods. 'Do you still read *Peter Pan*? You promised you would come here and read with me, but you never do.'

Meredith smiles. 'Yes, I must know *Peter Pan* by heart. When I'm up on the hills Peter is often up there with me. Sometimes I think I must be Wendy Darling.'

Myra opens her eyes wide. 'Does he fly about and help you round up the sheep? Is Tinker Bell there? Is Captain Hook chasing after you? Do you ever see Hook?'

'No, Myra, just me and Peter.'

Agnes reaches over to Meredith, picks up Jo and lays the sleeping baby back in the little wooden cradle that Reg has made. 'Captain Hook stays home I bet and drinks whisky in the whare?'

Meredith doesn't reply. It's time she's heading back. There are the dogs and chooks to feed, the cow to lock away from her calf and supper to be made.

oo*O*oo

Meredith carries a plate of stew out to the whare. James Stanley is snoring, his unshaven face turned away. She leaves the meal beside the bed, blows out the candle and runs back across to the house in the rain. In the morning she will take breakfast and tip away the uneaten meal into the chook bucket.

oo*O*oo

Agnes hugs Meredith. 'Why don't you come with us?' She grabs Meredith's shoulders and looks hard into her face. 'Our new place in Marton is going to have an inside bathroom, and we'll have the power on. The kids will be able to catch a bus to a school with proper classrooms.'

A truck stands already loaded with all their gear roped onto the back. Myra, John and Michael are excited to be riding on top of the load. They are already bouncing up and down on the mattress, which is roped down over the treadle sewing machine just behind the truck cab. Meredith passes them up the sandwiches wrapped in newspaper that she has made for their trip.

Myra hangs over the side to reach down for the parcel. 'Will you come and see us at our new place? Will you bring *Peter Pan* all the way to our new farm?'

'Only if you're not too big for make-believe.'

Jo is already tucked into a basket in the cab where she will ride jammed in behind the gear stick between Agnes and the driver. Reg will follow on his horse with a mob of sheep and his dogs. He is saddled up on Paddy, leading Ginger, ready to turn his small mob out of the yards onto the road once the truck has gone.

Agnes squeezes Meredith's arm one last time. 'No hard feelings, girl?'

'No hard feelings. This is exactly the sort of place that Peter would have brought me to.'

Neither of them mentions James Stanley.

Meredith stands in the middle of the road with Muriel McDonald alongside her, waving goodbye to her friend Myra. The truck disappears around the corner. They listen until the double clutching and laboured motor is gone from earshot, leaving another hole in the valley.

Meredith gives the nine-year old girl a leg up onto her horse and they ride together down the valley. Muriel is clutching the left-handed hand-shears that Reg has given her as a parting gift. As they ride side by side Muriel tells Meredith about the gifts that she had exchanged with her best friend for their last birthdays. A cake of soap from Myra and a carefully polished goose egg as a return gift from Muriel. An egg, large enough for Agnes to make a cake for them all to share. They will both miss the Andersons.

The silence settles around Meredith even more as she waves the little redhead away at the McDonalds' place and carries on down the valley alone. She passes the Bettjemans and then settles in for the last few miles.

ooOOoo

Meredith takes a rare trip to town with some pig snouts to cash in. There are sheep in the yards as she passes the McDonalds' woolshed. Muriel's red head pops up at the door and waves her into the shed where her sisters Ivy and Helen are hard at work shearing.

'Guess what? I shore nine sheep with Mr Anderson's blades, to show Dad. One sheep for each of my birthdays but it's pretty hard going. I'm not very fast.' She points at the catching pen behind the board and grins. 'Dad says I'm the best dagger.'

Meredith watches as the slip of a girl rushes into the pen to demonstrate how she can pull a leg out from underneath a woolly sheep, which looks to weigh as much as she does, roll the old ewe over and plonk herself down on top to hold the ewe in place while she crutches the sloppy green dags away from its tail.

Muriel's older sisters take a break from their shearing and Meredith stays for smoko in the shed to hear the girl's news. The McDonald family have finally bought a car. They have helped their father to cut a hole in the end of the Andersons' deserted house to garage it in the winter time when the track will be too slippery to drive up the hill from their own place.

Meredith rides away on her horse. There is no thought that the Stanleys will buy a car.

*ooOOoo*

Pat's car pulls into the Stanleys' driveway; right behind is a truck loaded up with all their possessions. He opens the car door for his mother.

Mrs Mowat climbs down off the running board and hugs Meredith one last time. 'Our little home is ready for you. I have even left our clock on the mantel. You deserve a proper stove and some home comfort after all these years. To think it's 1937 and you're still using a camp oven like some pioneering woman straight off a sailing ship.'

Meredith takes the warm wrinkled hands in her own. 'How can I ever thank you?' Tears are pricking her eyes.

'You get what you give in life and this is what you deserve. Can you please watch over my daphne bush? How I loved to pick those blooms to scent the house right at the worst of winter. Each year my daphne bush gave me hope that spring would come, and it always does in the end. Spring comes for those who deserve it.'

Pat takes off his hat. 'Is James out the back there?'

Meredith nods towards Jack Ward's old whare and Pat heads off around the corner of the house.

'Did you hear the news?' Mrs Mowat looks after Pat as he disappears past the tank stand. 'Pat's got a job down in Wanganui. I'd say it won't be long before there are wedding bells. We've met his young lady friend from up the river at Whakahoro. She's been coming over to the dances for quite some time. A nice girl. I'm sure they would have tied the knot already, if it hadn't been for Mary and I cluttering up the house.' She turns to Mary and they both laugh. 'Three women in one small house is probably more than any new bride needs. We're looking forward to getting back to town. We have a nice little place lined up. We'll have an electric stove with two hot plates on top and not too far to walk down to the picture theatre. Imagine that? You must come down and stay with us. We'd love that, wouldn't we, Mary?'

Mary nods.

Meredith drops her eyes to pat Spark, who is sitting at her feet. She says nothing. They all know that Meredith will never come to stay, just as she has never found the time to visit Agnes. But Meredith does find time to write letters to her departed neighbours and just an occasional day trip to Raetihi for supplies. With James Stanley the way he is, who would milk the cow and feed the dogs if she were to go away for any longer than a day?

Pat is back. He shakes her hand. They climb back into the car and the doors slam shut. Another family drives on out of the valley for the very last time. Meredith stands in the middle of the road and listens while the car and truck grind up the valley, around the first bluff and the next.

The silence is unbearable. Meredith claps her hands and Spark bounds over. She rubs the bitch's ears. Tomorrow they will be moving down to the Mowats' place. There's a whare out the back that will suit James, and good holding paddocks for the horses and the house cow. She must hide the whisky tonight so James will be in a fit state to help load their sled tomorrow.

*ooOOoo*

The Mowats' place is warm with well-fitted shingles on the walls and a watertight corrugated chimney that snugly fits around the little Orion stove and Mrs Mowat's clock, wound every morning, ticks on the mantel. The daphne bush greets each winter with fragrant flowers.

There's a mailbox out front by the track but Meredith is watching from the window and runs to the gate to meet Muriel McDonald as she pulls Starlight to a halt and takes a letter out of the canvas bag. She thanks the young girl who is delivering the mail now instead of Teddy.

Muriel drops the reins and gives the horse its head to eat. She tells Meredith about her trip south to stay with Myra in Marton. How she had just missed out on seeing *The Wizard of Oz*, which was due in the picture theatre the week after she had come home to the valley and about the latest accident. Another car nearly over the cliff. This time the McDonalds up past the trig on their way to town, two wheels over the bank and the car left teetering. How Muriel had climbed out onto the door frame to anchor the car until a truck could be found to tow it back onto the road.

Muriel pulls her horse away from its browsing and is gone back up the track at a trot, her fiery red hair clip-clopping out of sight around the first bend.

Meredith waves and looks at the letter. A white envelope written in a woman's hand, but it's not from Agnes. Meredith turns the letter over to read the return address – Whangamomona. The letter is addressed to James. She carries it around the back to the whare. James Stanley is lying on his bed smoking a rollo. There's a near empty bottle of whisky on the side table. Meredith hands him the letter. He turns it over and gives it back to her to open and read out loud.

*Dear James,* 7/9/41

*A strange request I know. You will not have heard of me for some years – indeed the last time I saw you was at our district farewell before you and Albie marched off to catch the boat to Gallipoli. That's a good many years ago now, and strange that my letter is on the same topic.*

*You may not be aware, but I have a son. His name is Toby. A quiet lad and big and strong for his years, not much between his ears, but good enough to be a farmer.*

*You'll remember my husband, Albie. He always spoke of you fondly. You may not know, but after Albie came home from the war, he was never the same. The gas got him. He lasted five years but could never do real farm work and we only had one child born, which is no reflection on me.*

*Albie wasn't made of tough stuff like you. Always sick, bad breathing and nightmares from the trenches, too soft to make it. But that's another story; he's been dead and gone a long time now.*

*Toby's finished with his books. He needs a boss with a firm hand and hard work on big country. He's a simple-minded oaf. The pity is he took after his father in that way, a bit soft, but he can ride a horse and work the dogs as well as any other man.*

*My worry is, all the time down here he's hanging around outside the local pub at Whangamomona. He's all eyes and ears, listening to the talk. He can't wait to sign up for this new war. I overheard that he is keen to forge his age and be off to Europe with the next intake.*

*You'll understand, having lost my favourite older brother and then poor old Albie after the Great War, I have no desire to see Toby go off to fight against Hitler.*

*The other problem is, I have no desire for Toby to take up the other option, which is working for my least favourite brother next door here either. My younger brother Joe was always spoilt rotten and now he's become a hateful man with the moral fibre of a flea. I don't know if you ever met my brother, Joe Ogden. He's still a thorn in my side, and no example to youth. He terrorises his poor mouse of a wife something awful. Joe is not a good man for Toby to learn his ways from. Even war would be better than Toby working for Joe. I worry he will poison the boy's mind against me, and take away my share of the farm.*

*If you will have Toby for a while in the back blocks, he won't end up going to war until he really is 18 at the very least, and, out of sight up there, maybe even longer.*

*Can I please send him up to you, James? Just feed him – God knows that'll cost you enough. He's ducking under the doorways already. Takes after my side of the family in that respect – big-boned you could say. If you can just keep him in hard work and away from the war, teach him to be a real farmer and send him home in one piece, all my thanks will be yours.*

*Yours sincerely,*

*Iris Dougherty*

*P.S. Sorry about this but things with my brother are getting worse. Toby will be on his way by the time you receive this letter. Please send him home if this is unsatisfactory. My brother, Joe, is forcing my hand. Blood is not thicker than ditch water in this situation. Enough said.*

*I will get Toby down to Wanganui and onto the riverboat as soon as I can arrange to get him out on a train to Stratford. They're clearing the slips, and I'm hoping tomorrow the line will be running again.*

*Joe Ogden is agitating to take him on. I want Toby out of here as soon as possible, so sorry about jumping the gun and not waiting for your reply.*

*I.D.*

Meredith folds the letter and hands it to James who twirls it around between his three hook fingers. 'Albie Dougherty dead and gone, huh.'

He crumples the letter against his palm. 'Albie Dougherty always did have the luck of the Irish. Pity it didn't rub off on me. Lucky bugger, dead and gone all these years and I'm still here.' James throws the letter on the floor, picks up the whisky bottle and gulps down the remainder.

Meredith picks up the letter. 'Did you ever meet this Joe Ogden that she speaks of? Her own brother – is he really that bad?'

James lowers the bottle from his lips, both his deformed hands clutching around the base as he licks the last precious drops off the throat of the bottle. He screws up his eyes to look at Meredith, trying to recall her question. 'Yep, I visited Albie when he was first working on Ogden's place. I met Joe Ogden. Just a boy then but already a nasty piece of work. His old man could see the flaws in Joe even when he was still a kid.'

Meredith presses him some more; he is not usually this talkative. 'How do you mean, a nasty piece of work?'

James rolls the empty bottle between his hands. 'Even back then, Joe Ogden had a mean streak and no stock sense. The old man caught the boy thrashing a dog to death when it wouldn't work for him. Take my hat off to Iris' old man though. When his favourite son died in the war he gave two shares of the farm to Albie Dougherty, who was just a worker there when he married old Iris, and only one share to Joe. Albie loved that woman; none of the rest of us could have stomached her. She was on the shelf, a huge horsey creature and bossy with it, but strong and keen on the farm. She could work like a man. Her old man had an eye for good bloodlines. Albie would have made a real fist of that farm if the war hadn't laid him down. Iris Dougherty though, she's made of stern stuff – with Albie dead, to have stood up to her brother all these years. Done well to keep her share of the farm out of Joe Ogden's clutches.'

James burps, then wipes his mouth on the stained edge of Meredith's quilt. 'The least we can do is have Albie's son up here for a while and keep him out of Joe's reach. What's his name again?' James lies back and closes his eyes.

Meredith uncrumples the letter. 'Toby, Toby Dougherty.' She glances at James, who's already snoring. She rescues the bottle from his hands. The chooks and dogs need feeding but there's no hurry to get the rest of her chores done. Mr Stanley won't be wanting any dinner tonight. She closes the whare door behind her.

The next morning the weather allows Meredith to air the bedding in the bunkroom. Toby Dougherty will be here to stay within a couple of days. It's a long time since anyone has shared her house.

ooOOoo

There's a knock on the door as Meredith is putting wood in the stove. 'Come in,' she calls, without looking up from her chore. A large bashful youth ducks his head under the door frame. He stands with his hat in his hands, eyes hidden by his shaggy white fringe. His face is broad and flat, pockmarked with fresh pimples that stand out against the flush of colour that has swept up from his neck and over his sparsely stubbled chin. He shuffles his feet and turns his hat in his dinner plate-sized hands.

'You must be Toby.' Meredith shakes the sticky hand, already roughened as only farm work can do.

'Pleased to meet you, Miss.' Toby looks around and Meredith indicates the side room with a set of bunks built into the wall. 'Put your trunk in there. Would you like a cup of tea?'

Toby nods and lumbers into the bunkroom, drops his trunk and returns to settle at the table.

'How's your mother?'

'Good, Miss.' He glances at the wood basket. 'Shall I fill that up for you?' He grabs the bin and flees outside.

At the door, Meredith watches the effortless rhythm of the axe, which slices the rounds on the chopping block exactly down the centre like a knife in warm butter. He looks more comfortable in the outdoors. A seventeen-year-old boy who needs a little space, she thinks.

That evening, Toby collects James' empty plate from the whare after dinner and helps with the dishes. Afterwards they sit at the table. Meredith hands over the *Weekly News* and watches the colour rise again in Toby's flat moon face.

'I don't read too good, Miss.' His eyes are cast down behind the fringe.

Meredith goes to the bedroom to get her book and opens *Peter Pan* at the first page. 'How about we read together. You can sound out the words you know and I can help with you the rest?'

He looks up and nods. 'I'd like that, Miss.' And so, Toby begins to read. '*Peter Pan was a st . . . range cre . . . at . . . ure, a be . . . twixt and be . . . tween. He was cer . . . tainly no or . . . din . . . ary boy, th . . . ough he looked v . . . ery like one.*'[4]

A pattern is set that they both come to enjoy, evening after evening. He can read whole passages now, only needing help to sound out the occasional word. Meredith's chin lifts as Toby's shoulders rise up from their slump. Pride is what she's feeling. Is this what it is to be a mother?

ooOOoo

Meredith hears it first from Muriel McDonald. There's a new shearer in the valley. Some say an itinerant avoiding the draft. He is shearing at the Bettjemans' place. Muriel passes on a message from Mrs Bettjeman who says he has good habits around the house and Fred is happy with his workmanship in the shed. He shears at a good speed, not too many cuts and he can also shear with blades. They all know that Meredith hasn't upgraded to a Lister engine in her shed.

Meredith nods. There's not much choice now anyway with the war going on and all the young men gone overseas. 'Tell Fred to send the shearer on down to me when he cuts out Bettjemans' shed.'

Muriel nods and rummages in the mail sack. She pulls out one handwritten letter – nothing official like the letters the other families in

---

4  The opening passage is from JM Barrie, *Peter Pan and Wendy* (Leicester, Great Britain: Brockhampton Press Ltd., 1962), 7.

the valley get. Only four families left now, counting the Stanleys, in the valley. But squatters don't count. At least that way no official letters come in the mail with summons for lease money or official-looking letters asking them to move on. The authorities are only counting the three families left in the upper valley. The Stanleys here in the lower valley are all alone. They don't exist. Fern is stealing back across great tracts of land. Pigs are multiplying and rooting up the deserted pastures. The pig fern comes first, followed by the bracken and mānuka.

The handwritten letter is from Agnes. Meredith reads quickly and summarises for Muriel. Reg and Agnes are well, still loving being closer to town, and their farm is taking off. Agnes is over the moon with her new refrigerator. Myra is doing well in secondary school in Palmerston North and Jo has just started in the primers. How can this be?

Meredith glances down at Spark and notices, for the first time, the grey showing around her muzzle. The grey is coming to her own dark hair as well if she looks closely at the ends when she pulls away the hair pins. Her hair is long enough so she can trim the ends herself, there is no money for the fancy cuts that she sees on the streets of Raetihi at her rare visits. She doesn't have a mirror. They say if you want your hair to shine you must crack an egg and rub it over your scalp. She never does this or rubs her feet with pumice. Who would ever notice if she did?

Meredith thanks Muriel and stands in the middle of the road, watching the young horsewoman canter out of sight, her long red hair beating in time with the hooves that fade around the first corner. Muriel is fifteen, she rides the four-hour round trip to collect and deliver the mail twice a week, a land girl who has stayed in the valley to help her father after her older sisters have moved away.

*ooOOoo*

On her way back down the hill, Meredith stands her horse, Holly, at the spot where her homestead first comes into view. The Mowats' old house is her home now. She often stops here to admire the big sky and the view down into the valley. Their place is just a doll's house from this distance, way down below the ridge. The house sits well, a snug fit between the creek and the steep upstand of hills behind. Holly nudges the reins and puts her head down to snaffle what there is between the pig fern. Meredith drops the reins down onto Holly's neck and looks about. A hawk circles above the near hills, which show new scars from the latest storm with fresh grey slips across the face of her land. Her life's work, for what it's worth. Meredith is covered in blood but she has two more pig snouts to hang up to dry in the chimney and a good supply of meat draped across the front of Holly's saddle.

Down the hill no smoke is rising from her chimney. James Stanley seldom moves from the whare these days and she isn't expecting Toby back from fencing out in the Wards' back paddock until it's nearly dark. More work lies ahead of her. She gathers up the reins and makes her way home. There's meat to chop for the dogs, the pork to put in the meat safe and the house cow to shut away. She lights the fire, makes a pot of tea and then carries more wood inside.

As she kneels to stack the logs by the wood stove there's a loud knock on the door. She's not expecting anyone. She rises to her feet as the door is pushed open. A man is standing there; she cannot see his face in the gloom. This must be the shearer.

'Mrs Stanley, I presume?' He ducks his tall frame under the door without waiting to be asked. His hair is tousled and his eyes twinkle as he looks her up and down. 'Peter – I don't think we've met before.' His eyes pause on her breasts longer than they should. 'Or shall I call you Bloody Mary?'

Meredith gasps and looks down. She has forgotten her shirt, blood-stained from pig hunting. She turns to face away. 'No, Meredith is fine. I don't always look like a butcher.'

'Shall I put my horse in with that pretty mare of yours in the paddock?'

Meredith nods and stands on the step while Peter strips his gear off a gelding, which is young and black and stamping his foot with attitude. Holly is watching with interest, her head hanging over the gate.

Peter dumps his shearing kit in the lean-to and carries in his swag. Again his eyes drop from her face to her chest.

Meredith crosses her arms over the worst of her bloodied blouse. She glances down at the table. 'Can I get you some tea before I change?' Peter's eyes move from her breasts to the teapot and then to the book, which is lying open where Toby has left the story of Peter Pan.

Peter picks up the book. 'No hurry for a cuppa. Can I look at this?' He turns to the pictures, richly coloured, noticeable even in the dimness of the room. 'When I was a kid, this was a favourite. I used to pretend I could fly just like Peter Pan. Did you ever think you could fly like Wendy Darling?'

Meredith inhales and turns to look closely at this man. Can this really be Peter? She glances away, confused for a moment, then remembers her blood-covered blouse, clutches her bosom and turns away from the shearer. 'Please excuse me.'

She fills a basin with warm water from the kettle and rushes to the bedroom to peel off the bloodied shirt. What should she wear? What a thought, she has not cared about what she should wear since her wedding day over ten years ago now. She chooses her best white blouse for Peter. How strange, another Peter, not at all like her Peter, but how would she know? She tries to remember her Peter but only his official war photo comes to her, standing to attention in his uniform, hat pulled well down over his ears, not smiling. She thinks instead of the picture with the green velvet dress and her Peter's face comes back. This Peter is quite different, not so tall, and a lazy slurring in the way he speaks. Not at all like her Peter. So why is she smoothing back her hair and biting her lips to make them redder? This could be any man and certainly not her Peter. She looks around the room, wishing she had a mirror.

Back in the kitchen she hands Peter a cup of tea. He reaches with both hands, cupping her fingers for just a moment. His touch is warm and seeps through her, which is a surprise after all these years. They drink in silence. He insists on pouring her a second cup. She places her empty cup on the table and pulls her hand away before he can touch her again. She watches his long tapered fingers turn the pot. He stands to pour the tea over her shoulder. He is closer now than any man has been for a long time. She holds her breath as he finishes the pour, puts the pot down and comes to sit in the chair across the table. She notices his teeth when he smiles, white and even, perfect eye teeth sitting lower than the rest on each side of his generous mouth, his tongue licking the very tip of the beautiful tooth on the left as he hands her the sugar bowl.

The door pushes open and Toby comes in. Meredith turns and smiles at the bashful youth who reddens in response.

'Come on in, Toby, you must be famished. Meet Peter, here to do the shearing. You two will be sharing a room.'

The smile leaves Peter's face with this news, but reappears as Meredith turns back to complete the introduction.

'Peter, this is Toby, the son of James' friend Albie Dougherty. His mother, Iris, has kindly sent him up here from Whangamomona to help me with the shearing and to get some lambs out to the Raetihi stock sales.'

Toby drops his face, which colours again. He says nothing.

Meredith watches as Peter takes in the tall gangling lad with his flat face, not yet fully grown but already over six feet, the shock of coarse blonde hair and the acne standing out.

Peter moves to shake his hand. 'How old are you kid?'

Toby shuffles his feet and looks at the floor. 'Almost eighteen.'

'Pleased to meet you, boy. I can see you're too big to be a toy soldier but not yet man enough for a real gun.' Peter laughs. 'Don't be in too much of a hurry to sign up. No panic to take yourself off to Europe just to get shot to pieces.'

Toby nods but doesn't take the hand offered. He picks up the wood basket instead and makes for the door.

Peter shrugs and picks up his swag and puts it in the bunkroom that Meredith indicates he will share with Toby.

Meredith busies herself, scraping and cutting more carrots to add to the stew pot. Lucky thing that she has made extra bread. She gets out a cloth that she's never bothered to put on the table before, and sets for three. She makes up a fourth plate, which Toby takes out to James Stanley.

Meredith and Peter sit at the set table waiting for Toby to return. Meredith stares at her plate of food, unsure how to talk about the weather with this new Peter.

The door bursts open. James Stanley sways slightly in the doorway. Toby is behind him, still holding the plate of food. James crosses to the table and crashes down on a chair. 'You never told me we had company.' James is staring across the table. 'But I saw that gelding of yours out there – nice piece of horse flesh – and thought I'd join you for dinner.' He indicates for Toby to put his plate of food down on the table in front of him.

'Are you man enough to shake my hand then?' James stands and leans forward across the table. He sways again and doesn't seem to notice that he's planted his left hook hand in the centre of his dinner plate as he thrusts his withered right hand across the table at Peter. His right thumb is opening and closing like a deformed crab with only one claw. James is unshaven, his caked hair standing on end and his shirt discoloured down the front.

Peter hesitates for a moment before grasping the hand offered.

'What? Scared of a wet fish? A codfish to be sure.' James Stanley roars with laughter. He bangs his hook hand down on the table again, sweeping his plate of food onto the floor.

Meredith and Toby both rush to clean up the mess. James doesn't notice. He proceeds to shake the shearer's hand up and down within both of his deformed mitts. James tightens his left hook grip, crushing the shearer's knuckles. Peter tries not to show his pain.

The rain pours on the roof that night. There will be no shearing tomorrow. Meredith turns in her warm bed and listens to the rain. She is not unhappy about the delay; they needed this rain. She whispers goodnight to Peter. He is closer now than he ever was. Or is he? She thinks of the new Peter, the shearer – is he asleep yet? She reaches down and touches what is stirring deeply inside her. Maybe this rain will last for a couple of days before the sheep are dry enough to start. That would be a good thing. She whispers her final goodnight to both Peters.

# Twenty

# Beanstalk

The game of cat and mouse continued. Jane would move the hope box but Beanstalk always found it, with Ernie's help of course. Did she know he read her poems? Of course, she must. Was she teasing him? He believed she was. At night now when he thought of her he was moved to dispel the cursed ache that he had seldom felt for any woman. He was revolted by his lack of self-control. He no longer a young man and Jane an ugly monster who ignored his very existence and yet he felt the pull of a string that tied them together. Each time he washed his sheets he would chastise himself. Of course, he should have handed her over to another doctor and forgotten her, but each week without fail he would invite her back into his office and watch her in silence as she sat for the full half hour and stared away from him at the wall. He had given up on words. It was enough for him to have her close and, of course, to seek out her poems.

In the patient notes he wrote that her therapy was progressing well. Occasional brief updates were all that was required to be written up in the files of long-term patients. *No changes to treatment, no medication required. Weekly reviews with Dr Bean to continue.*

**Waiting For Rain**

We wait for rain
The land is gasping
We both know it will come
That smell before rain

The land has body odour
In anticipation

First drops
Dent my scalp
Drop by drop by drop
Spots will appear
Virus from the earth
Or a salve from the sky

Merging clots

Link hands
To clothe the parched
Rivers of flotsam
Drill our brains
Dripping off our hair

Upward faces
Our eyes are closed
We want to eat the rain
You see through me
I see through you
The land is slipping away

# Twenty-One

# Kate

It's Ginny who insists that I must come. 'Families are always there for family – Whytes stand together.'

I take a deep breath and step out of the bedroom that still has my childish dreams on the wall: a poster of Andy Gibb and a photo board. There we are, Ian and I, or was that Ursula? The two of us, even then me a full head taller, Agnetha and Frieda standing proud singing 'It's a rich man's world' into broomstick handles. Or were we Bay City Rollers, conning Ginny into making us both matching checked trouser cuffs? I rip the photos from the wall.

Ginny gives John's suit jacket a final brush. It's the same suit that John wore to their wedding forty years ago, the one he always wears to funerals.

John Whyte raises his voice above the music as we join the queue outside the entrance to the hall down at the port, which is done out in brightly coloured balloons. 'Bloody hell, trust Ursula.'

Ginny pats his shoulder, which is straining against the old suit jacket. 'Those mothballs needed an airing and besides, I know you, John Whyte – you wouldn't have missed this one for the world.'

A big man nudges John's elbow. 'Kia ora, mate. How's my old coach?'

'George Ngatai, by gum – you could still toss a football around.' John shakes the hand of the towering man who stands behind us. 'How the hell are you? Have you met my daughter, Kate?'

I can see my father's mind ticking over as he appraises George's physical proportions.

George nods briefly in my direction and turns back to John. 'Not too bad, and yourself?'

'Fit as a bull. Trust Ursula to drag us all out, but does she really have to bury him? Ian wasn't a bad bloke.'

'Nope, a handy winger, I recall. Good enough on a handpiece and humdinger on a board when the surf's up at the port.' George gives me a further nod.

The queue moves and we file in under the banner, which reads: *Dressed to Kill on Roller Skates*. Ursula is everywhere, not just in the large pictures of her that hang from the walls.

Our queue snakes past the welcoming committee, who are wearing several of the outfits that have previously hung on the racks in Ursula's showroom. Feathers and glitter feature above all else. The outfits are introduced as Trudy, Matilda, and Maxine. They all hug me. I come away wrapped in an array of their competing perfumes.

Maxine gives me an extra hug and whispers.'Ursula's given us lots of instructions. Me and the girls are doing our best and you should see her dress.' Maxine whistles through her teeth as she turns away to hug Ginny and John and then to greet the next guest.

We move on through to where the local PTA fundraising girls, resplendent in Torvill and Dean Outfits, are handing out roller skates.

'Cor blimey, there's a first time for everything.' John buckles on his skates. 'I hope there's an ambulance standing by.' Two sturdy Torvills in short skirts link John's arms and whisk him off out into the crowd. An attentive Dean holds out an elbow for Ginny and they set off together at a sedate pace over the floor.

I tiptoe out into the hall where the disco ball is throwing ever-changing light over the whole arena and more Torvills and Deans are moving around with trays of pink champagne. I push off and glide out onto the floor. The DJ is playing *Tears in Heaven*. Someone hands me a glass. I take a sip and gasp at the smooth speed, cool air and the sparkle of bubbles in my nose and slipping down my throat. Glittering peahens and shearers wearing Swanndris glide past. My brothers are all here, and there's Ian's IT boss. Perfect, Ursula. It's all bloody perfect.

I pull up by the coffin that stands open at the centre of the floor. It's bright, glittered with hand-painted flowers on the outside and there is Ian. He lies on pink satin. Am I the only one here in mourning? The death mask is an uncanny resemblance, spread out over his face and then lifted away and left to set hard.

Up on the big screen random shots of Ian are coming up from slides on the projector. I have seen them all before: the laughing handsome boy holding his mother's hand, me and Ian holding up the eels we have caught, Ian doing a wheelie on a motorbike, Ian feeding our pet lambs, dressed for rugby, hanging ten in Speedos surfing the port, dressed for work, both of us sitting with coffee cups on the sagging couch in our flat, he and Ginny holding up the first dress he ever made. The boy and then the man who was always there for me.

Bloody Ursula. I sip champagne and glide around and around, my head spinning.

The music stops. Maxine is on the mic, welcoming us all. There's a show to watch: Ursula walks out on stage wearing a stunning white gown with huge teardrop filigree earrings. She sings *Don't Cry for Me Argentina*. We raise a toast to Ian.

I take another glass and whirl some more to the music. *Don't Let The Sun Go Down On Me*. Ursula is everywhere; the perfect hostess, our paths never meet. Rodney grabs my hand and we move to the shadows. It's getting late; the music and lights fade out.

The Torvills and Deans lift the coffin high and we gather around and watch Ursula, a white silhouette, lead them in the moonlight as they make their way down to the beach. She strikes a match and the surfers are standing by to push the coffin out through the shore break on a small wooden skiff that John has made for the occasion. It kindles and lights up the sky. Fireworks are rocketing up to touch the Milky Way. Ian is no more. Tears are pouring down my face. Rodney's rough hands are crushing me against his jacket. We move outside to his ute.

*ooOOoo*

The shingle road peters out, a no exit, just a farm gate saying *No Trespassers*. I turn for home. Back down through the Waipoua Forest, I'm watching the logging trucks approaching at speed. My eyes are drawn into the solidness of each approaching front grill. An easy bullseye spread between the headlights.

'Look where you want to go.' That was one of the first things John Whyte had taught me, age fifteen, learning to drive in Ginny's Mini. 'You must physically force your eyes away from the obstacle and always look for the gap.' He had beaten his hand against the dashboard for extra effect. 'It's why so many folk die hitting power poles for no good reason. They get a little out of control, look around for the nearest power pole, can't take their eyes off the damn thing and the rest is history.'

I drag my eyes away from the truck and aim for the gap on my side of the empty road ahead. My bike takes me home to our empty flat.

Ursula has gone to Australia, for good. She didn't say goodbye.

*ooOOoo*

*I'm swimming with Ursula, deep in the sea. She is beckoning and I am to follow. My long, blonde hair is swimming away in all directions. I can't see. Where is Ursula? Hair is in my mouth. I can't breathe, I can't cry out.*

I wake and untangle my mouth from the hair that threatens to strangle me. Now that's a headline:

*'Teacher found strangled by her own hair in her own bed. No suspicious circumstances.'*

Not one of my limbs is offering to be the first one out of bed, and my head isn't offering to help either. Maybe I could just pull the covers over my head? But my limbs can't even do that. It's all her fault.

*'Teacher found paralysed, held hostage by her own bed. "It's the bed's fault," she said. "No matter how much I pleaded, the bed refused to let me get up."'*

Look at the time: late, late, too late. One final effort, I raise my foot and bring it down hard on the bed. The bruised bed lets me go. I stumble to the bathroom. Don't look in the mirror. Don't look in the kitchen; it's a mess. Flies are walking over the concrete set on yesterday's plates. Or was that the day before? No time for breakfast.

Every day the same small catastrophes of eight-year-olds have lost their fascination. I go back to bed and pull the covers over my head instead and imagine the day ahead. Did I remember to ring to say I'm too unwell to come, maybe ever?

*Hurry into Room 3. The bell has gone five minutes ago and the classrooms on both sides are settling to work. My room is exploding. Hapless Harry has just spilt his jar of tadpoles all over the mat area where the class should be sitting. There are wriggling black taddies all over the floor.*

*The Dirty-Kneed Boys are picking up the tadpoles and chasing the Frilly-Socked Girls who have found the perfect excuse to scream.*

*Responsible Rebecca is charging in from the locker room with a new jar of water for the tadpoles and collides with Obese Oliver who falls backward onto the nature table.*

*Ernie, the white mouse, is crashing to his near death in splintered glass. I stand in the middle of it all and do Munch's scream as the principal walks in behind me.*

After the third time I forget to ring in sick the principal asks for a meeting.

She pulls out a letter she's received from one of the parents, along with a homework sheet headed up:

*My Teachar.*

*My teachar is Miss Whyte. She is reilly tall. She is the bigest teachar in the whole school. She cries alot. Her tears are huge. A tear fulls down on my writing book and I can not rub out my mustakes any more. She says don't worry about the mustakes. She is reilly nice. She rides a big motabike too. She lets us go out to play time early and cries some meow. Sometimes she does not come to school and we get now play time while the Prince pull does a ring a round – not the roses.*

The principal gives me time off; she tells me to go home. Back at the flat I ignore the flies on the dishes, pull the curtains shut and climb back into bed. I pull the covers up over my head and close my eyes.

It's my mother, Ginny, who pulls the curtains open. She tells me she's done the dishes and there's coffee on the stove. She's filled the script that Eric has written. I don't take the tablets she holds out to me.

Ginny pushes the hair off my face, pulling apart the knotted ends. 'It's your choice – play the victim if you must but come home when you're ready. There's a letter here for you.' She walks away.

'Bloody Ginny.' I hear her closing the door to the flat. Her footsteps disappear down the stairs.

The bed doesn't put up a fight this time. The floor claims my feet and walks me to the bathroom. I turn on the shower and let the water drum down on my forehead. Where's the towel? I step out of the shower and grab a towel, but don't dry my feet. Ian hates wet feet on the bathroom floor.

Standing in the kitchen, water is dripping off my matted hair, which hangs about my limited view. What's this? I push my hair aside and drag my wet feet to the table. A letter, addressed with purple ink. Ginny must have brought it in from the box. I snatch it up and sniff for any familiar smell.

To:  Kate Whyte,
     2nd on the Right Street,
     Neverland

Returned to Sender: Kate Whyte . . . At our usual mailing address here at the flat. Bloody Ursula.

*Dear Kate,*

*By the time NZ Post returns this to sender all the way from Neverland with their usual efficiency, a little time will have passed. Ian will now be well despatched and you will be wallowing, playing poor-little-me, as you are prone to do. How do I know this? Maybe I have known you too long. Maybe I have been too free with my advice. But you can be rest assured I will stop meddling in your affairs unless, of course, you ask me to.*

*My reason for writing? I called Beanstalk. Jack Bean in the phone book at Clarks Beach. He's not hard to find.*

*I shouldn't meddle, but he knew your mother. I pretended to be you and told him about the Veto on your B. Cert. Told him he was your only hope. Grumpy old thing, but he did agree to meet you. I left it a bit vague as to when . . . I know you too well . . . Some excuse about a trip.*

*P.S. You can thank hunched over Ian for this. It was he who found this information for you long ago . . . not me. Maybe he should have told you this sooner, but were you ready, Kate? Are you ready now? Or are you still 'unsure'? Still heading for Palmy North?*

*Take care, darling, and know that I have always loved you.*

*Ursula*

I crumple up the letter and throw it into the bin. I can't face another dead end, just like that deserted green valley beyond the Bridge to Nowhere. Maybe I'm better not to know.

Nausea rises in my throat and I run to heave, then finger again my tender breasts and stare down into the bowl that never shows red. On the toilet floor I cry for Ian and clutch instead the porcelain bowl, which is cold and hard against my cheek, and go back to bed.

ooOOoo

Ginny comes again and takes me to Dr Heng; I stare at the wall and refuse to speak to him. Diagnosis of anxiety and depression, treatable with medication. He gives Ginny another script. Ginny moves into the spare room. I tell her nothing. At least I have stopped heaving now. I start to take the pills and convince Ginny the farm needs her more than I do. She leaves me alone and I remain in bed hoping the pills will flush this thing away. But the lump inside me is starting to push upward toward the bony point where my bladder used to be.

I reach for the phone and ring the number that was given by the pharmacy who sold me the kit. The woman on the other end is matter-of-fact and uses the word termination. Too late for a pill, too late for a simple termination, I will need a general anaesthetic and have three weeks left to make my choice. Three weeks to find out the truth about who I really am. I uncrumple Ursula's letter.

# Twenty-Two

# Beanstalk

Beanstalk had almost hung up on the unknown caller. Since retiring he seldom got calls apart from strangers wanting him to give money, but this was not a charity call. The gravelly voice had compelled him to listen at the mention of Jane Stanley's name. Was it Kate? Is that what the man-like voice had said her name was? Of course he should have expected that small baby would one day want to know about her mother. He had wanted to decline, but couldn't help listening all the same, trying to connect the voice to some small part of Jane. The perfect unburnt part of Jane he had never known. Did this Kate look like how an unburnt Jane would have done back then?

His mind far away, he had missed some of the garbled message about a trip to Palmerston North. Kate would ring again sometime soon, when she got back. Afterwards, he thought how vague and unsatisfactory the whole conversation had been. He had stared down at the beeping phone. It was too late now. He'd said yes and the caller was gone but yes to what? And when would she call again? And where would they meet? And what would he tell her? And what did she look like? His thoughts returned to Jane.

The poems had started to take on an agricultural bent. He had met Jane in his office as usual and they had both stared at the wall. Beanstalk had said nothing. There was nothing about agriculture he could add to a conversation that they weren't having, on the taboo subject that constantly filled his mind. No words had passed between them for the entire hour.

## **Wool Girl**

The shearer tips the young ewe back against his pen-stained pants

Her world inverts, leaning back in his arms
Beautiful with youth, he drags her from the pen
The shearer's moccasins glide backward across the polished floor
She's wedged between his knees
His hands momentarily free
One to pick up the handpiece, the other to pull the cord
The shed comes to life, the throaty machine ricochets off the tin walls
Urging the shearer on
The comb vibrates against the young ewe's brisket bone

This part is tricky, the yellow curly grease is chipped away
Exploring her soft warm belly, a hand finds and shields her teats
A ewe is useless if her teats get cut off
The handpiece runs once over the outside of her right thigh
It then dives between her legs and busies itself with the nether end
The dags are chipped away from around the fanny
Which becomes swollen this close to lambing
And then closes down again to a small pout
The dags sometimes stick in the cutters, this is a matter of fact

Life and birth and death on a farm, are all matters of fact
The young wool girl stands by with the wooden boards
Taken off the side of an apple box
She uses the boards to scoop up the dags
Green and shiny, large grapes between her boards
Sometimes wet and sloppy, the broom rubs the residue away
The wool girl understands these things
The wool girl understands all things

The handpiece reverses and swings up the left thigh
Then pushes down towards the young ewe's tail
The shearer lays her back, grips her nostrils, extends her neck
He runs the comb into the wool below the throat
Feeling his way blindly upward
Jabbing through the thick wool that lies there
An act of faith, the cutters run up her windpipe
The fleece is parted directly under her chin
One slip and it's over, the life blood will leave her body

The shearer grabs her left ear

The handpiece is running in gentle strokes over the neck
Removing the fluff from her woolly left cheek
He folds her ear down to shear the back of her head
And then he takes her top knot
The head is lighter now, exposed to new ideas
The handpiece slips the wool off the point of her left shoulder
Then he lays her body gently down full length on the board
The long blow is the best bit
The shearer hits a rhythm and each stroke rocks her

Soothes her, gradually lifting her up off the floor
Carving down over her ribs, peeling the last of the fleece off her rump
Tossing the final tuft off her right hock
Into the waiting hands of the wool girl
It's over, the young sheep scrambles to her feet
Unpeeled and naked she plunges head first down the port hole
Knowing things that only a wool girl can know

# Twenty-Three

# Meredith

Droplets hang onto the bells of pink foxgloves and fill out the cobwebs between the wires on the fence. They glimmer and reflect in the early morning light. The drops are intent on holding place as long as they can before smashing to the ground. It only takes the slightest movement. The drops will soon disappear anyway. The sun coming up over the eastern hills will gobble them up.

Toby is mending the yards; the sheep are still too wet for shearing. His hammer bangs down hard. Each strike rings out a hollow boom. The hills seem to press in closer and watch with interest as Meredith saddles Holly. Peter is astride his dark gelding, which is toe-heeling round the paddock in anticipation. The rain has left everything fresh and wobbling.

'So, you haven't been down to the new bridge yet?' Meredith walks Holly around Peter's prancing horse. 'Race you then.' She takes the advantage – already facing towards the river track, she spurs away ahead. His black hooves are thundering behind.

Meredith stands in her stirrups, pushing her knees into Holly, throwing her weight on the corners, ducking under low-hanging limbs and urging Holly to jump across the slips and washouts that mar the narrow track. There's no room to pass; she keeps her lead.

Breathless, Meredith pulls up and walks Holly out onto Battleship Bluff. A towering white papa cliff with just a narrow track cut into a shelf across the sheer face that drops away to the creek below. Man's arrogance to think that he could tame this place. Pebbles tinkle onto the track from way above their heads, and far below a boulder splashes into the creek.

This place is breathing in and out on its own.

Peter pulls in close, his horse unnerved. Another rock leapfrogs from above, getting louder, closer, then bouncing only once on the ledge before spinning on down to a quiet, final splash. 'Let's move on.' Peter walks his horse across to the quiet safety of the regenerating mānuka on the other side.

Meredith laughs. 'Welcome to our paralysed valley held together by bluffs that never sleep.' They walk their horses on down to the new bridge, which arches with concrete precision up out of the uncertain green bush. The tinkling creek is an age below them.

Tethering their horses, they stroll across the bridge and back to the centre. Peter slides to sit and pulls Meredith down beside him. The concrete is warm against their backs, their knees bent up, shoulders almost touching. A fantail is sitting on the opposite railing. *Cheetah, cheetah, cheetah.* It flits and turns and foils this way and that, preening, laughing, strutting, and showing off. They watch in silence. The small piebald fantail flicks her tail and shows her breast.

Peter reaches for the knapsack that lies at Meredith's feet where he dropped it. He is lean from shearing, his well-muscled forearms show below his rolled up sleeves. His eyes are blue and clear with 'trust me' smile lines at the corners. He turns to Meredith, he knows that his teeth are beautiful and he runs his tongue along his full bottom lip as his thigh touches hers. He doesn't take his thigh away.

Electricity is warming Meredith's leg and other places as well, an ocean rolling over a forgotten swimmer. She moves her leg away, crosses her ankles and slides her knees down flat, tethering her thighs together and to the bridge, but her knee, unbidden, falls outward and touches his.

Peter grins and pats her knee. He discards his bag, reaches for her chin and pulls her face towards him. His lips are warm and part easily over those fine teeth. His tongue is in her mouth. His hand, undoing her shirt, is now on her breast, reaching for the nipple that has never stood up and betrayed Meredith in this way before. She stumbles to her feet and buttons her shirt.

Peter holds up both hands. 'Sorry.' He's on his feet and his hands are in his pockets now. 'No harm done – I forgot my manners. Please forgive me.' He grins and doffs his hat in front of Meredith and then holds it over his heart. 'I am here for you, Wendy Darling. Your wish is my command.' He is waiting for her, seeking out her eyes, watching her cheeks turn redder and the tear that she brushes away.

He drops his hat to his side. 'Sorry.' He moves to take her hand. 'It's like you've never?'

Meredith does not raise her head.

'Not even with Stanley?' He watches as Meredith shakes her head and more tears form in her eyes. 'I understand.' He lifts her chin and kisses her cheek. 'I think I understand exactly.'

Meredith nods and extracts her hand to wipe her eyes.

'Let us be off then, to see the rest of Neverland.' He takes her elbow and they walk together down to the landing and gaze into the slow, deep Whanganui. He makes her laugh, touching her occasionally, inviting back the warm ocean and then sending it away again with confident control. He whispers the answer to a riddle, brushing his lips against her ear, his warm laughing breath caught within her head, leaving her wobbly in a way that not even her Peter had ever done. He wins the race home, his black horse thundering ahead, hurtling back across Battleship Bluff without even a sideways glance.

James Stanley does not appear at dinner. Meredith tiptoes out and leaves his meal by the bedside. There's an empty bottle on the floor. She picks it up and puts a full one in its place.

After dinner, the fire flickers fun and laughter even into the deepest shadows. Meredith brings out her book. She explains to Peter, how, of an evening, she and Toby have been working on his reading, taking turns aloud.

Peter takes the book. 'What a splendid idea. Let me choose a place.' He opens the book with a flourish. 'I, of course, will be Peter Pan.

Meredith, you will take the part of Wendy Darling, and,' he pauses and glances at Toby, 'maybe you can take the part of the Lost Boy, Tootles.' Peter finds his place and begins to read.

> *But there was the arrow. He took if from her heart and faced his band.*
>
> *'Whose arrow?' he demanded sternly.*
>
> *'Mine, Peter,' said Tootles on his knees.*
>
> *'Oh, dastard hand,' Peter said, and he raised the arrow to use it as a dagger.*
>
> *Tootles did not flinch. He bared his breast.*[5]

Peter reads on. Meredith finds his stockinged feet under the table and invites his legs to close around her knee. She no longer hears the words, just the lips moving over those beautiful teeth.

Toby breaks the spell as he mumbles something about bed and stumbles away.

Meredith stands and reaches for the book that Peter is offering her. It tumbles between them to the floor. His lips are on her now. The hexagons on her bedspread are drawing Meredith towards her bedroom as they have never done before.

Peter is kissing her cheek, her lips, her neck. His lips brush her collarbone. He pauses and pulls himself away. 'Not here, dearest, not now.' His hand is moving through her hair. He leads Meredith to her bed, sits her down, kisses her cheek and tiptoes from the room.

Peter whistles as he readies himself for bed and squints up at Toby who lies rigid in the top bunk with his eyes on the ceiling, close above his head.

'Have you ever had a woman, Toby?'

Toby's face colours; he shakes his white shaggy head and pulls the blankets up to his chin.

---

5  JM Barrie, *Peter Pan and Wendy*, 77.

Peter whistles some more as he climbs into the bunk below. 'Do you know, Toby, I've never had a woman in a woolshed.' Peter blows out the candle.

*ooOOoo*

Before dawn, Meredith lights the lamp and looks out. The sun is coming up in a clear sky. The light wind will be drying the sheep nicely. She stirs up the fire.

The shearing will take four days. Toby scouts the hills and brings the sheep down. Meredith's in the shed; she dags the sheep and picks up the wool for Peter on the shears. James Stanley remains sober enough, emerging from time to time from the whare. He stamps down the wool, tips the wool press over, cranks the handle and stitches up the hard pressed bales with his right hand crab, before stumbling back to the whare. And so the pattern is set.

In the shed the air hangs between them. For three days Meredith watches the sweat slide from Peter's muscled shoulders bent over the sheep. Three days he handles the white flesh of freshly shorn ewes. Three more evenings of sharing the reading, with Toby retiring early to avoid the storm that is building over the kitchen table.

Peter leads her towards her bed on the third evening. He pulls her down onto the bed and his lips linger too long for her to say no, should he have chosen to stay. He pulls himself away. 'Tomorrow in the shed,' he whispers. 'If you choose it to be so,' and he is gone to the bunk room.

Wendy Darling pulls the hexagons over her head and falls asleep with *Peter Pan*.

On the fourth day, the bales are mounting up, most of them already on the sled by the woolshed door, ready to be taken down to the landing before the rain comes. There's a change in the weather. The last of the sheep are dagged and stand ready for the shearer in the catching pen. The heat before rain becomes oppressive.

At lunchtime, Meredith collects the pail of sandwiches she has prepared in the early morning. It's hot. She slips off her trousers and sheath knife in favour of a simple cotton smock to pick up the last of the wool. She washes herself with a cold wet cloth and smooths the soft fabric down over her stomach and thighs, assuring herself she is only doing this because of the heat of the day. The rain is overdue to come; the land is waiting. It will soon be over now. Once the shearing is done, she knows that Peter will be gone out to Raetihi for his next shed. He will leave tonight to ride out of the valley before the rain closes the road.

Between sheep, she stands by the door of the woolshed and watches the clouds building. Everything is changing, not just the shearer leaving. Toby is going to war. Muriel has delivered the official-looking letter, which Mrs Dougherty had hoped would not find its way to Toby here in the valley. He is already taking the last big mob away to the back paddock. Then he'll be packing his trunk to catch the boat out with the wool clip.

Meredith looks out over her land. Tomorrow, once more, it will be just her and James Stanley here in the valley: she in a quiet house, he in the whare. She turns back into the shed. Just the tail enders left. How will she cope when Toby and Peter have gone? She straightens her shoulders. She will do her best.

But Peter. Meredith can hardly bear to watch the shearer. His muscled arms move so surely through each fleece with only the snip, snip of the hand shears and the tick tick of the clock breaking the badly contained silence between them. His hands move over the body of each ewe, his tapering fingers glistening with their sweat, his sweat, their lanolin, his life blood moving under his skin next to their skin. She can hardly breathe.

The shearing is almost done, another old ewe slips down the port hole. Meredith steps forward to pick up the fleece and Peter rests his hand on the catching pen door. She knows he is watching her as she bends over to gather the fleece and turns away to hide her hot, flushed face.

The last ewe stands alone in the pen, a reject marked with raddle. The door slams shut as Peter enters the pen, pulling the old girl over onto her tail, towing her out of the pen. Meredith throws the wool quickly, sorting the skirting, the belly, the neck and soft cheek fluff. She rolls the fleece in on itself, lifting, carrying, and pushing it down into the wool press.

She turns to watch the last sheep being shorn. Peter is already on the long blow. Her heart aches to be that sheep.

His hands are on her neck, the last shoulder, the last thigh. The last sheep flies away down the port hole with a skitter of hooves on wood. The shed is silent, apart from the clock ticking.

Peter leans on the door of the empty catching pen. He watches as Meredith steps forward and bends over to gather up the last fleece. Peter steps close behind her. He reaches down with his shears and snips the band that holds her hair back. The dark, damp locks fall around her face and forward over her eyes. Peter reaches down and takes her hands away from the wool and pulls her slowly upright. He draws her back towards him, his groin cups her buttocks, his chest against her shoulder, his sweat washing through her thin cotton dress. His arms criss-cross around her.

Meredith's hair is flowing down like a curtain between them. She is motionless within the circle of his arms.

His lips are next to her ear. 'For every woman there is a time to choose.' He lifts his hands away from hers and steps back. 'You understand that I will be gone tonight.'

Meredith nods beneath the veil of hair which covers her face. 'I understand,' she whispers. Her hands seek to find his and pull the shearer close again, wrapping his arms low down across her belly. 'I understand that I must stay and you will go.'

'Thank you,' Peter whispers. His moccasin-covered feet glide backwards across the polished floor. He steers her back and lowers her down onto the soft white fleece that is still lying there on the shearing board at his feet. 'Thank you with all my heart.' He bends over her.

Meredith can feel his breath through the curtain of her hair. She tips back her head and her hair falls away.

He finds her lips. His lanolin-covered fingers work the buttons and hooks, deft hands used to parting wool from naked skin. He eases her dress and undergarments away to find her breasts, her buttocks. He runs his hands and lips over every part her. Long strokes with a practised hand.

He gathers Meredith up off the fleece and carries her to lay her down on a wool bale. He stands between her thighs, her calves over his shoulders. His pants are gone now. Her ankles tighten around his neck, lifting her hips free of the bale. Her hands are gripping his buttocks, guiding him forward into the rising slap-slap. Pieces of her are drowning. Her body is begging for less air. Meredith's hearing is leaving her as has never happened before.

The air is broken by the high-pitched, unstoppable wail of a hurt animal. Meredith is hardly aware of this but her ears are unplugged by the fall of the axe on something hollower than the chopping block. Her feet are falling to the woolshed floor.

She cowers on the wooden boards, her back against the wool bale, arms crisscrossed to cover her nakedness. Drops are forming on the floor between her feet.

James Stanley howls again, looking down at the wetness that darkens the floor. He throws the axe down across the unmoving form of the shearer who is sprawled out beside him.

James is howling at Meredith. He reaches down and flings her back onto the wool bale. His right deformed hand is on her neck, the long disused nails on his left hook hand are raking her body. Pausing only to rip open his bulging fly, the gouging continues until he is spent.

# Twenty-Four

# Beanstalk

Now it was the thought of Kate that kept Beanstalk awake at night. What would he say? Which bits would he leave out? She hadn't rung back yet. Why had she disturbed his peace if she didn't mean to come after all? These were the thoughts that circled in his head. So many of Jane's poems seemed to have double meanings or were unfathomable to him. What would a modern young woman make of them, he wondered?

His games of cat and mouse had continued but each poem he had found was less fathomable than the last. Why would Jane write in riddles about a story that she had shunned and refused to read? He had taken down the beautiful volume of *Peter Pan* that Jane had refused to open and checked what he vaguely remembered about the boy from Neverland. The boy who had given his acorn button to Wendy Darling instead of a kiss. He had crowed with delight at this small discovery.

Another doomed avenue for his therapy awaited him. He could not tell Kate these things.

**A Button's Fate**

Given not taken, an acorn instead of a kiss
Taken not given, an arrow removed from a nut
Given not taken, a new life falls from the tree
Taken not given, an oak tree growing within

# Twenty-Five

# Kate

Beanstalk lives at Clarks Beach. He's in the phone book under the name Jack Bean. I don't ring the number. I don't ring the number. I do ring the number. I hang up before he answers. I do ring the number, I don't hang up. He remembers that I have called before. His voice gives nothing away. I hang up. I call again. He gives me directions, then I hang up. I ring back and say sorry for hanging up.

Do I take the right turn off the motorway at Papakura, or straight ahead to Palmy North? At the last minute I swerve onto the motorway off-ramp. I will do it. I will turn right to head west past Kingseat Hospital, right to Waiau Pa and then on down to Clarks Beach. The directions I know by rote go slowly round in my head.

At Kingseat, I slow down at the first big bend and roll through the village, if you can call it that: a takeaway dairy, a couple of houses and on the right tall trees that flank a formal driveway. This must be Kingseat Psychiatric Hospital. A man stands by the entrance way; he is waving to each car as the traffic goes by. He sees my indicator blinking for a right turn and grins, showing all his teeth and most of his gums as well. As I pull into the entrance to the hospital he does a little dance on the spot then trots along beside my bike. His elastic pants are tucked in up to his armpits above his oversized shoes and high-lifting knees. He grins again and twists his right hand in space, urging me to rev the bike, to lift up the front wheel. If I were Ursula, I would oblige him, riding the long straight into the hospital grounds on my back wheel. I am not Ursula. Bloody Ursula. Where is she when I need her?

I choose first gear to idle down the avenue of phoenix palms. There is not much to see. The two-storey brick villas are set well back, each in its own dignified isolation. In the no-man's land at the centre are playing fields with deserted rugby posts, football goals and tennis courts with sagging wire. Everything needs paint; they say the place will close down in a year or two. Some of the buildings look like they've been mothballed already. I don't stop at reception, just drive straight past and turn the bike at the end of the avenue and then gun it back down the long drive of phoenix. It's the same route that Ginny and John must have taken with their carrycot in the back of the station wagon twenty-four years ago. This is where I was born. I don't feel a thing.

Charlie Chaplin at the entrance has given up on me. He stamps his foot as I approach and turns his back on purpose to look for cars coming from the opposite direction. I turn right and head on out to Clarks Beach.

Right off Torkar Road, down an access way that leads to the water, I find the huddle of old baches that sit right down at the harbour's edge. I pull in at Beanstalk's place. It's small – a corrugated iron affair held together with layers of paint over the rust spots, forever braced against the northwesterlies under the overhang of pōhutukawa wreathing the whole place in pockmarked red and golden-brown leaves. The harbour is just across the grass reserve. The tide is currently sucked away. Tiny dots of people walk across the grey-riveted sand, way out towards the near rise of Awhitu, and the far dark hills of French Bay on the other side of the Manukau entrance.

Jack Bean sits with a pipe in his mouth, under the trees, on an outdoor chair that's large and wooden with broad arms like a throne. He rises up unsteadily, pushing down with both hands. He's very tall and very old. A towelling hat is pulled well down over a long nose; his eyes are cut glass blue and look directly at me. My hands are shaking as I undo my helmet and slowly take off my dark glasses. He reads my thoughts as I raise my eyes from the huge hand he holds out for me to shake and rudely scan every detail of his face.

'I am not your father, if that's what you are thinking.' He takes my hand. 'Jack Bean, Dr Jack Bean.' His grip is still firm.

There's a pause as I try to figure out what to say. Neither of us speaks.

He walks back to the chair and waves me to an uncut circle of firewood alongside. I perch at his knee while he relights his pipe and puffs slowly.

'You knew my mother?'

Beanstalk puffs for a moment. 'Yes, I knew Jane Stanley.' He puffs some more. 'Jane Wendy Stanley.' He turns his startling blue eyes towards me.

It all blurts out. 'What was she like? Did she look like…?'

Beanstalk looks down at my hands, which are bloodless and fastened onto the arm of his chair.

'You need to understand something. I don't know what the poor girl looked like.' He turns and gazes at the mudflats as he speaks. 'Before she came to Kingseat she'd been burnt, badly burnt.'

Beanstalk stares out across the harbour. 'Her face…ears melted and glued back to her head. She had no hair, just a few golden wisps. Jane's face…' He pauses and swallows. 'Her face burnt flat, no nose, just small angry holes where the surgeons had opened up the scarring for her to breathe and slits for her eyes to pop through. And a mouth, just an angry oval shape, and rattled breathing that was horrible to hear. Her teeth awry, terrible scarring.' He pauses again and pulls on his pipe and turns back to look down at me. 'Your mother looked at the world through a dreadful mask and the world felt sick to look back at her.'

I swallow hard and we both think about this thing. 'Is that all?'

Beanstalk slowly takes the pipe out of his mouth. 'She didn't speak – burnt throat. She refused to communicate with sign language or a pointing board despite us thinking her more than capable.'

'Is that why she ended up in a nuthouse?' I think of the picture shown to me by the nuns: a small, determined girl refusing to hold hands with the other children in the picture at Jerusalem.

Beanstalk ignores my question and continues as if he has rehearsed what he is going to say and needs to get it out.

'It became my habit to take her outside. I would talk to your mother about what we saw. I named the plants. We watched for birds. We'd take the small boat and I would row her on the creek when the tides were right and she would dip her hand in the water. We developed a language of sorts.'

'What about me?' I'm carving a hole with my nail, digging into the arm of his chair.

'Ah, you.' Beanstalk rubs his nose. 'Your mother Jane must have been pregnant before she came here.' He pauses for a moment. 'When it became…apparent…the next of kin, a Mrs Dougherty, suggested that a farming family would be best for the baby.' Beanstalk glances at me. 'Was this ever discussed with you?'

I shake my head. The words blurt out. 'She didn't want me?'

Beanstalk shakes his head. 'It wasn't her choice.' He looks away from me and bows his head. I can't see his eyes.

'I remember the day your new parents came to collect you. A blonde-headed baby.'

He reiterates the timing of the thing. That Jane must have been newly pregnant before she burned, before she came to Kingseat.

I busy myself removing whole, splintered strips of wood off the arm of his chair.

'So, she wasn't a nutter then.'

Beanstalk stirs in his chair and brightens a little. 'A little depressed, yes, but no, your mother was actually a very intelligent woman. She became a poet.' He glances at me and then his eyes drift away to the receding water across the mudflats. 'She wrote well for someone with no training.'

Beanstalk stands up. 'I can show you.' He pushes up from his chair, clomps into the bach without taking off his boots, and returns to place a small box in my hands. Wooden, with yellow metal beaten around the corners held in place with tiny nails.

My fingers fumble with the catch. Inside, a white feather and a notebook. I lift the notebook out and run my fingers over the soiled cardboard cover and woven cloth on the spine. I brush the feather across my face and hug the book to my chest. My mother Jane feels bony and all angles but she has touched these things as well.

I open the notebook slowly and look first at the writing, which is in pencil, small and cramped, raked forward with 0s like oval-shaped eggs. Just like when a choir sings the *Hallelujah Chorus* at Christmas. All standing in a row with lipstick oval mouths all opening at the same time. 'HARR lay lu yar, HARR lay lu yar, hallelujah.' My hands shake as I stare at the oval shaped oOOos, written just the way I write my oOOos. I read the poems, Jane's poems.

Her words are circling around in my head; some of them make sense and some do not. On the first page I read of the white heron and stroke the white feather that Jane once held, rubbing it the wrong way then smoothing each white barb back into its rightful place. Beanstalk smokes his pipe and watches me read. His answers to my questions are brief and abrupt when I press him for details about Jane.

'How can I possibly remember? There were 800 patients in Kingseat at that time.' He waves his pipe at me. 'I can't be expected to remember them all in the detail that you are demanding.'

Beanstalk puts his hand out for the book and the box. I tuck the feather inside the book and place it back inside the little wooden box. His watery blue eyes give nothing away as I zip the box under my jacket. Jane's words sit uncomfortably hard against my ribs and the bottom of the box is cushioned by her grandchild deep within me. I take courage from this, rise up, and step away from him. I clutch the bulge under my jacket that is now my hope box. He grips the arms of his chair as if to rise up, but makes no move to stop me.

'So what happened to her in the end?'

He shrugs. 'Don't recall. Must've happened while I was away in England. The long-termers died here, of course. This place became her home.'

'And my father?'

He shrugs again. 'Who would ever know?'

'Toby Dougherty,' I whisper. Beanstalk makes no response.

At Clarks Beach the tide is still going out as I'm leaving. The tide has also deserted the mangroves that have now choked the creek behind Kingseat Hospital. The ugly mangrove roots are visible above the pools of muddy water that are left behind on the low tide. There is no space anymore for a rowing boat in this creek.

Charlie Chaplin is still out by the main gate as I pass. He refuses to wave.

Where to go? A left turn onto the motorway will take me back to the flat, where I can pull the curtains again and climb back into bed. A right turn will take me to the farm.

I stop and sit. The bike hums obediently but doesn't help with the decision.

Left for sleeping pills, enough there at the flat to finish things if I want to. Right to Ginny for a cup of tea.

Left to the flat, I can destroy the poems and pretend they don't exist. Right to steady myself, make plans to head down country to finish what I've begun.

Left to drown myself in wine and make arrangements to destroy the life I carry inside me.

I choose right.

Ginny hugs me. We drink tea.

'After Luke was born, the only way I tossed this thing was through hard work, making myself do something, anything, every day.' Ginny has tears in her eyes. 'The shed is full of sheep and they could do with a wool girl. It'll do you the world of good.'

There's the rhythm of the shearing, the action of picking up the wool, the smell and touch of lanolin, the perfect pitch of the machine bursting into life over and over each time a new sheep is dragged out onto the board. The rythm of the shed calms and then, with repetition, it retrofits my brain. Suddenly I am not unsure – in fact, it is all very clear, and very simply spelled in my head.

T O B Y D O U G H E R T Y
TOBY DOUGHTERTY    TOBY DOUGHERTY

# Twenty-Six

# Beanstalk

Jane's tiny baby phoned again. Kate's voice was not as gravelly as Beanstalk remembered. This time she was not so self-assured. It had taken Kate three calls to make the arrangements to meet and a fourth call to apologise.

Beanstalk was not ready, only part way through ordering his thoughts, but what else could he do? Her voice, on the phone, indicated to the professional in him that her visit was urgent and her state of mind unclear. He sighed and backed down, resigning himself to listening.

Retirement be damned. All the damaged beach folk around these parts seemed to find a reason to come and visit Beanstalk. An old man with time on his hands, he would listen to their woes in a confidential manner. They would depart his bach with a lighter step, leaving him with nothing but the burden of their sad words and his advancing years.

How much would he tell Kate? The night before her visit, he'd lain awake. The professional in him had been taught long ago to leave none of his own skin in the game. Or so he had thought, until the whole debacle of Jane.

The girl arrived on a large motorbike. Kate was tall, with strong limbs. She climbed off the bike and reached up to lift off her helmet. A striking profile with shoulder-length white-blonde hair tied back, her skin pale and green eyes turned towards him. This girl had Jane's hungry eyes and a full mouth that wasn't smiling. He could see her question there already as she looked at his hands.

'No, I am not your father, if that is what you're thinking.'

The girl was different to her mother. How could a perfect baby have grown so awkwardly tall? Beanstalk remembered the little farmer's wife who had taken the tiny baby away from Kingseat that day. He remembered her being a good woman; she didn't deserve this sullen daughter.

It seemed all wrong. Kate's voice was hard. He had always imagined Jane with a melodic voice and a neat and graceful demeanour. Apart from her green eyes, there was no resemblance to the mother. Kate was not his type at all.

He decided not to take her inside his bach. Perhaps better to talk outside under the trees where the words could waft away rather than hanging in claustrophobic tendrils from the fly spots on the ceiling. After all, he was a bachelor. There was not much time for cleaning the place.

Beanstalk was ready for her first question and told her straight up about Jane Stanley's scarred face. He watched her recoil, just as people always did when they saw Jane for the first time, just as he had done.

What should he say? There was so little he could tell this girl that wouldn't incriminate. He started with the day her new parents had come to collect her, a tiny, perfect blonde-headed baby. He reiterated the timing of the thing; that Jane must have been pregnant before she burned, before she came to Kingseat.

He didn't tell her what an odd couple they had become, he and her mother Jane. The staff hadn't seemed to notice; they were all known to have their favourites back then. Human, after all, and nothing unprofessional happened between him and Jane.

But worst of all the hope box. Why had he shown her the poems? An explosive was now waiting to blow back in his face. He should have helped that girl, Kate, to understand that Jane's poems weren't real, just a patient being manipulative. That notebook, a time bomb of make-believe. Or was that just the feeble man in him unable to face the reality in Jane's words that had hurt so much? Some of the things written there, so sad, that even he the professional, or should he say smitten professional, had chosen not to believe.

Why hadn't he thrown the notebook away when he'd had the chance? Or taken it away from Jane, stopped her writing? Instead he had sought out the hope box from every hiding place and coveted each poem, like the small taste of nectar he remembered from his boyhood when he had peeled back the blue petals to find a fairy paintbrush at the centre of a wild flower.

Jane's poems were her gifts, given only to him, but of course he didn't admit any of that to Kate. Instead he told her there had been 800 patients at Kingseat at the time. A doctor could not be expected to recall one specific patient. He'd told her it was a long time ago and Jane must have died while he was away studying in England, because she wasn't there when he'd returned. That much was true. Lots of patients had died unexplained deaths at Kingseat Hospital. They just wrote pneumonia on the death certificates. That was also true, but he hadn't mentioned that to Kate.

She had stood to go, her green eyes on him, and a twist in her mouth that was hard to defy as she zipped the hope box inside her jacket. He'd held his breath; part of him was leaving with Jane's poems. He'd made no move to stop her.

And now the book was gone. As a younger man he may have jumped up and wrestled it back, but he had just stood and watched with empty hands.

It was only after she had gone that he realised the hope box was nothing to him now. Each poem written in the notebook was still burnt into his brain. Word after word, her poems continued to vomit out of him. In the dark of the night, he found he could still recite each one, in the same order that she'd first written them down.

He hadn't told Kate how he had continued to try and help her stubborn little mother. He hadn't mentioned the time he had sat her down in his office and forced Jane to listen while he read to her from *Peter Pan*.

But of course it was Jane who won. Blackness had settled over him when he had read her next poem. He knew then he could never please Jane, nor stop loving her. He was caught with his feet stuck firm in her sticky web, hating Moonface all the more.

## Been Stalked

Beanstalk looks through my mask and asks me who I am
He looks through my head and asks me where I'm from
My father is Peter Pan, my mother still waits by the window
She holds his shadow and a needle in her hands
Waiting to cross again the bridge to Neverland

Beanstalk looks through my mask and asks me where I've been
'Second to the right, and then straight on till morning'
My mother is Wendy Moira Angela Darling
She sewed my heels to the eiderdown and named me Jane
I shan't cry, I can't cry, tears will never come

Beanstalk looks through my mask and asks me how I feel
When I touch my face the surface is numb
Scars burnt deep, even before the fire
Two souls unable to give or receive a mother's love
Not even a thimble dressed up as an acorn

Beanstalk looks through my mask and asks me how she died
I tell him that it was Peter's fault
Wendy Darling who never speaks with her candle by the window
Always open a crack, in case Peter should come back to her
Did Tinker Bell knock the candle or was it just the wind?

Beanstalk looks through my mask and speaks to me of love
A tide on a muddy creek, I think of Colossus
A flea in his ear and his feet, gnarled roots exposed in mud
I vomit over the bow, a rainbow spreads over drab grey
Only Moonface can truly know these things in a faraway tree

# Twenty-Seven

# Toby

It wasn't my fault. I have never been the sort of man to snoop about, but the door was ajar. I had come back to the house to pack my things. I hadn't expected anyone to be there, thought Meredith was still at the shed. I had a war to go to – planning to leave from the landing on the riverboat that day as soon as the shearing was done.

I pushed the kitchen door wide. I can see her still; Meredith standing in the metal bathtub by the wood stove, red marks scouring the length of her back, her buttocks.

'Toby.' She turns and pulls a towel around herself but not before I catch a glimpse of her breasts. 'A pig, Toby, a pig got me.' She rushes to her room and closes the curtain.

I walk across to the bunk room and fumble to pack my things. I call my farewell through the curtain. What else can I do? I tiptoe out the kitchen door and close it behind me.

At the woolshed, old man Stanley's pressing the last bale. I avert my eyes from his deformed hands fumbling at the simple task of sewing down the top. I am not sure why, but his hands and dirty nails disturb me, like the smell of decayed meat. Push the needle in, pull the needle out, push the needle in, and pull it out through the rough, jute sacking. When he is finished I help him roll the last two bales onto the sled and throw my trunk on top and a shovel as well. One of the bales is smeared with blood and the floor of the woolshed is damp.

His eyes follow mine to the mess. 'Killed an old ewe with bad flyblow,' he says in a way that dismisses any more questions.

Old man Stanley is never this sober. For the past three months he's hardly spoken a word to me. It wasn't my idea to come up here. Damn my mother for that one. Would she have sent me up here if she had known how low Stanley had sunk? Most of the time, holed up in the whare out the back, talking to his whisky, Meredith making excuses for him. Meredith in the bathtub, the red welts – I try not to think about the deep, red gouges.

We walk along the track, me and Stanley, towards the river. One of us on each side of the horse, neither of us speaking. Me, smoothing the track from time to time, shovelling away the slips, easing the sled over the washouts.

'Off to earn yourself some glory for home and country?' James Stanley snorts. 'Good luck to you, boy. Killing gets easier. After the first one, it's a piece of cake.' He tips back his head and laughs. His voice booms down the valley.

The day is hot. There is no air in the valley today. The clouds that have been threatening all morning are getting closer, closing in. The sun is gone. The tui that have been chattering and darting about in the flax flowers have left as well. Mr Stanley's laughter ricochets back up the valley and leaves again. We walk on through the silence.

We get to Battleship Bluff. There's a slip well across. I take the shovel and start to scrape what I can over the edge. Rocks bounce and splash, filling the air with echoes as they tumble over the side and down, down into the creek.

Behind me there's a crashing, smashing, booming splash. I spin around. Mr Stanley is standing on the sled where the last bale had been. He's shaking his fist in the air and his laughter is booming and returning. I look down. The bale has split wide open and there lies the shearer, all smashed up in the creek amongst the wool.

I run back to the sled, my mind not yet processing what I have seen, shouting at Stanley. 'Peter, fallen in the creek…needs our help.'

James Stanley throws back his head and laughs again. 'He helped himself. Let this be a lesson to you, boy.'

As I reach the sled, my brain catches up and my world contracts. All I can see is Stanley's laughing chin. I swing the shovel. Stanley sidesteps the shovel and falls off the sled. I'm onto him and we're at it like a pair of wild boars. I have the height and weight but even with all his drinking, the strength of the man is colossal. He's getting the better of me, flipping me over onto my back. His hook is at my throat. His hook is taking my air. He's edging me towards the bluff side of the track.

'Toby, Toby.' He kept repeating my name. 'Toby, so much to learn, kid, easy meat, and here you were, ready to fight someone else's war.' He is laughing as my vision tunnels in. All I can see is his chin rising and falling and even that is fading into blackness.

A terrible cry. I can't see. Everything is red and wet and salty and warm and I'm breathing again. I sit up and wipe the blood from my eyes. Meredith is there; she has flipped Stanley onto his back. Her knee is on his chest. She has cut his throat, and is still hacking away. Stanley's head is cut nearly clean off. I take the bloodied knife off her and fling it wide into the air. Cartwheeling, it goes over and over, down into the creek.

The rain is starting now, big spots hitting us on the head, spotting the ground, a virus spreading, banging my brain, running all over me, dripping off my chin. The rain mingles with the blood that covers us both, running red, running rivers. We stand there and look at each other as the rain runs away. Is Meredith laughing or is she crying? I can't tell. I hold her shaking body against my own. A puddle is forming around our feet. We can't stay here. I unbuckle the horse and we push the remainder of the wool over the bluff and the sled as well.

I nod to Meredith's pinched white face; she understands what must be done. We pick up a boot each and tow James Stanley back up the track. Tomorrow I will bury him, but not now. We leave him where the bush meets the clearing on Ward's Flat and walk back to the house in pouring rain.

We close the door, cannot speak and cannot hear. The rain beats down on the roof like a madman drumming on a tin can. Meredith drops into a chair; her hair flops forward only for a moment across her face. She tucks it back behind her ears, steadies her hands on the table and raises her chin. She doesn't speak but out she goes into the pounding rain to drag in the tin bath. She lights the fire to heat water and then indicates my turn first. I face away to pull off my bloodied wet clothes. She helps me step into the bath, and washes my back as a mother should. Not that mine ever did.

I can't stop thinking about the deep red welts I had seen on her back and buttocks, across her ribs, scratches on her chest and on her breasts. I'm crying now, as I have never done before and tears and bath water are running down my face as she tips billy-can after billy-can over my head. When I'm spent, she towels me down, guides me to my bunk and places a cool hand momentarily on my hot forehead. She pulls the curtain across before tending to her own bath. The rain is deafening. I can't think or make sense of anything.

# Twenty-Eight

# Kate

Below the hospital there are joggers in the Domain. They take the path beneath the oak trees, their feet crunching on acorns, twigs and flotsam that need to be swept away. A strapping young chest with well-muscled thighs is striding towards me. His silky shorts are riding up at the front as his thighs inch the material upward. I watch his future sliding from side to side. This is an Ursula moment but wasted without her commentary. I look around for her, but she's not here.

I close my eyes.

*Eric appears — he strides down the hill, his arms swinging as carelessly as those of the young running god. His white coat sails out behind him like a warrior prince. I look again. Maybe not quite as careless as he once was. Are his shoulders starting to set? I dare not take my eyes off Eric, in case he grows old and crumples before me.*

*Eric sets himself down on the bench. He looks me over with his doctoring eye, no doubt looking out for any sign of the V for victim on my forehead. I try not to think out loud. 'Damn you, Eric.'*

Ursula would have liked this, drawn in, sitting on the couch, wanting to hear more. Of course, I would have hammed it up for her.

*Eric smiles broadly. I flash him a V for victory, just like the young boys do in his homeland, Cambodia. He takes my hand, rubbing the small muscles between the bones as only he knows how.*

*I tell him about Beanstalk and the masked woman who is my mother. A horror story with a dead end, not of Jane's own making: a mother who had no choice but to let me go. Was my mother a victim or a heroine? Eric says nothing, just nods for me to continue the way that doctors do.*

Ursula would have had an opinion. It would have been something about slaying the monster that still lurks out there somewhere.

*Eric listens with his head on one side. He lowers his chin into his hands and looks away. 'Be careful, it's not your job to judge.'*

*I lift his chin and turn his head back towards me. 'So what is my job then?'*

*Eric's molten brown eyes don't blink. 'That's simple: to come out of this thing whole.'*

*He stands and bends forward. He nearly kisses me on the tip of my nose, but catches himself. 'Just like you can never fix Jane, who could never fix Meredith.'*

*The cold metal of the stethoscope that hangs around his neck is touching my throat. I grab both ends of the thing, and pull it tight around his neck.*

*'They found the doctor on a park bench in the Domain, strangled by his own good advice. There were no suspicious circumstances.' I kiss his lips.*

*Eric pokes out his tongue and mocks choking, rearranges the stethoscope around his coat collar, pats my knee and is gone back up the hill towards the tall building that blocks out the sky. The hospital is white and square, softened only a little by the oak trees that are readying themselves to lose their leaves.*

*I don't tell him about the baby inside me, my breasts bursting over the top of my bra, my morning sickness and no Ursula here to hold my head.*

I open my eyes. I'm alone. The runner is well gone. White butterflies fly around but what's the point with no Ursula to share them with? I stand up, crush an acorn under my foot and wonder how long it would take to ride to Palmerston North. Maybe I will go to Whangamomona. I pick up my helmet. Bloody Ursula.

*ooOOoo*

Long distance – I call the number that Ginny has given me. There is no reply. Bloody Ursula.

*ooOOoo*

The sign at the start of the Forbidden Highway reads *No petrol for the next 148km.* Less than half a tank. I turn back and fuel up in Taumarunui and walk into the garage to pay.

'How far to Palmerston North?' I ask the gum-chewing fringe that shields the eyes of the attendant behind the counter.

'That depends if you're taking the scenic route.' He thumbs towards the Forgotten Highway. 'Are you heading down through Whangamomona?'

Bile rises in my throat. Am I ready? Will I ever be ready? My bike chooses the route through National Park instead. A good road, with long straights and weak, scrubby stuff that grows in shades of black and grey along both sides of the road. I can smell the dampness of wet wood. My tears are whipped away by the wind that taunts me. I close down my visor. Why does this not feel like the easy option?

On my left, Ruapehu and Tongariro are sitting proud in a clear sky. I wonder which of the smaller bumps is Pihanga and where Taranaki originally sat on this great plateau. Bloody Ursula. I hunch lower on my bike and let the white dashes in the middle of the road blur as my speedo inches around requiring all my attention to make it through the corners at the ends of long, forgiving straights.

At Palmerston North, the clock tower in the square is as disappointing as the rest of this flat inland city that feels like a country town with nothing to remember it by. The Manawatū River is small and sluggish compared to the great, wide, dirty Whanganui. I press on south with no thought as to where I am going until I take an exit arrow that says Cook Strait Ferry. I ride up the metal ramp and tie my bike down with the oily ropes, which the stevedore points out hanging on the wall. Most of the bikes are tied down with their own fancy ratchets. I do the job and wipe my hands on the back of my pants. The bowels of the ship smell sweet with stock-truck effluent. I stumble up on deck and watch the North Island disappear. No point going up the other end of the boat. I have no clue what lies ahead and am hardly interested.

The steel ramp deposits me on a new land. It is all the same to me. I have no clue who Queen Charlotte was, but I take her scenic route, with corners and green bush crowding in. Soon it's behind me. I sit at the sign board where a decision is required. My bike turns west and then east again. The Lewis takes me zig-zagging through the beech trees, following a bouldered river up and over the pass and then down to a broad valley between dry majestic hills. My first view of the flat lands sees me looking to turn right, hugging the foothills, seeking a road that will lead me back to the mountains and the next pass.

Again I ride west, rising up above the green bush line, pinned to the black tarmac between the hot rocks. As I ride over the apex of Arthur's Pass, the sun picks me up through the wrong end of her binoculars. Soft bitumen cakes my lungs. I breathe in and take up the challenge. Just me and the late afternoon sun racing each other down the other side of the pass. Who will be the first to touch the Tasman Sea? I pull up at Kūmara Beach just in time to see the green flash as she disappears over the horizon. Only now do I feel alone. The sun has followed me all the way from one side of this vast range to the other but now she has gone on, beyond where I can follow her. Sweat cools inside my leathers with the first hint of evening. I zip up my jacket to the chin, turn my back to the beach and gun on down towards Ōkārito.

In the softening light, I lift my visor and let my nostrils take pictures of things I cannot see. Cows after milking walk the lanes between ragwort paddocks. Beech trees rub their heads together and speak of rain that will not come tonight. I hold my breath to pass a smoky diesel and then settle in on the empty road south. Now it's just me with the mighty Alps hanging over my left shoulder and salt somewhere to my right.

It feels good. I tip smoothly into the gentle corners and check the rear vision mirror. No Ursula. Bugs hit my face so I lower my visor again. There is only me and my own familiar breath, which warms the small world inside my helmet. I press on.

Too late to make Ōkārito, I pull in when I see a backpacker sign. The cross-sawn timber buildings stand together in a bush clearing. I sit out on the deck and order dinner. I'm the only guest tonight. I drink beer and talk to the lonely woman who runs in and out, preparing her speciality dish. Her man is up hunting somewhere in the hills. The possum burger is meaty and delicious with a garnish of wild blackberries, a sprig of lavender and homemade chutney. I eat slowly, cutting small portions, making my lips and tongue savour each forkful, making it last.

Like so much of New Zealand, this place is picture perfect but so alone. How does this woman survive the winter in this clearing when the sun is gone by three o'clock and no one comes? She has no child.

A baby deer reaches its long ears up over the table edge. The woman rushes out to retrieve her pet. Her husband had brought it down from the hills for her after he shot the mother.

'No, no, it's no bother.' Quite the reverse, I am staring into big brown eyes, which in turn are staring at the greens that accompany my perfect burger. I gently manoeuvre my elbow between this baby and my plate. The deer springs up into the air and lands one petite hoof in the middle of my burger bun. Then it's gone, skittling away on long wobbly legs. The sudden movement is startling in this place that seems to stand still. The young woman bursts forth again to make good. Can she get me another burger? I wave her away, pulling the food back onto my plate, honoured to eat around this perfect imprint on my memory.

Up early, birds are tuning up for the approaching sun, still stuck somewhere on the other side of the range but I'm not waiting for my companion of yesterday. The bike coughs and then wails like a woken baby, until warm. I put the choke to bed when the throttle begins to respond the way it should, bungee on my gear with cold fingers, pull on my gloves and swing my leg over the dewy seat. Clonk. The cold gear box hesitates a small protest but finds first gear and we're on the road. The only noise now is the wind inside my helmet and a positive well-timed song as the bike lifts up through the gears. I think of the silence I am leaving behind, the woman and her quiet deer. Will she get more visitors tonight? Will her man return from the hills?

Ōkārito at last. I swap my bike for a canoe – the first one out on a perfect lagoon of early morning glass. I paddle hard upstream to where they say the sacred birds have their nests. Carefully I ship my paddle and glide in towards the kōtuku, magnificently offset above the picture postcard perfection of their reflections. Elegant white herons against tree green, against the grey Alps and sky blue…then again, all inverted to look…almost too perfect. I send a ripple with my paddle across the reflection to make it real. Is it really this silent or has the vista magnified so much that this is all my brain can take in?

A white feather floats past my canoe, perfectly positioned like a sculpture in this vast gallery. Turning in a gentle spiral it's mounted by only two points on a molten pedestal for my pleasure. I reach and scoop the feather up away from its reflection. A keepsake from the kōtuku. They have spoken and I have heard.

I tuck my feather into the hope box against my heart, alongside Jane's feather. They nest together well. My bike is gunning north. This time I will not be stopping in Palmerston North.

# Twenty-Nine

# Beanstalk

Kate was well gone but his mind still fizzed and replayed their brief meeting. He should have been more the professional – impressed on Kate his efforts to help her stubborn little mother.

He thought of Kate riding away with the hope box bulging under her jacket. How could this serious girl be Jane's daughter? Not at all the way he had imagined Jane to be, apart from the same green eyes boring into him.

Why had he never shown the poems to anyone else – never mentioned their existence in his hospital notes? Another part of his mistake, his guilt. Not ethical. Damning now, if someone was to read all those poems and connect them to him. His guilt and Jane's guilt, there for all to see… or was it? What was real and what was make-believe, tucked away in the hope box that was no longer his? Surely Kate would see Jane's fantasies for what they were.

He should have told Kate that the poems were of no consequence, a school girl's verse full of fairy stories. He hoped she wouldn't read them too deeply. He consoled himself with the thought that some of them, at least, were only nursery rhymes. Just nonsense and silly verse. He recalled how angry he had become when Jane had taken to writing in nursery rhymes. His frustrations boiling over in his little office. He trying to help and Jane's response to ply him with make-believe and goad him with Moonface. Jane's next poem was another silly verse just to spite him.

## There Was a Man Lived in the Moon

There was a man lived in the moon
It wasn't Aikendrum
Mary's little lamb was never snowy white
Born yellow and bloody
Mud-stained in spring storms
Lavender's blue dilly dilly
Never saw it green in our garden
Hickory Dickory Dock
No self-respecting mouse
Would bother to climb our clock
Ticking metal on the mantle
We used tin cans to block
Holes in dark cupboards
To keep the vermin out
Together we did these things
Me and the man who lives in the moon

Still now it upset him to think of Jane's fairytale stage but, looking back, it had led to a small breakthrough. Her poems still a web of fairytales but finally more details that could be related to an actual event. Had she really visited her father's grave at Jerusalem or was that some misplaced metaphor for what? Like Plath and Sexton had she been missing a daddy figure? For psychotherapy to be effective he would have needed more details. He had written again to Mrs Dougherty. But of course, there had been no reply. Maybe he should have told Kate these things.

## Carsick on River Road

Carsick on River Road
Moonface drives us both through dust

My father lives at Jerusalem
I knock three times on his slab
But he isn't home

Can I climb down
Beneath the ground
The way the lost boys do
Where's my hollow tree?
A perfect size for me

We put flowers in a vase
My mother nods and smiles
She spreads her arms wide
Does she see Tinker Bell
Or just a fantail flying by

The sister gives me a peach
For the long road home
The juice runs golden brown
Forever staining the front
Of my best white shirt

# Thirty

# Toby

It will take four days for the flood to drop enough for the riverboat to run. On the second day I set out to bury James Stanley. It's still raining when I take a spade and shovel from the lean-to and walk to the edge of the bush. The pigs have beaten me there. Water drips off my hair, down my neck, into my eyes, which are leaking again and mixing with the mud and water that gather at the bottom of my hole as I dig. Only parts of the man are still there. I roll the whole sorry mess into the grave that I have created. No words are said before I cover him over.

Meredith has the water heated for my return. Without saying a word she cuts my hair and readies me for war. She sews a button back on James Stanley's best shirt and lays it out for me to wear and packs her own small leather case, just a few clothes, her sheath knife, three books and the metal clock that Mrs Mowat had given her. Neither of us speaks a word of what has been done.

It is left to me to raise the alarm in the valley. James Stanley is missing, lost in the flood along with a sled load of wool. Only Stanley's horse spared but not Peter's. I had led Peter's gelding to the cliff edge on a side creek where no one ever goes and shot it in the head.

I watch as Meredith takes each article from Peter's swag, holds it to her nose for a long time and then stuffs it into the fire box. She doesn't cry. The bloodied knife in my mind is always turning, end over end, off the edge of Battleship Bluff.

There is nothing left here for Meredith. The neighbours are kind. The McDonalds will take the stock. Muriel rides down to collect Holly and

Stanley's horse too, loading them up with Meredith's chickens and drives the house cow back up the valley. Mrs Bettjeman sends baking for our trip down the river.

I tell them that Peter must have ridden out to Raetihi before the rain got going. None of the neighbours saw him go by. No one asks any questions. They all know he was dodging the war. A man like that may not want to be found.

On the fourth day we walk down to the landing. The house is properly swept, and the door pulled too. Ready perhaps for the next hunter or squatter looking for shelter. The quilt remains on the bed.

Neither of us stops at Battleship Bluff. There's a new slip across the track. We climb over the tangle of fallen trees and papa rock, which now covers the spot where Stanley had lain. The creek has been swept clean by the flood. Peter, the sled and the bales of wool are gone. There is nothing to see here except the bloodied knife tipping end over end whenever I shut my eyes. I glance at Meredith. She has her hat pulled low across her face, looking straight ahead. Her leather case bumps against her leg as she walks. Spark is glued to her side. She never speaks.

The Whanganui River is still running high. Dirty brown water swirls past with debris caught up at intervals. There are no tourists today and most of the papa landing is still submerged. We scramble on board and the riverboat is let loose to travel down with the fast moving current. No rapids today. All eyes are required to watch out for sunken logs that have been caught up in jams.

The captain is the one who tells us a body had been found, blown up, unrecognisable, draped over a willow branch at Jerusalem. The eels have taken what they will. Word has spread that the missing body of James Stanley has been found. We take the bus down River Road from Pipiriki. The nuns are there to welcome Meredith at their mailbox. I don't get off. Meredith walks away, flanked by a black clad nun on either side. She doesn't look back.

I travel on down to Wanganui, already late for my war. I can't get there soon enough.

The nuns arrange the funeral for James Stanley. Meredith never speaks. They take her in as they would an orphan child.

*ooOOoo*

Three years at war. I write to Meredith but she never replies. They send me to the Solomon Islands to stalk the Japs who are holed up and hiding out in the jungle. If I'd had a pig dog it would have been easy. We could have baled them, before they peppered us with wild shots. Weeks and months spent walking through the wet, clinging jungle, rattled by snakes, rattled by desperate Japs gone mad in the steamy heat. But in the end we rounded them all up. Shooting Japs – no different to shooting pigs. Do it cleanly.

A long war on a small island, glued to the radio the odd time we had batteries. Both Churchill and Meredith are a world away from where I am. The men complain when their cigarettes and matches are too wet to light and hang out for leave in a town where a woman can be found. Me, watching that blooded knife arcing over Battleship Bluff, over and over and over until I wake clawing holes in my own mosquito net. I need to get home.

*ooOOoo*

Home to my sour-faced mother in the house on top of the hill. Her albino hair is pulled severely back off her face and tied up. Her features have not weathered well. The frown between her eyebrows has turned from a crevice into a glacial valley. I move into the shepherd's cottage on the flat below and try to make peace with my uncle, old Joe Ogden, next door. He's been running our share of the farm as if it's his own while I was away. Ogden, holed up in his own private war, still terrorising that small mouse of a woman, Mrs Ogden, my aunty, but I never call her by that name. She smiles bravely and waves out when I pass. My mother's feud with her brother Joe has spread long ago to include this feeble woman who apes her husband's words. The only friends Mrs Ogden has are the sows that she raises. She tends her pigs with the love she still harbours for the children she never had. The pigsty is close to the house and there are no lawns. They say that old Joe Ogden would never let her grow flowers. The pigs raise their snouts from the trough and flap their sunburnt ears at me whenever I drive by.

*ooOOoo*

Up River Road, it's polite to toot on one-way corners. I pull in at Jerusalem. The nuns tell me Meredith is away in the hills. They say she's often gone all day with a knife and dogs, chasing the pigs. They tell me that Meredith never speaks.

The nuns have gone to make me a cup of tea. They return with a moonbeam, a small golden red head fresh from sleep, the mark of the coverlet still showing on her peach-cream cheek. They place the tiny hand in mine. I am looking down into huge, green eyes. Those eyes are staring up at me and blinking slowly, eyes that give nothing away. Jane needs a father. Meredith needs a home; she's a mad woman who hunts pigs by day and returns with blood dripping down her shirt to sit by the open window at night, reading of Peter Pan. I tell the nuns a white lie, that Meredith is my sister. They are glad for me to take her home. They say they will remember us in their prayers. They give Jane a Bible.

Meredith comes without a word. She stares out the window, all the way down River Road, measuring the hills with her eyes. Downcast, over the flat lands to Stratford, then perking up again when we hit the bush on the first saddle as we head for Whangamomona. She bridles my horse as soon as we get home and is gone up into the hills, leaving me to lay the golden head down for a sleep and to find a biscuit and a makeshift toy to amuse Jane on her waking. I go to town and buy some things a small girl can use: gumboots, a good coat, a book of nursery rhymes and the tales of Hans Christian Anderson to read when she's fractious.

My mother doesn't approve, ruling her roost from up on the hill in the villa that looks down on us all. Meredith and Jane are now installed in my shepherd's cottage. From above, my mother thunders and rumbles doom. Satan and hell are on her lips. She doesn't understand why I choose to live in the whare out the back of the cottage, just like Stanley, but without the whisky. Watching over them both.

*ooOOoo*

Jane runs to me in the whare on nights when there's a big moon. Meredith walks the floors, opening the windows, as if waiting for Peter Pan to come back to Wendy Darling. On these nights Jane climbs into my bed and I tell her stories until she falls asleep. Up the magic faraway tree, to the lands of make-believe. I feed her Pop Biscuits; she calls me Moonface. She helps me on the farm, following me everywhere like a long-haired red setter puppy, always willing to please. I teach her to ride, to mend a fence, how to lamb a ewe, how to run a trapline for possums and kill humanely, how to be a wool girl in the shed – everything except pig hunting.

My mother, Mrs Dougherty, sets forth from the big house on the hill to lay down the law. But Meredith confronts her with a sheath knife and we all know she can use it. Mrs Dougherty stops coming down and even Jane and I, we keep our distance from Meredith, just in case she mistakes one of us for Captain Hook.

# Thirty-One

# Beanstalk

Beanstalk thought of Kate reading the poems. Her accent had not been well schooled. He doubted a higher education, just a basic rural upbringing without any exposure to poetry beyond nursery rhymes and maybe some old English standards – nothing more than Wordsworth's *Daffodils* and Coleridge's *The Rime of the Ancient Mariner*.

What would a woman like Kate make of the poems? He should have made more effort to impress upon her the truth he had always wanted to believe himself. He should have told her to dismiss the ramblings of her damaged mother – poor, burnt, Jane. After all, Plath and Sexton never told the truth. They overplayed their hands – accusations against fathers and lovers never substantiated. Why would Jane be any different?

Back then he had been tormented by these things going round and round in his head. His life had become a dedication to this demented woman. He had still played cat and mouse with Jane and the hope box, finding it next in the laundry tucked behind a stack of worn out sheets. But his heart had gone out of it. Her poems remained fixated on silly children's stories. Was this also his fault? After all, he had brought those books to her. Or was he really just wanting his own part in her make-believe, because it hurt too much to think otherwise? Forever climbing the beanstalk.

## Why

Why does Wendy wait by a window?
For Peter Pan
Why does Meredith, wait by a window?
Never closed
Why does my father lie dead in a grave?
Never discussed
Why does Moonface bury his face?
Whispering sorry
Never saying why
*The Faraway Tree*
No longer makes it better
We move on
To read from the *National Geographic*
Instead

# Thirty-Two

# Kate

Clouds block the sun and first rain falls. The sign at the start of the Forbidden Highway still reads *No petrol for the next 148km* but this time my tank is full and I push on. Huge spots start to splash down around me. I think of Jane's rain poem and stop on a short straight between corners to put on my wet-weather gear to protect myself from the gathering virus of drops.

As I climb back on my bike, a magpie oodles from a pine tree, which shelters an abandoned house with faceless eyes, looking out from windows, once cleaned, to keep up appearances for neighbours who seldom called. Some lonely woman would have shaken out the mat and rushed to get the black singlets and work pants off the line before the rain shower wasted her day's work. Hay sticks out through the orifice that would have been a doorway, hacked larger now by a chainsaw with no thought to appearances. A rose has survived, grown taller than the stock can reach. It scrambles up the decaying wall with one jubilant flower waving a spot of cerise under the gathering cloud. The Zephirine Drouhin is a long way from home. I start my bike, pleased for the engine noise drowning out the magpie.

The shingle greets me like a friend. The road is newly graded with a thousand grey marbles beneath my knobbly tyres. I stand up and clear my mind of everything except keeping upright and looking ahead, leaving the bike to slide and skate across what is here in the now, fixing unfocused eyes on the middle distance. What will he be like, this Toby Dougherty? I make up my mind not to like him.

At the Whangamomona Pub, I back my bike in against the corrugated side wall of the hotel. Around the front there are wooden posts holding up the balcony and an open trapdoor in the pavement. The wooden trapdoor hatches lie back on either side like a gaping mouth with the lips pulled away. Beer kegs are standing by, ready for their trip up or down into the bowels of this place. I put my head over, just in time to catch a coil of dirty hemp rope that is hurtling skywards. A ruddy upturned face glows in the gloom below.

'Mate, can ya help pull up a few empties?'

As instructed, I haul up the fat metal cylinder, untie the knot, roll the beer keg to the side and send the loose end of the rope back down again into the deep, dark hole. 'Thanks, mate, next one ready, heave-ho.' Five empties later we reverse the process, me rolling the heavy full kegs to the brink, tying them one by one to the rope and then bracing my legs and easing the rope, hand over hand, while the keg slides down the steep wooden ramp, disappearing into the black hole to the waiting hands below.

'Thanks, mate. I owe you one. Step into the bar there.'

The pub has a heavy door. I step into the warm smell of spilt beer. The odour of men and well-worn work boots rises from the patterned carpet – circa seventies imitation Persian. There's no one behind the bar. The high-studded walls are covered in memorabilia and quotes that usually culminate with advice to drink more beer. Above the bar are fancy silver cups and shields for local rugby, with the glorious team photos of years past all around the walls and a line-up of dead heads, a tatty deer head with a full set of points, the wide horns of a goat and a grinning pig with large tusks. There are T-shirts to buy and a poster about the newly-formed Republic of Whangamomona. The handles on the counter that pulls beer from the kegs are shiny with use.

The publican walks in, rubbing the dust off his apron with a dirty tea towel. He looks around. 'Where's the bloke who helped with the kegs?' He glances over my shoulder towards the toilets.

I raise my eyebrows and flex my bicep.

He grins as he reaches below the counter, his cheeks bulging like ripe tomatoes. 'I'd expect no less from one of my own daughters.'

I indicate the lemonade and he hands over a brimming handle.

'You must've grown up rural. City chickens can't even lift their own powder cases. Where're you from?' He puts out his hand and crushes my knuckles in a way he never would have done if I was a townie. 'Are you staying tonight? I'm Mac.'

Settled at the bar, I sip my drink while he empties glasses out of the dishwasher and rubs off the grey smears.

'What brings you to the Republic of Whangamomona, home of the Bridge to Somewhere?'

Mac's head disappears under the counter so I talk to his bald spot. 'Just looking up some family history.'

Mac's head re-emerges and he squints at me with one eye shut. 'Let me guess – you'd be a dead ringer of old Mrs Dougherty.'

I spill some liquid down my front and Mac hands the dirty tea towel over the bar so I can mop at the dark stain spreading across my stomach. I put down my drink and steady my hands, crushing the tea towel into a wet lump. I look down at the shiny rail that runs around the floor in front of the bar. 'Sounds like the ones I might be looking for. Do they live around here?'

'Not too far up this road beside the pub here. So how are you connected to the Doughertys?' Mac grins at me as he lifts my drink, wiping under my handle. 'With the families around here, they say it pays to check the fingers and toes before you marry in.'

I look down at my huge hands. 'So, what about the Doughertys?'

Mac stops rubbing and looks at me. 'Do I give you the squeaky clean tourist version or do you really want to know what the locals say?'

'Something about a fire?' I take another gulp and put the handle back down on the bar top and grip the front edge with both hands.

'That'll be the mad woman that young Dougherty brought back here after the war. Managed to burn his cottage down.' Mac goes back to rubbing the smears off the glasses.

My stomach heaves, but I shrug my shoulders as if this is nothing to me.

Mac stops rubbing. He raises his eyebrows and I nod for him to continue. 'Not long before that, funny thing happened on the place next door. Old Joe Ogden lived there, unpleasant sod, wife clears out and then old Joe disappears as well. They never found him, just a whole lot of his wife's sows locked in the house. His sister, Mrs Dougherty, she got to inherit the lot.'

I nod my head as if I know these things. 'So who's up there now?' I try to make it sound casual, picking up the lemonade again with both hands and steadying it between my teeth but I don't drink any more.

'Just Toby Dougherty left up there. He's an old fella now – and maybe a ghost or two. The locals talk, of course, but none of us ever get to see.' He rubs the bar with the dirty tea towel. 'Funny fellow, Toby, living up there in Mrs Doughtery's old homestead. Owns near half the valley, but you never see him down here. Never spends a bean at the pub.'

Other guests are arriving. Mac heads outside to help a woman with her smart city suitcases and matching pink powder box balanced on top.

Leaving most of the handle, I sling my gear over my shoulder and climb the main stairs and then on up the narrow steep flight to my room in the gods of the building. I pull the curtains closed to cut out the west lying sun, climb into the narrow bed and pull the covers over my head.

# Thirty-Three

# Beanstalk

Beanstalk lay in bed and stared at the ceiling. Would Kate ever guess how close he had come to loving Jane? Did his unconventional behaviour show in any of the poems?

Clearly not ethical, but he had concluded that the silent stand-offs in his office with Jane had achieved nothing. Instead they resumed walking the grounds, down through the gardens to the orchard where the Trusties waved out to them. Trusted patients who were busy harvesting, or tending to the orchard, which produced boxes of sale-grade apples, pears, plums and even quinces each year.

Walking side by side they were more companionable, even if they didn't speak. They had crossed the road one day and walked amongst the autumn calves being hand-reared on the dairy farm by patients who worked the land.

Together they had skirted the bull paddock and kept a wary eye on the inmate holed up there. A large Ayrshire bull shut away from the herd. Beanstalk pretended not to look at the wet pink tip, which was showing below the bull's belt line as he stood with his muscled neck on the top barb of the fence. A precarious arrangement of posts and wires that was supposed to hold him back from the heifers on the other side.

Beanstalk hadn't dared to glance at Jane. He wasn't sure if she had noticed; he had never spoken of it with her. Surely there was nothing in the poems to alert that girl Kate.

## Young Girl

Pink the nipple standing forth
White the raw-edged cotton pad
Pink the colour of the pain
Red the blood runs down my leg
Black the make-believe that's lost
I weep for Moonface
But he doesn't hug me anymore

# Thirty-Four

# Toby

Jane doing her correspondence schoolwork and in the holidays, running wild on the farm. Those were the best years, always laughing, always mischief, coming to me in the nighttime. But I swear I never touched her, I swear I never did. I only ever comforted her as a father should.

I order the *National Geographic* and we pore over the pages each month when it comes. Jane writes her correspondence school assignments longhand onto ruled paper with large sloping *oOOo*s and we pack them off in the mail. A smart girl, running to the woolshed when her work books come back to show me her marks.

Her legs are long and brown. Her shorts are getting tight across her rear, making the shearers whistle. I take her to town and ask the woman in the sewing department to help us choose a pattern that comes to her knees with space for growth. We choose a bigger size, which should give ample space. The lady explains how to fold the fabric with the salvages together and lay the paper tissue pieces down.

Jane running, screaming, to show me the blood between her legs. I take her up the hill to my unsmiling mother who issues rags and shows her how to wash them out.

Fresh buds forming on Jane's chest, far too visible to the shearers under the simple cotton shirts she wears in the shed. I take her back to town and hand her over to the matron in the women's department and stand watch outside the door.

Me watching over Jane, who is watching the sweat pouring off the bare, glistening shoulders of the shearers. I don't dare send her down to their quarters with messages anymore.

Wool girls know how a ram will sniff and chase one ewe after another until he drops down panting and spent. How can I explain to her that, with humans, it doesn't need to be this way? Not all men act in that way. I send her to muster instead of working in the shed. We both hug and pat the dog, the warmth and touch that I cannot give her.

I no longer invite her into my bed on the long nights when Meredith is disturbed. Instead we sit in the bentwood chairs in front of the wood stove in my whare with a hot drink to warm us. I take her down to Wanganui and drop her at the boarding school but we both know it won't last. I am pleased to bring her home and back to the correspondence school.

Jane learns to work the dogs and becomes my single shepherd. She can bring in a mob of sheep and work them in the yards. Calm and gentle when they go the wrong way.

Both of us, too, watching over Meredith. A woman who hunts pigs by day and sits by her window at night, sometimes even forgetting to wash or remove her blood-stained shirt. It's Jane, the single shepherd, who leads her mother to the bathroom, helps her with the buttons and soaks away the blood in cold water before the wash. There is never a word from Meredith for poor Jane, never a hug, never even an acknowledgement of their kinship.

It's Jane who cooks the endless pork into roasts or stew, makes us cakes, writes the list, rings the store order through each week and puts away the groceries when they arrive on the truck.

It's Jane who looks through the catalogue and sends away the order forms. The Wentworth parcels arrive with the fabric she has ordered: yards of cloth for shirts, corduroy for winter trousers and the right fabric for my shearing pants. I buy her an electric Singer machine that has a reverse lever, a light that switches on above her work and spare bobbins so she doesn't have to rewind the cotton every time she wants to change the colour.

It's Jane who builds a fence around the garden to keep the rabbits out.

She plants carrot seed, humps sheep manure from under the woolshed for the pumpkins and harvests the rhubarb for stewing a sweet bitter red.

Meredith takes to eating by her window. Jane brings our plates of food out to my whare and we eat together then sit by the fire in my bentwood armchairs. She reads to me from the papers. We keep up with what is happening in the world around us but neither of us go there in person. Just to Inglewood, or Stratford for the odd thing. But most times we order in on the mail truck.

The phone seldom rings. The young stock agents come and go but know better than to ask to take my Jane down the road to a dance at the hall and never to the pub. They know we don't do these things. Jane has no pattern for a dress. I can't believe it when she turns 21. There is no hope box to fill with linen, no celebration at the local hall. Our birthdays quietly come and go.

*ooOOoo*

Ogden's wife disappears. She must have shot through, that's the whisper in the district, finally had enough of living with Joe Ogden. Jane is worried for the pigs. Will he remember to feed them? I tell her not to go near the place. But does she listen to me? Those big green eyes blink slowly, her red setter lashes behind her long fringe giving nothing away. A month later they can't find him either. Old Ogden clean vanished. We don't even notice until the stock agent spots the pigs locked inside his house, lapping water from the toilet, no sign of any food, but not hungry either. No sign of Ogden and the place a stinking mess. We never find out who kept on feeding the pigs.

The police are no help. After a long while they close the case and we burn the Ogdens' house down. I bulldoze the site – push what's left over the bank. My mother and I, we're the only next of kin. Jane takes over caring for the pigs, crooning and scratching their ears. We build sties and move them closer to home.

*ooOOoo*

There's a huge moon the night I hear the shrieking. I run from the whare, into the house. Jane is flying towards me down the hallway, her beautiful hair burst full of angry flames. Meredith stands behind her framed in the doorway to her bedroom, arms raised up, a pillar of flames, reaching up and melting down.

I take Jane to my chest. I carry her outside and roll her over and over on the wet grass. Over and over I squashed the flames with my hands but it's too late, her hair is gone, her face blackened, her body limp. My charging mother binds my hands and my head so I can't see what happens next. Meredith is dead, Jane gone in the ambulance.

My mother's accusing face, spitting fury, tells me that Jane is dead.

*ooOOoo*

Long years, my hands heal but not my heart.

Grey years turn to black, when I discover the truth. Hidden until my mother dies and her papers come to me. It still plays on my mind. Would it have been different if we hadn't lost those years? Could I have saved Jane?

I get to read the letters that sit in my mother's desk, unopened, clamped together with a large metal clip. Several from Dr Bean at Kingseat Hospital, suggesting it would be helpful if he could have some background information about Jane.

I drive there, of course. My heart thuds as I turn through the entrance beneath the phoenix palms and then skirt the playing field.

At reception, the woman is programmed to smile but not to help. She shakes her head. No one here by the name of Jane Stanley. When I ask after Dr Bean, she shakes her head again and tells me he must be long gone, before her time. No, she does not have access to any records. She shouts out 'Ernie' to an old guy mopping the floor. 'Did we used to have a Dr Bean here?'

Ernie nods his head. 'Yep, gone from here a good few years'

I ask where I can find him now.

They both shrug.

I ask where a long-term patient may have been transferred to.

The receptionist looks up at me over her glasses. 'I'd try the undertakers if I were you.' She hands me a card and gets back to her work.

My darling Jane, just a dust-covered box when I find her on a shelf at the undertakers behind the main street of Papakura. I pay him the money owing and bring my darling home. Buried her under the peach tree where I like to sit.

My hands have healed long ago with angry scars, but never my heart. I never did look to find Dr Bean. Afraid that my strong fingers may have torn his limbs apart if I had not liked what I had found.

# Thirty-Five

# Beanstalk

Kate had asked Beanstalk how it ended. He had told her about his study break in England. That much was true; he wasn't there at the time. It was also the truth that he had missed Jane, but couldn't hurry home. There was learning to be done, and exams to sit and an interminable voyage home on a passenger ship full of beautiful women, and him with only eyes for the horizon, looking into the mist for his ugly, green-eyed monster. Had the Medical Superintendent guessed? Had he sent Beanstalk away on purpose?

When he did get back six months later, he had hurried straight to the ward, but Jane wasn't there. The medical notes in the storeroom were brief. Jane went alone to the tidal creek. Was she looking for him? The boat untied. Jane found half-naked in the mud once the tide receded. The hospital notes had ended at this point.

Beanstalk had turned away and hidden his grief from the nurses. Medical Officers shouldn't cry. How could he explain: that he was broken in half by a green-eyed monster who had showered him with spiteful poems?

Of course, he had rushed to seek out the hope box. Ernie had indicated his cleaning cupboard. Her final resting place for the little box was in full view on a shelf amongst Ernie's dusters. Jane must have known all along about Ernie; she must have wanted Beanstalk to find her final poems. He had grasped the hope box and crushed it in his arms in a way that he had never held Jane.

Would her final poems absolve him? Had she missed him? He had hurried to a quiet place to scan her four final poems, but he didn't even get a mention.

## If Only I Could See Her Face

Put an apple on my head and fire the arrow
Prepare to miss and crack this old mask through
Like giggling girls would we gobble the flesh
Comparing faces, using our thumbs
To measure each other's noses

But silly me, my face has rotted away
This mask is no rosy apple to wet her lips upon,
Whatever is left inside this tainted skin
Collapses inward, if only I could close my eyes
If only I could see my baby's face, just once

My starboard lights burn green
But sink low to the horizon now
A burnt-out sun that no one can look upon
Oh to submerge my head, in the coolness of the sea
How long must I remain, suspended here?

I hide behind the rotten pulp of this thing.
This branded fireball is no apple
No ears, no expression, nothing here
My lid is ugly, I cannot show my daughter this.
My treasure is gone to a place that I cannot follow

# Thirty-Six

# Kate

Mac says it's easy to find. 'Take the road up the side of the hotel. It's the only mailbox left up there on the right. If you get to the Bridge to Somewhere you've gone too far.' He glances out the window at my bike. 'Road's not much chop. Good to see you've got knobblies.'

I nod my thanks and strap on my gear.

There's a derelict church amongst a handful of houses and then the road passes two neglected graveyards on the right. The Catholics are on higher ground, separated from the Protestants by a rugby field. The mown green field has newly-painted goalposts which stand proud, a church of sorts that still functions in this small village.

The road drops down to single-lane gravel. The fences are old but tight, the stock well fed but suspicious. They raise their heads and watch me ride by, a sign that not much traffic comes up this way. I follow the river, which has cut down deep into the papa rock on my left. Similar to the Mangapurua, but still farmed with grass between the slips coming off the ridges and scrub returning to the gullies. If Meredith had come here, maybe she'd have felt at home.

I pull up beside what was once a substantial mailbox. In its day a mailbox like this would signal a big station where the kids were shipped out to boarding schools and trips home to England would be in a cabin with a proper port hole. But those days are long gone. The paint has peeled off and the door of the mailbox hangs awry. The starlings have moved in. There's a large river rock to stop the mail blowing away.

The driveway is just two wheel ruts with grass tufted down the centre and dotted with sheep droppings. The cattle stop rattles me across. I follow the driveway which runs across the small river terrace and then disappears on up the hill into trees. Part way across the flats, there's a line of overgrown macrocarpa, a tell-tale sign of a derelict house site hidden from the road behind the overgrown shelter belt. I pull up and flick down my bike stand. A brick chimney stands alone. A small whare is still here, bearing witness to where the house once stood. The door of the whare is hanging open. Sheep have been camping inside, and it smells sweetly like a woolshed.

The garden fence is gone now. Nothing to mark where the front lawn must have been, except an old lilac that has grown above sheep height, and a totem pole.

Is this Jane's totem pole? I know her poem by heart, and here is the totem pole that Moonface made her, tall and straight, casting a long shadow across the space where the house must have stood. On top, there's a carved hawk's head with a huge beak jutting forward. The hooded eyes are watching me take off my helmet and follow me as I walk across the site.

There are depressions in the ground where the wooden house piles must have been and a tangle of rusting pipes. I look up at the totem; the hawk's beak is directly above me now. I wrap my arms around the warm solid wood, made from old tōtara posts, carved and stacked in interlocking pieces three high, taller than the chimney. Lichen grows like grey wool in the carved sections and a bright orange birthmark is spreading over the face of the bird. I smell for linseed oil but there is none. My cheek is pressed against a split in the timber. My tears are drawn away before they fall down my cheek. The wood is parched and cracking open. My hands run down over the carved form. For the second time in my life I'm hugging something that my mother Jane has hugged before me. The hope box is pressing against my gut and separates me from the totem. I whisper Jane's poem that I now know by heart.

## Totem at the Sarjeant Gallery

You call this art, girlie? He steps back
Squints one eye at the totem
Checking that it's straight
Just like the fence posts I rammed with him
All summer long

Look at the price, girlie
All that money for some old tōtara post
Ten minutes and a chainsaw
I'll knock one up for you
He moves on to the next exhibit

Don't look . . . the totem has taut sinews
Don't smell . . . linseed oil on wood
Never cracks . . . you know that, girlie
Don't touch . . . I put my ear to the post
Don't listen . . . I only ever hear the sea

Don't taste . . . I bite my tongue
Don't feel . . . not this rigid form
Don't hug . . . his arms are bolted to his sides
Don't cry . . . we both know that totems never do
Righto, girlie . . . he leaves me at the boarding school

He's gone all the way back to the faraway tree
Don't cry . . . you know I never do
It's just my eyes . . . how dare they break open
Tiny shards dripping glass that don't stop
Moonface comes back and takes me home for good

'Ouch, bloody totem.' I pull away and suck the splinter that has driven into my thumbnail. It's too deep to pull out. I'll need someone to help me with a needle.

Back on my bike, I drag my eyes away from the totem and look on up the driveway where it disappears between trees at the base of the hill, up to the big house that must have always looked down on what was once the shepherd's cottage.

'*Look where you want the bike to go, Kate. You must always look where you want the bike to go.*' Right up the hill to that old homestead. I can just make out a small piece of the corrugated roof and two square brick chimneys, built the old fashioned way, only just showing above dark trees. Clunk. I put my bike into gear and ride on up. I don't look back. '*Only look where you want to go, Kate. Look for the gap.*'

The driveway up to the house is bulldozed into a clay bank, held up on the topside by old man pine trees, which have dropped their needles onto the track. They deaden the sound of my tyres but not my motor, which vibrates off the side of the narrow gut.

The old villa needs paint; it sits on a ledge carved out of the hill. The veranda is on the cold side; the large front door is too imposing to use. I ride straight past up the side where hydrangeas push outward, covering most of the double-hung windows.

Around the back is the usual jumble of sheds, outhouses and a farm ute. I pull up alongside and cut my engine. Clunk. I lean my bike into the silence that surrounds this house and climb off. A magpie sets up a cry followed by a gust in the upper branches of the pines.

The back door is hidden by a fig tree, which hangs over the path. I brush past and step up into the back porch. A dog uncurls from a hessian sack, black with faint marks of tan and a slash of white across the chest and neck. A heading bitch, she cowers her tail and creeps past me. I knock. No response. I knock again and listen for footsteps. Is that a shuffle I hear behind the door?

Crunch, gumboots on the path behind me, I turn and there he is. A giant of a man. His arms hang down like wet washing beneath his wide shoulders with red angry scars showing on his hands and forearms below his rolled up sleeves. The heading bitch moves to stand at his side. This must be Toby Dougherty.

He doesn't offer to shake my hand. Instead he nods his huge flat face just once.

He moves forward. I hold my breath, but up close he's like a Clydesdale, trusted to manage his bulk and not crush a man in a confined space or startle a child.

It blurts out of me. 'I'm Kate – my mother was Jane Stanley.'

His head snaps backward, his eyes widen and he sways for a moment. The whine in the trees goes up an octave then drops away again as he regains his composure. His mouth gives nothing away. He does not speak.

'You're Toby Dougherty?'

He nods his head. 'You'd best come in.'

Toby knocks off his gumboots on the step and leads the way inside. The heading bitch settles back on the sack in the porch; I step over her and follow him into the big square kitchen. There's no one there. A clock ticks time on the far wall. A plastic affair, the minute hand moving in a jerky fashion around the clock face with each tick.

He motions me towards the kitchen table, square, oak, orphaned at the centre of the room. On one side of the kitchen there are ceiling-high cupboards with metal catches that you sink your fingers into. At the far end of the room, a bench with a view down the valley from a window seldom cleaned.

Toby makes tea in a tall enamel pot. He reaches into a high cupboard to bring down fine china cups with saucers and wipes off the dust. This is not normal. I can see the single stained mug, tipped up in the dish rack on the bench.

Where to start? It seems ridiculous to talk about the weather.

Neither of us speak, both observing the similarities. Our height, our lack of small talk and my large man-like hands, which reach for the saucer he offers. Strong blunt fingers, the same square nails. Both of us careful not to crush the delicate cup.

He looks at me for a long time without saying anything.

I avert my eyes to the clock. Both of us stubborn as well. The second hand makes four circuits before he speaks.

'What do you know?' He looks away, intent on manoeuvring the tiny spoon between the sugar bowl and his cup. We both count his third spoonful and stare at the vortex, which threatens the gold-painted rim as he stirs.

My words stumble out, the deserted valley up the Whanganui, the nuns at Jerusalem who gave me his name.

Through it all Toby continues to stir his tea round and round the cup. When I finish, the clock ticks, louder than it should.

An electric oven is squeezed in beside the bench but the old wood stove is still in place, set back into the wall with two easy chairs pulled up in front; bentwood arms with buttoned-up fabric that shows wear. Each of the seat pans is covered over with a sheepskin from a newborn lamb.

Toby raises his head and removes the spoon. 'I'm not your father, Kate.'

I leap to my feet and bang my fist down hard on the table in a way that rattles the roses on the cups. Hot tea spills down my cheeks. I unzip my jacket and take the notebook from the box, which rests against my belly and open it at the poem about pigs. I slam the notebook down in front of him.

'My mother – this terrible thing she wrote?'

I watch as he fumbles for his glasses. The pages are spotted brown but the lines of poetry are still clear enough, even for an old man to read. His finger shakes as he points to each line. He pauses at the word Moonface.

'That's you, isn't it?' I watch him choke a little. 'Keep reading.' My tone is nasty. Ginny hates it when I speak this way but I don't care. I stab at the last verse of the poem and then sit back again in the chair opposite, my arms crossed on the table and watch his slow progress until the last line is read.

He drops the notebook, which falls flat on the table between us. 'Jane never told me this.' He pushes his palms down against his thighs to stop the tremble and makes no move to hide the tears that fill his eyes.

'It's not what it seems, Kate.'

'So why was my mother in a nuthouse?'

My voice is low and guttural. 'My father, a monster?' I cradle my belly and watch his eyebrows rise. 'This child?' I prod the bulge. 'Still time to get rid of it.'

'Please,' he whispers. 'Please give me a moment.' He pushes up from the table, picks up the notebook, turns his back on my green eyes and moves to sit by the fire.

He stares for a long time into the fire box where the door of the wood stove stands open. I can see it's unlit; the inside is black and cold with a layer of grey ash lying there.

# Thirty-Seven

# Toby

This girl is thumping on my kitchen table just the way my mother used to. She has the same long limbs, the same sharp tongue, coarse blonde hair and accusing eyes. The shocking thing is that she is so much like my bloody mother, not like Jane at all. Which bits do I tell her, which bits do I leave out? It's all such a complicated mess.

Kate has some sort of box stuffed inside her jacket. She pulls it out and opens the lid. Inside is a notebook, handwritten on yellowing pages but the words still plain to see. She's stabbing at the page.

'This terrible thing she wrote?'

She thrusts the book at me and I fumble to put on my glasses. The pages are spotted brown but the pencil marks are still clear. The passage she has indicated is a poem, written in Jane's hand, a poem about pigs, Mrs Ogden's pigs. This girl is watching my response, an old man gawping and spluttering. I clutch the book closer to make sure it really is Jane's writing, her cramped sloping hand, with those distinctive shaped *oOOo*s. I pull the book hard against my belly to stop the print shaking and read my dear Jane's words out loud. I pause with my finger on the word Moonface.

'That's you, isn't it?' There's a nasty twist in her mouth. 'Keep reading.' She's leaning over the notebook, stabbing at the last verse of the poem.

The final words dissolve into a salty blur that merges with the dreadful things written there on the page.

## Mrs Ogden's Pigs

Mrs Ogden loved her large whites
Carefully tended, staggering about heavy in-pig
Or squalling with a new litter hanging off
Well fed and always mucked out

Did you know if you scratch a pig
Just above the tit line, it flops to the ground
Playing dead, just keep rubbing the tit and you can
Tickle its bristles or pick flakes off its sunburnt skin

I didn't really spy on the Ogdens fighting
Just a country kid playing in their pigsty
Watching and learning, I already knew a lot about death
How to do it cleanly

With a possum, you stay away from the claws and grab the tail
Stretch it out full length from the gin-trap jaw
The leg bloody and ripped to the bone
Dong it on the head – clunk, it's dead easy

Sometimes death is unexpected, like the time
I found the dog, dead, hung by its back legs
From a hole it pushed through the kennel, or my pet lamb
Only its teeth ever found, after it strayed into the pigpen.

With a sheep, pull the neck way back, ears laid flat
Mouth clamped shut, eyes wild and blinking,
One sharp knife stroke, do it clean, no sawing or hacking
The eyes glaze over quick and the jerking stops

I liked to watch the blood arc up the killing house walls
Stomach and intestines spilling over
I know where the organs lie, waiting for Moonface to hand me
The heart and liver to take home for dinner in a steel bowl

It wasn't always about death; I saw how Jack the stallion
Takes the old mare, draws blood and bruises her neck
With similar interest I watched Mrs Ogden
Wash the red from her torn white shirt

Moonface tells me not to go over
He says that Mrs Ogden has gone away
But I know better, I'm grown now, of course I go
The pigs are hungry, I check their pen for Mrs Ogden's teeth

Mr Ogden sits in the dark, catches me looking
Hurts me bad, leaving blood on my ripped-up pants
But I get him back in the end, clunk, dead easy
No one ever asks me, how the pigs got into his house

Why didn't Jane tell me this? The book falls flat onto the table and I hold my shaking hands flat against my thighs. How could I have missed this thing? My head is whirling as chess pieces move and leave the board.

Kate is watching me, just as Jane used to, wanting me to make everything better with Pop Biscuits and a made-up story. Jane never asked me to make this better. There is no better.

'It's not what it seems, Kate.' My voice sounds old and waspish. Just the way a condemned man must sound. 'This thing is not what you think.'

'So why was my mother in a nuthouse?' Her voice is low and guttural. She cradles her stomach. 'Still time to get rid of it.'

'Please, Kate,' I whisper. Pushing up from the table, I pick up the notebook, turn my back on those accusing green eyes and move to sit by the fire. I need to rest. My heart is lumpy and missing beats here and there. My dear Jane is in these pages, back in my hands. Some of her story is here at least.

I stare into the fire box where the door stands open on my wood stove. Unlit, the inside is black and cold with a deep layer of grey ash. I picture a younger Meredith. It's a long time since I have thought of her this way. I never knew her when she was truly young but I imagine that she was handsome. She is coming back to me now, how she was when I first met her, silver threads only just starting to show in her long black tresses, standing by her fireside, sitting at her kitchen table as she taught me to read from Peter Pan.

I glance at Kate; I need time to think about these things.

I look away and leaf through the book of Jane's poems with my trembling hands. I need my old ticker to slow. I breathe and read the poems. The presence of Jane here in these pages helps to calm me. It takes time; my old dog creeps in and settles beside the girl. I let them be.

Finally I'm done and signal for her to sit beside me on the same bentwood chair that Jane used to draw up to the fire in my whare all those years ago. Kate sits upright; her legs are threaded tightly around the legs of my chair, fit to break the thing. The girl begins working her thumbnail back and forward along the arm of my chair, working a sliver of wood away from the smoothly bent arm, lifting my own skin.

I motion for Kate to rest her hands still and watch as she places both her palms on her stomach. I look at the striking profile of this girl who is Jane's stolen treasure and see a strength that I have known before. 'Is there a father for this child?'

She shakes her head.

'Another misplaced man?' Words, which shouldn't have been said, have slipped out.

'It's not that simple,' she whispers. Her hands are trembling now.

I reach as if to pat her hand but don't quite connect.

She pulls her hand away.

'Look at me, child – you can't be brave if you only ever have wonderful things happen to you.'

'Was my mother brave?'

'Yes, girlie, never met anyone braver than my Jane.'

'You'll tell me about her?'

'Aye, soon enough,' my voice cracks. 'Maybe you're braver than you think.'

Her green eyes are locked on me. She nods her head. We both see the tear I wipe away. I clear my throat to start. 'Your grandmother, her name was Meredith.' For the first time in my life it starts to make some sense. Meredith's story must be told before it will be my turn to speak of Jane.

Truth and Justice are crowding in on me now to listen. Their stories are flickering up the walls of my chimney as sadness folds its wings around me, but I grasp their hope for the future. If God really did have four daughters, Meredith would be Truth and Jane would be Justice. But can Kate and her unborn child find it in their hearts to be Mercy and Peace?

I light the stove. Our words stretch across the afternoon and well into the evening, backward and forward. I stir up the wood stove to heat stew and butter bread. The words keep coming, waves of words.

The night is nearly gone when at last it's done. We both stare at the small flicker of flame behind the open door of the wood stove. The clock is ticking close to dawn, which brings with it a certain coldness before first light. But my heart has steadied now to a regular tick. There is no more that I can say. Weariness has settled over me.

Kate has the notebook in her hands; she flicks to the pig poem. She is rereading it through.

I bow my head and watch the bloodied knife rolling over in the small flames.

Her reading is done. The book drops to her lap. She raises her head and resets her shoulders. She looks at me, her green eyes locking me in, daring me not to look away. Her hands fumble to find the page she has just read. She rips the pig poem from the notebook, crumples the page into a tight ball and tosses it into the fire. She does not miss. Our gaze is broken. We both watch as the flames in the fireplace flare up green to eat what's left of Mrs Ogden's pigs.

Kate speaks to the fire. 'Can I choose who I want my father to be?'

I rise up unsteady on my feet and nod my head.

She rises and turns to face me. 'Moonface, I would like the grandfather of my child to be Moonface.'

For the first time I see a glimpse of Kate's teeth. She has Jane's beautiful even teeth with a perfect eye tooth on either side of her wide mouth and just the small beginnings of a smile.

We stand facing but not touching. Our heads are nodding up and down in unison, our arms hang useless by our sides. We grin dumbly at each other, both using muscles that have lain dormant for a long while.

Deep in my heart I know that this is true. Kate is the rightful daughter of Moonface.

She snaps the notebook shut and glances at the phone on the wall.

'Can I ring Australia?'

I nod my head. She reaches for the phone on the wall and dials a long number. I try not to listen.

'This is Pihanga calling. Is that Mount Taranaki?'

There's a pause and then a chuckle.

'No, this is not the Neanderthal woman and I'm not sitting on the couch.'

Another pause. 'No, I'm not in Palmerston North. I'm here with Toby. Yes, Toby Dougherty.'

There's a longer pause.

'Of course I'm sure. It's time for Taranaki to come home to Pihanga. We need to talk.'

Another pause, so long that I wonder if the person on the other end is lost.

'Maybe I can love you too.'

Kate places the phone down and smiles across the kitchen at me with all her beautiful teeth showing this time. She comes back to warm her hands, standing tall beside the fire.

I would like to hug Moonface's daughter, but I've never been any good at that sort of thing. I fill the jug for another cup of tea instead.

# Thirty-Eight

# Beanstalk

Funny thing, since the hope box has gone I can breathe better at night. I didn't tell that girl Kate how I used to lie here in my bach, Jane still watching me, green eyes like starboard harbour lights in the dark. Never showing emotion to a sailor in the water, neither pain nor pleasure at my fate. Just her green eyes standing between me and the rocks.

But now the hope box is gone I can sleep at last. And one morning soon I may not wake, out there in the ocean, dissolving in foam.

**Ariel So Loved the World**

God so loved the world
He gave his only son
That whoever believed in him
Would not perish
But have eternal life

God so loved the world
He gave his four daughters
That whoever believed in love
Would not perish
But have a daughter too

Ariel so loved her prince
She chose to leave
Dissolved in wordless foam
Only three hundred years
Watching over them all
To find her human soul

## Acknowledgements

While *The Strength of Eggshells* is a work of fiction, I have tried to maintain it within an accurate historical context and I have located the fiction within real geographical New Zealand landscapes and locations, particularly the Mangapurua Valley, which was part of the largest and last of the WW1 Returned Services Settlement Schemes. Ninety-six farm blocks were surveyed off in a remote location of virgin bush over three valleys, which run from the hills behind Raetihi down to the middle reaches of the Whanganui River. The Mangapurua Valley was the central of the three valleys and was settled by 36 returned soldiers and farmed between 1917 and 1943, when the government closed the road and the land became forest park.

I would like to thank the descendants of the original settlers of the Mangapurua Valley who shared their families' memoirs and memories. Special thanks to Wayne Bettjeman, Muriel Roberts (nee McDonald), Tom Mowat, Jane Voon and Bruce Sandford who met/spoke with me and shared their families' stories, documents and photographs. Also, special mention to May Bettjeman and Agnes Anderson who wrote marvellous accounts of their families' times in the valley and to Sam Whitburn who reviewed my story on behalf of the Anderson Family.

I have depicted the way of life in the valley as accurately as I can and have used many of the original settlers as secondary characters in this fiction. A summary of their history and my sources are detailed in the chapter notes and references following. The characters of Kate Whyte, the Whyte Family, Meredith Stanley (nee Innes), Jane Stanley, Ursula, Ian Dunn, Mr Dunn, Eric Heng, Toby Dougherty, Iris Dougherty,

Joseph Ogden, Mrs Ogden, Beanstalk, Mac and their families are entirely fictional and bear no relationship to any person, alive or dead.

I acknowledge quotes and or references to the following authors: JM Barrie – *Peter Pan and Wendy*, Enid Blyton – *The Magic Faraway Tree*, Hans Christian Anderson – *The Little Mermaid*, James K Baxter – *High Country Weather* and *Haere Ra*, Arthur Bates – *The Bridge to Nowhere* and Sylvia Plath – *Ariel.* I thank Kate Renowden for posing for the cover photograph.

I would like to thank my family and the folks who helped me with the writing: Witi Ihimaera who lectured me in 2014 on the Diploma of Creative Writing at MIT and encouraged me to write this novel. Thank you to my 2015 lecturers at AUT on the Creative Writing Masters Programme, my 2016 Alumni Group and Manuscript Editor Chris Else.

A big thank you to my long-suffering critical readers who encouraged me along the way, particularly Rachel Houlbrooke, Wendy Davidson, Michele Laing, Basil Connor, Andrea Moses, Alison Schofield, Jacquie McRae, Michael Giacon, Helen McNeil, and Raewyn West, whose comprehensive book *Remembering Them,* published in 2017, is a wonderful new resource for folk interested in the history of the Mangapurua and Kaiwhakauka Valleys.

I would especially like to thank Diane Sparkes who, as a transsexual woman, shared her own journey, parts of which are reflected in Ursula's story.

My heartfelt thanks to Cloud Ink, particularly Dione Jones and Helen McNeil, for seeing this book through to publication.

Thank you one and all!

<u>Chapter Notes</u>

## Meredith's Chapters

Meredith sets forth from the provincial city of Wanganui, which is located at the river mouth of the Whanganui River. Aunt Gwyneth's house is an old wooden villa in Wicksteed Street, which runs parallel to the main street in Wanganui and down towards the river.

Meredith, Aunt Gwyneth, Phyllis, Edwin, and Richard Mason are all fictional characters. Agnes Anderson is a real person who, along with her husband, Reg, moved to the Mangapurua Valley, as she describes in her letter to Meredith. Details in the letter of hanging yellow sheets to protect her house from dripping water after frost and Reg building a bath, are taken from descriptions written by Agnes and transcribed by Arthur Bates and JM Carver. Agnes and Reg brought their three children, John, Myra and Michael as a 16-day-old baby to the valley, and baby Jo was born at home as described in the story.

The description of the trip up the Whanganui River on the *Wairere* and *Ongarue* paddle steamers are taken from Agnes Anderson's account of her arrival at the Mangapurua Valley in 1931. Descriptions of the passengers and landings reflect the account written by Robin Hyde of her trip up the river, which was written for the 'Ladies' Page' of the *Wanganui Chronicle*, published in 1934. Kenny Stewart and Jumbo are both real characters who worked on these vessels in 1932. Mrs Nancy Bettjeman is a real life character. Her descriptions of coming to the valley and the history of her sister Mrs Bolton are accurate and taken from the account of her daughter, May Ross, who was the first child to arrive in the valley, along with the dented Tilley lantern. The descriptions of the weekly work undertaken by Agnes and Meredith are also from May's recollections of the weekly chores in the Bettjeman household (JM Carver 1998).

The account of the woolshed dance at Bettjemans' woolshed is from a description by Agnes Anderson detailed by Arthur Bates. These dances really did go all night and the musicians and calling details for the square dance are accurately reflected along with details of the decoration and toilet/changing facilities. All characters described in the early scenes in the valley are real apart from Meredith Innes and James Stanley, whose interaction with the real characters in this book is entirely fictional. Descriptions of trips from the Mangapurua Valley to Raetihi on the mail bus are taken from an account by Agnes Anderson, as detailed in Arthur Bates' book.

All details of the meeting, romance and wedding of James Stanley and Meredith Innes are entirely fictional.

The novel covers the fictional life in the valley of James and Meredith from 1932 to 1942. During this time, families continued to pack up and leave, with the Andersons going in 1936 and the Mowats leaving in 1937. The bridge was finally completed in 1936. This is also the year that Phil Bennett, the last settler in the lower valley, left the valley, leaving only three families remaining. The bridge was built by Sandford and Brown. Bill Sandford owned the joinery business in Raetihi and his son David (Dave), a keen photographer, took a wonderful series of photographs of the Bridge to Nowhere during the construction phase. His father Bill and brother Doug both worked on the bridge. The pictures of the bridge construction on the front cover were taken by David Sandford in 1935/6 – thank you to the Sandford family for sharing these with me. The men standing on top of the bridge are David's father William (Bill) Sandford and his apprentice Jack Lynn.

Following a 100 Year Flood Event in 1942, the government closed the road and the three remaining families had to walk off their farms. Muriel Roberts (nee McDonald), now in her nineties, was born in 1926 in the valley and lived with her parents in the valley until it closed in 1943. She has an excellent recall of their daily lives including such details as the names of the horses owned by the McDonald and Anderson families. Ginger, Paddy and Starlight were real horses, while Holly was a fictional horse character. At fourteen, Muriel rode a round trip of four hours to pick up the mail for the three remaining families in the upper valley until it closed in 1943. She and her three older sisters worked with their father (Hugh McDonald) on the farm with horses, dogs and handpieces. Muriel really did shear nine sheep with a pair of left-handed hand shears given to her by Reg Anderson at age nine and recalls she was better at dagging sheep than shearing, never finding a satisfactory left handpiece once the switch was made to machine shearing. Muriel recounted the story of her family nearly losing their car over the bank and her role in weighing down the door until a tow could be arranged.

After the 1942 road closure the McDonalds continued to lease land and run stock in the valley for a further three years. Muriel regularly rode alone back into the valley after it had been abandoned by all other families to check on the stock that remained there. She reports the valley was overrun with wild pigs at this time and she feared her fate, should she have fallen from her horse. When the McDonalds' stock finally left the valley, after failing to reach reserve at the Raetihi Sale Yards, Muriel and her father drove the flock all the way to their new farm in Otorohanga.

Of note, Peter, the shearer, and Toby Dougherty are fictional characters.

## Beanstalk's Chapters

Kingseat Hospital was a government-run psychiatric hospital situated on Kingseat Road in South Auckland. It was opened in 1932. By 1947 there were over 800 patients, including children. The hospital was sold into private ownership in 1996 and the last patients were relocated away from the site in 1999, as psychiatric care moved to a community-based model. The site is now used as rental accommodation and is the home to Spookers, a haunted themed attraction based in the Nurse's Home, which some believe is still haunted by the Grey Nurse.

While the character of Beanstalk is entirely fictional, in the late 1950s and 60s, Robert Lowell, in Boston, was encouraging the confessional poetry movement. His students included Sylvia Plath and Anne Sexton. A Boston psychiatrist, Martin Orne, did encourage his patient Anne Sexton, to express her inner feelings through poetry. Sylvia Plath's book *Ariel* was published in 1965 after her death to much acclaim. Janet Frame was similarly encouraged in her writing while under psychiatric care in Dunedin.

Clarks Beach is a small harbour-side settlement where some of the Kingseat staff chose to live close to the hospital. The hospital setting is accurately described. The hospital grounds back onto a tidal river, which, by the 1990s, was largely overgrown with mangroves. However, in the late fifties and sixties, this was a clear waterway and staff at the hospital did take patients out on the river and harbour by boat.

## Jane's Poems

All of Jane's poetry depicts fictional characters and events.

## Kate's Chapters

Kate's story begins in Auckland and the North Waikato, New Zealand. All characters are fictional. Kate's flat is located on Dominion Road in Auckland. She travels to her fictional family farm, 'West Hills', which is located on Waikāretu Road beyond Port Waikato. Her motorcycle ride over Klondyke Road is accurately described and remains today a narrow metal road still dearly loved by gravel riding motorcyclists. Descriptions of farm life at West Hills are fictional.

The action moves to Auckland City Hospital, Albert Park and Piha Beach, all located accurately in the greater Auckland area.

The Māori legend of Taranaki's fight with Tongariro over Pihanga and his subsequent escape to the sea forming the Whanganui River is detailed by Arthur Bates (*A Pictorial History of the Wanganui River*, 14).

The town of Whanganui (previously known as Wanganui from 1854

– 2009 so this spelling is used for the town throughout the book) is accurately described, including the restored *Wairere*, which still takes visitors for short excursions on the Whanganui River and is managed and maintained by a keen team of volunteers.

The trip up the River Road is very scenic and historic. The papa rock cutting above the river is a great place to stop and look at the soft oyster shells embedded there. Bates' 1986 *A Pictorial History* describes the Whanganui River Valley as, *A relatively recent addition to the New Zealand land mass. This explains the soft papa banks, which tend to wear down to gorges and the resultant papa sediment carried in suspension in the river water* (15). The ongoing slipping of narrow roads as described in the Mangapurua Valley is clearly evident on the River Road, which is frequently blocked in winter or after heavy rain.

The Kāwana flour mill was proposed by the local mission and donated by Governor Grey to local Maori in 1854. It was operational intermittently until 1912 and restored in 1980. It is well worth a visit if touring this area.

The mission at Jerusalem was first established at Hiruharama in 1883 by Sister Mary Aubert. At this time approximately 600 Maori lived in the surrounding area. A church was built and Mother Aubert established a home and school for 'foundling children', which continued until 1963 for both Māori and Pākehā children. In 1891, Sister Aubert had a contract to supply nine herbal remedies to the company Kempthorne Prosser & Co. Her cherry orchard was another successful enterprise.

In 1969, poet James K Baxter established a community in Jerusalem. He died in Auckland in 1972 but had requested to be buried at Jerusalem. Today there are two nuns still tending the church and convent, which has now been turned into backpacker-style accommodation. On the wall of the convent is a copy of Baxter's poem *Haere Ra*, which was written for Sister Sheila when she was leaving Hiruharama in 1969.

In this story the interaction between Kate, Ursula and the nuns is entirely fictional, however the church, convent and description of Baxter's grave are accurate. One of the highlights of my research for this book was visiting Sister Suzanna and Sister Louisiana at Jerusalem, enjoying their warmth and learning first-hand how they continue to care lovingly for this unique community and its slice of history.

Kate's trip to the museum is entirely fictional. A museum was set up at Captain Andy Stewart's home, which still stands at Pipiriki alongside the derelict rebuild of the Pipiriki Hotel. The museum is no longer open.

The direct quotes from Bates (1981), summarise the ill-fated history of the settlement of the Mangapurua Valley and the detail of the government act that closed the valley down after the 1942 flood when it was no longer financially viable to maintain the road to the valley.

Today, jet boats offer sightseeing trips to and from the Bridge to Nowhere, which is a short walk from the Mangapurua landing. Kate's interaction with the passengers and the jet boat driver is entirely fictional. During her walk up the valley, Kate visits the makeshift camp of Tom Mowat. Tom is the real-life son of settler Pat Mowat; he was not born in the valley but has become a regular visitor over his lifetime. Tom's makeshift camp at the McDonalds' homestead is as he describes camping in this area in the early 1990s. In more recent years he has moved his camp up to Johnson's Flat. The descriptions of running stock in the area during the '70s are as Tom describes.

Descriptions of pig hunting are with acknowledgement to the recollections of Doug Houlbrooke and a superb little book on the subject written by Peter Sorensen called *Rippers & Grippers*, written about his pig-hunting experiences in the Wairarapa. This privately published book is available on request from the Pongaroa Hotel. It is well worth the read, as is the pub a visit.

Descriptions of the Mangapurua Valley are from my own visit to the area on a mountain bike ride from the trig to the landing in December 2015, as well as descriptions and the private photos of Clarice Clark who tramped in this area in the early 1990s. Of note, foxgloves and birdlife are still prevalent today, as they were in the 1930s as described by Agnes

Anderson (Bates 1981).

The route to Okārito in the South Island and Whangamomona in the north are accurately described. The Forbidden Highway from Taumarunui to Whangamomona is picturesque, as is the Whangamomona Hotel, which continues to thrive and still shows old-style New Zealand country hotel hospitality at its best. They offer accommodation and hearty meals to strangers passing through, many by motorcycle. If you ever have the opportunity to visit, ask the friendly publicans to show you their cellar, which opens up in front of the hotel for the kegs to be lowered to the cellar under the hotel. The character of Mac, the publican, is fictional.

## Toby Dougherty's Chapters

The character of Toby Dougherty, his family, homestead and Mac at the pub are all entirely fictional. The Sarjeant Gallery is an iconic art gallery in Whanganui; it has recently been removed from its hilltop site for earthquake strengthening of the historic building. The sister bridge to the Bridge to Nowhere is known as the Bridge to Somewhere. It is located off Whangamomona Road at Strathmore, with access now via the Makahu Road. However, previous access to the bridge was via the old road from the Whangamomona Hotel, which is now a scenic walking and cycle route. This bridge was built in 1937 with a grand plan of connecting a road across the Whanganui River and over the Bridge to Nowhere and then on up the Mangapurua Valley, connecting Stratford to Raetihi. This route was never completed. Today both bridges are tourist destinations in their isolated environments and well worth a visit.

# References

Barrie, J.M. (1962). *Peter Pan and Wendy*. Leicester, Great Britain: Brockhampton Press Ltd. (first published 1915).

Bates, A. (1981). *The Bridge to Nowhere: The Ill-fated Mangapurua Settlement*. Wanganui: Wanganui Newspapers Ltd.

Bates, A. (1986). *A Pictorial History of the Wanganui River*. (2nd edition). Wanganui: Wanganui Newspapers Ltd.

Blyton, E. (1943). *The Magic Faraway Tree*. London, England: George Newnes.

Carver, J.M. (1998). *Combating Isolation – The Women of Mangapurua 1917–1942*. M.A. thesis, Massey University. Palmerston North, New Zealand.

Frame, J. (1994). A*n Autobiography*. (Vintage collector's edition). Auckland, New Zealand: Random House New Zealand.

Hunt, J.K. & Hunt, S. (2009). *James K. Baxter Poems – Selected and Introduced by Sam Hunt*. Auckland, New Zealand: Auckland University Press.

Plath, S. (2015). *Ariel*. (Restored edition). Wolfeyes Books. London, England: Faber & Faber.

Sorensen, P. (Undated). *Rippers & Grippers*. Palmerston North, New Zealand: Stylex Print.

Spivack, K. (2012). *With Robert Lowell & His Circle: Sylvia Plath, Anne Sexton, Elizabeth Bishop, Stanley Kunitz, and Others*. Boston, USA: Northeastern University Press.

West, R. (2017). *Remembering Them – The Settlers of the Mangapurua and Kaiwhakauka Valleys*. Raewyn West, Taumarunui. (westandwest321@gmail.com).

Kirsty Powell grew up east of Eketahuna in an isolated rural community and loves to write strong New Zealand characters into her fiction. She has published short stories, poems and her debut novel *The Strength of Eggshells*. She is currently working on a sequel which revisits Kate, Ursula and their daughter Ariel 20 years hence.

Kirsty lives in rural South Auckland and spends her spare time helping to solve the erosion and marine plastic problems on the Awhitu West Coast. She also likes to get away to various parts of the world on a motorbike or a bicycle.